CHENOO

AMERICAN INDIAN LITERATURE AND CRITICAL STUDIES SERIES

CHENOO

A Novel

Joseph Bruchac

UNIVERSITY OF OKLAHOMA PRESS : NORMAN

This book is a work of fiction. Names, characters, places, and incidents are either the product of the author's imagination or are used fictitiously, and any resemblance to actual events, locales, or persons, living or dead, is entirely coincidental.

Library of Congress Cataloging-in-Publication Data

Names: Bruchac, Joseph, 1942– author.
Title: Chenoo : a novel / Joseph Bruchac.
Description: First edition. | Norman, OK : University of Oklahoma Press,
    [2016] | Series: American Indian literature and critical studies series ; 68
Identifiers: LCCN 2015038310 | ISBN 978-0-8061-5207-3 (softcover : acid-free
    paper)
Subjects: LCSH: Private investigators—Fiction. | Abenaki Indians—Fiction.
    | GSAFD: Mystery fiction.
Classification: LCC PS3552.R794 C48 2016 | DDC 813/.54—dc23
LC record available at http://lccn.loc.gov/2015038310

Chenoo: A Novel is Volume 68 in the American Indian Literature and Critical Studies Series.

The paper in this book meets the guidelines for permanence and durability of the Committee on Production Guidelines for Book Longevity of the Council on Library Resources, Inc. ∞

1 2 3 4 5 6 7 8 9 10

Preface
Behind the Monster

Chenoo. It's the name of one of the mythic—or perhaps not so mythic—creatures from our northeastern Algonquin cultures. Formerly a human being, it was transformed into an insatiable cannibal monster by its own greed. The fact that such a creature figures into the plot is one reason why I call this novel by that name. But this is not just a story about a monster. It's also about Native American rights, about the power of tradition and story, about martial arts—all rolled up into what is ostensibly a sort of detective story.

When I was an undergraduate student at Cornell University several decades ago, I took a fiction writing course from a truly wonderful author named James McConkey, who became a lifelong friend. One piece of advice Jim gave us during that course I took to heart and have always remembered.

"When you write a novel," Jim said, "put everything you know into it."

Of course, that is not literally possible. But in those books of mine that are not historical fiction, I always invest the action, plot, and main characters with aspects of my own life, my own experience, those things that I have attempted to learn and have come to know well enough to talk about in a fairly intelligent way. Thus, if a character in one of my stories makes a fire with a bow drill, he or she is doing something that I know how to do and have done numerous times before. And if I am talking about historical events or aspects of a culture—such as that of my Western Abenaki ancestors—I do my best to stick to well-documented facts, to avoid distorting or changing events and traditional practices, beliefs and stories. I am not saying that I am always right. Like everyone, I have made mistakes, but I am always trying to do my best to be true to things.

So how does this apply to this book, whose first-person narrator might be seen as fitting somewhat into the mold of such ironic, wise-cracking, hard-boiled detectives as Philip Marlowe, Sam Spade, Spenser, and Elvis Cole? Before I go further, I need to acknowledge the influence of Raymond Chandler, Dashiell Hammett, Robert B. Parker, and Robert Crais. I've been reading their particular genre since I was sixteen years old. I suppose the first thing I could say is that my main character, without being as world-weary as Chandler's and Hammett's heroes, knows and has experienced a lot of the things I have.

Like Jacob "Podjo" Neptune, I'm a student of the martial arts. When he refers to someone such as Musashi Miyamoto, the legendary samurai author of *A Book of Five Rings*, or to a particular style of fighting, he's talking about a warrior way that I've spent more than four decades following, and I'm still learning. I hold the rank of Master and 5th degree black belt in Pentjak Silat, the martial arts of Indonesia. I've also been devoted to Brazilian jiu jitsu and achieved my purple belt and Instructor's rank in 2015. And I've studied a number of other disciplines. When my main character engages in any sort of combat during the course of the novel, the techniques he uses are ones that I've absorbed, used, and know to be effective. Each chapter begins with a brief quotation that is derived, in one way or another, from master teachers and oriental philosophy. Take the quote at the start of chapter 4:

> Teeth are hard and decay
> Tongue is soft and remains

That was said to me in 1976 by my master, Gison Tenaga, when I first began studying Pentjak Silat, and the saying can be interpreted in several ways, touching on the lasting power of words and memory and the fact that a soft approach may be better than a hard one.

A few years ago, at a public reading, I was introduced as a poet who knows a hundred ways to kill you with his bare hands. To which I responded, "Well, I do write poetry."

And so does Podjo. Though poetry is more of a sideline for him than for me. (And, unlike my main character, I have yet to kill anyone with my bare hands.)

Another example of our shared interests is in woodcraft. I was raised in the Adirondack mountain foothills and learned forest ways from my Abenaki grandfather, Jesse Bowman; my taxidermist and hunter father Joseph Bruchac, Junior; and from a great many other elders and friends over the years, such as John Stokes, founder of The Tracking Project. My sons followed that way as well. James Bruchac, my older son, has now co-written several popular books on animal tracking, including *Scats and Tracks of the Northeast* (Falcon Guides) and is the director of our family outdoor education facility and nature preserve, the Ndakinna Education Center (which is also the site of our dojo, where Jim teaches Koyukushin full contact karate and my other son, Jesse, is the head jiu jitsu instructor). So, when Jacob Neptune is in the woods, he is making use of some very old knowledge that is part of Abenaki culture and is being preserved and taught by our family. He's not engaged in the kind of faux "Indian tracking" made famous in the early nineteenth century by James Fenimore Cooper in books like *The Last of the Mohicans*, where improbable things occur, such as characters finding their way back to a fort by following the tracks of a rolling cannon ball that was fired from said fort. What Podjo does is real deal.

I mentioned above that Jacob Neptune might be seen as fitting the mold of a number of famous fictional tough guys. At this point, I want to address a few ways in which he may be seen as different and unique.

Numero uno is his sense of humor. Wise-cracking is, I know, characteristic of the main characters of such icons in the detective genre as the late Robert Parker and Robert Crais. And, like them, J. J. Neptune appreciates his own jokes, even when others don't. But I would like to think that Podjo's humor is different in that it truly is "Indian humor."

Indian humor? What, pray tell, is that? Well, there's a brilliant chapter on Native American humor in the groundbreaking 1969 book *Custer Died for Your Sins* by Vine Deloria, Jr. Vine firmly believed that humor was an index to understanding a people. He described humor as the "cement by which the coming Indian movement is held together." And, the son of a Native American minister, Vine truly practiced what he preached. He never forgot the power of humor. Every now and then the two of us went to lunch with Robert Baron, the founder of Fulcrum Books, one of our mutual publishers. And at those lunches—and any other time I saw Vine—he always told a joke, or two, or three.

Three decades ago, Robert Conley, the Cherokee historian and novelist, suggested that he and I should co-author an anthology of Indian humor. We put a few things together, but other projects got in the way. I have to admit that I was influenced to think twice about the project when one of my friends and mentors, N. Scott Momaday, said to me, "Joseph, as your uncle, let me caution you to be careful. Indian humor is a very serious thing."

And indeed it is. Serious and hard to explain, perhaps, to a non-Native. But, at the risk of sounding ridiculous, let me point out a few things I've observed over the course of many years. One is that Native American humor does not tend to be angry, to be mean or demeaning of others, either groups or individuals. In fact, it is often self-deprecating. The butt of the joke may be the teller and not someone else. It doesn't victimize. Probably the best-known professional Indian comedian was Charlie Hill. One of his frequent jokes went like this: "I'm Oneida Indian from Wisconsin. We used to be from New York, but we had a little real estate problem."

What I've always noticed about jokes like that, or the jokes that Vine used to tell, is that they are always grounded in reality. There's an awareness of history in them and also an attitude that avoids self-pity or falling into "Lo, the poor Indian." Through laughter we are able to present, to interpret, and to control our own history.

Many Native American jokes are like our traditional tales. They serve two purposes. They amuse you, but they also make you think. At times, after Vine told me a joke, I'd walk away trying to figure out just what lesson he was trying to impart to me—not by hitting me over the head with it, nor by criticizing something I'd done or said—but in a funny way that, when I thought about it, made the point in a better, more lasting fashion.

And it is in that peculiarly "Indian" humor that Jacob Neptune and his big buddy Dennis are constantly engaging. I hope you enjoy the jokes.

Numero dos concerns my novel's difference in connecting the main character to his traditions. Especially as conveyed by the stories. The novel is interspersed with tales—all of them, I have been assured by various Abenaki elders, are at least hundreds of years old. And here is where I need to credit two of those teachers in particular: Maurice Dennis/Mdawelasis of the reserve of Odanak, Quebec, Canada, and Old Forge, New York, and Stephen Laurent/Attian Lolo of Odanak and Intervale, New Hampshire. There are not enough words in English or Abenaki to thank them for their teaching and their encouragement at crucial times in my life. *Ktsi wliwini nidobak!* They were the real-life equivalent of the Tom Nicola character in this book.

Stories count. In this novel I've tried to make them serve as counter-points or guideposts to the main narrative as Jacob Neptune remembers them. I've been a traditional storyteller myself—or at least called one—since the mid-seventies. I have tremendous respect for all that those stories contain and have always tried to share them in the proper context and with the right words. A knowledge of the Abenaki language has been crucial in this, and my family and I are devoted to its preservation. My younger son Jesse is a fluent speaker and has raised my two young grandkids, Carolyn and Jacob, in the language. When the four of us perform together we use both languages. (As I write this, Jesse is in Cape-town, South Africa, spending eight weeks on the set of a major National Geographic/Sony film called *Saints and Strangers*, which tells the story of the Mayflower and the Plymouth Colony from the dual viewpoints of the English and the Native nations of the time. Jesse's job has been to translate ninety pages of script for the Native actors from English into Abenaki and to serve as the language coach during filming.)

That Abenaki storytelling tradition leads back to my title and to saying a few more words about the being called the Chenoo.

It's a creature known by several names among the Algonquin-speaking nations of the Northeast. The best-known name is probably Windigo or Wendigo, as the Ojibway and Cree and other northern peoples call it. Abenakis know it as the Kiwakw or the Chenoo. (And here I must confess I chose to use "Chenoo" in part because it is easier to pronounce in English.) My son Jesse is the author of a bilingual telling of a story called *The Woman and the Kiwakw*.

The Chenoo is an embodiment of greed and selfishness. Formerly a human being, its twisted behavior transformed it into a giant cannibal monster. One of the messages of the traditional Chenoo tales is that out-of-control selfishness and greed create monsters. While the murders that take place in this book may be suspected to be committed by a monstrous being, it's worth noting that Chenoo or Windigo behavior is common in seemingly ordinary human beings—or in modern western cultures. It's evident in the motivations of those antagonists Podjo must face in the course of the story.

And, though this tale unfolds two decades ago, that kind of greed and selfishness is a problem for all of our Native American tribal nations to this day. It might be manifested within our nations—when high-stakes gaming leads to disproportionate wealth being vested in a few individuals or when tribal membership is revoked so that there will be fewer people claiming their share of casino revenues. Or it may be external—in the form of governments and corporations replaying that old game of "Take Native Land." That's happening in Canada in this year of 2015, and many in the First Nations of our northern neighbor have been attempting to fight back through the Idle No More movement.

Which brings me to another concern of my novel and a major plot point—the use of civil disobedience by Native Americans. Beginning with the 1969 occupation of Alcatraz Island by the "Indians of All Tribes," the tactic of taking over property to draw attention to legitimate Native issues has happened all over the continent. Perhaps the best known was the February 1973 seizure of the hamlet of Wounded Knee on the Pine Ridge Reservation in South Dakota when members of AIM (the American Indian Movement, founded in 1968) and local Lakotas opposed to the corrupt tribal government held off a heavily armed federal force for seventy days. Though some have said that both those takeovers ended in seeming failure, it can be argued that the public awareness raised by the events was a factor in creating the Indian Self-Determination and Education Assistance Act. That 1975 legislation ended policies of terminating tribes and provided not only greater support for economic development and education but also made self-determination a much more realistic goal. And even since 1975 there have been many actions of civil disobedience by tribal people in Canada and the United States. Mohawks of Oka in Quebec trying to stop the building of a golf course on land sacred to their people, Onondagas in New York State preventing the widening of an interstate through their small reservations, Abenakis in Vermont engaging in fish-ins and blockading Brunswick Springs, and so on. On the other hand, perhaps "civil disobedience" is not the right term when talking about such indigenous actions. Rather, they may be seen as *obedience* to treaties and promises to Native nations that have been broken by the United States and Canada.

So, although the Children of the Mountain takeover of a state campground in *Chenoo* is entirely fictitious, it is very real.

The last thing I'd like to say about this novel is that I really enjoyed writing it. I became very fond of my main character and hope to tell at least one or two more stories about him—or rather with him. And, just as our traditional tales succeed in getting their deeper messages across only if they are interesting to hear, *Chenoo* was written to be an entertainment—which also has points to make. With that in mind, I hope you'll find this book fun to read. *Wlipamkaani nidobak.* Travel well, my friends.

CHENOO

1

Awake, less than awakened
Sleeping, almost awake

Breath burns in my throat like acid. My legs are numb and heavy as clay. I struggle up the slope, seeking the safety of the pines. My heart seems ready to burst, but I can't slow down. It's too close behind me.

I've run at least two miles since I first heard that blood-stopping howl. First distant, then closer. Silent now. But the silence doesn't give me hope. It may only mean it's no longer following just my scent—that it's now seen me.

Is that drumming my pulse or the sound of heavier feet than mine striking the earth as it lopes closer, closing the gap between its thirst for my blood and my thirst for life?

The mouth of a small cave is just ahead. There at the base of the cliff. I might reach it! The bracelet on my wrist catches on a branch. I don't remember that bracelet. Where did it come from? I reach back, open the clasp. The heavy silver band falls to the ground, glitters in the moonlight. But in that moment, just as I free myself, something darker than shadow looms over me. Twin reflections of the moon glint from the ancient cold of its dead eyes. Lightning strikes inside my skull. I start to fall, my ears ringing from the killing force of that blow.

And then I was awake.

I sat up in bed. The full moon was filling the one window in my bedroom, set high on the wall above me and in front of me. But no one other than the oldest celestial grandmother was looking at me now. The sense of someone—or something—watching, watching with malevolent intent, was gone, though I felt as if I'd walked through a spiderweb.

3

The first five chords of "Custer Died for your Sins" sounded from the red cell phone on top of the old wooden soft drink crate I use as a bedside table. I wiped my face and picked up the phone.

"*Kwai, kwai*, Dennis."

"Podjo!" Dennis Mitchell's voice roared back at me, not quite loud enough to explode the electromagnet inside the earpiece. Long ago, tradition goes, back when animals and people looked even more alike than they do now, his people were bears. Get one of those Mitchells excited, they tend to lose their quiet tone of voice and start roaring like bears. Uncle John Neptune told me that and, like most of the things that old muskrat taught me, he was dead right.

"J. J. Neptune, P.I.," I replied in my most formal tones. Then I held the phone a foot farther away from my ear to avoid more permanent hearing loss.

"How?" Dennis bellowed. Then, in a more normal tone of voice, "How you always knows it's me when I call?"

As if he had to ask after all we've been through together? I didn't answer. Anyhow, it was not really a question. Dennis knew two things. First, that I do not have caller ID, and second, that I have this way of knowing things that most folks do not.

"Okay," Dennis finally said.

"It's the middle of the night. Where the hell are you?"

"Penacook Tribal Office."

"Why?"

On the other end of the phone, four hundred miles closer to the dawn than upstate New York, my best friend sounded like a whale in an echo chamber as he took a deep, deep breath.

"Podjo," he said, pausing between each word to emphasize his seriousness, "we . . . got . . . trouble."

"I know. I saw the piece on the news when I was down at the store yesterday. Caught Mikwe's sound bite and noticed just how noble he looked. 'Chief' Mikwe as they're calling him now."

Though I was joking about it, I actually had been impressed by Mikwe's response to the reporter asking if the tribe's takeover was an act of disloyalty at a time when all Americans needed to unite against terrorists. It matched the post-9/11 mood while conveying the legitimacy of the claims being made by the Children of the Mountain in taking over the thousand-acre abandoned state campsite that had been put up for auction by the state.

"We're the opposite of domestic terrorists," Mikwe had said. "We're loyal Americans, loyal first Americans. Every person in our ranks has either served in the armed forces or has a family member who served or is on active duty. We're just asking the government, our government, to honor some of the promises made to our people. Such as the promise that this sacred land we're occupying would be returned to our people if it was no longer being used by the state."

Impressive, indeed. But I wasn't about to admit that, which was why I then added, "Amazing what a few turkey feathers on your head can do for a man's image, eh?"

A sound like someone turning on a grinder filled the earpiece. Dennis's chuckle. But his voice was deathly serious when he spoke again.

"It's not just the standoff."

Another pause followed, the kind of long pause you get only when you're talking with another Penacook over the phone. Clam up with someone who isn't Indian and they start to get nervous. Real nervous. Have to ask if you're still there. And when you just say "*unh-hunh*," and nothing else, they get more nervous. Great way to spoil a telemarketer's day.

But Dennis and me were both Penacooks. Being Penacook meant never having to ask if you are still there. We are and we aren't going anywhere. Which, in itself, has been a source of consternation for those individuals, governments, and organizations that have tried so hard to eradicate our presence over the last five centuries.

Seconds silently ticked away as the digital display of the battery-powered clock by my bed reminded me it was now 4:15 A.M. There was no electricity in that little cabin of mine. Thus no TV, no air-conditioning, no computer. Just my two rooms, and my woodstove for heat. For entertainment, I had the picture window looking out over the high mountain meadow, the woods, and the hills rolling down to the Hudson River, which, though concealed by the trees, often reveals itself some mornings as a lazy *S* of fog rising above the green.

I was not a total whatever-ist. My windup radio, my cell phone, and that clock were concessions to the fact that "This is 2004, for Christ's sake!" Fred down at the store said that yesterday because I had no idea what he was talking about when he referred to the last episode of *Lost*.

That clock now read 4:16. But I only noticed its small glowing face out of the corner of my eye. My real attention was fastened on a brighter, more lasting keeper of true time. It was one reason I cut that southeastern window so high on my bedroom wall, perfectly placed for me to look up from my pillow and observe not just the swirl of stars across the firmament but also the passage of Nanibonsad, the Night Traveler, Grandmother Moon. She'd moved a bit since the phone woke me, walking her slow stately way across the heavens. I was willing to bet that Dennis was also watching her back there on the Island, his thick glasses reflecting Grandmother Moon's journey toward the promise of another dawn.

My cousin Dennis and I had both loved the moon since we were little kids. Batteries ran out, power failed, people changed or disappeared to never come back again, but not her. She was always there. Even when her face was hidden, we knew she was watching, would always be reliable, always return her light to us. We learned early in our troubled younger years that we could count on her to abide, to tell the truth, unlike some people or some nations. The faithful moon—the only grandmother that both of us orphan kids ever had.

"So tell me," I finally said.

Dennis sighed. "Podjo . . . ," his voice was weary, worried. "It's something that's . . ." he hesitated, trying to find the right way to put it without saying it straight out, "just something we can't talk about over the phone."

Another long pause. I listened to Dennis breathing and to the familiar, soft rhythmic sound I could pick up underneath it. It told me he was using a headset so that his hands could remain free. Thwick, thwick, thwick. Whittling. Thwick, thwick, thwick, small curlicue shavings of pine being flicked off the wood held in his left hand as the lock-blade knife in his right sought whatever shape was held within the grain. It was amazing just how delicately he could shape things with those huge lineman's paws of his. It reminded me of one of the things Uncle John taught me—that you can never judge people just by their looks. There was a lot more to Dennis than met the eye and people usually got the wrong impression when they first met him, especially when they were not, as the politically polite would now have it, Native Americans.

Both Dennis and I had spent more time than most Penacooks in that not always politically correct, bleached-out civilization. In college we were both Indians. By which I mean we went to Dartmouth and played football there. Back before he became the world's slowest suicide,

Dennis was pretty much unstoppable. Even today, at six feet six inches and 320 pounds, Dennis still looked like the NFL lineman that a good many experts thought he might have been—playing the same position of monster right tackle he nailed down for the three years we spent in Hanover. As the starting right linebacker for two years, I learned what it was like to get blocked by him in practice—less pleasant than being buried in a rock-filled avalanche.

I was almost as good at my position as Dennis was at his, which led to sportswriters in the '90s dubbing us "Dartmouth's Two Big Chiefs," despite our being from a contentiously unrecognized tribe. Some envisioned us making the jinx-ridden cover of *Sports Illustrated* and ending up being taken in at least the third round of the NFL draft. Maybe higher if our senior year stats improved the way everyone expected.

Someone, a psychology professor I liked, once told me, that we human beings can recover from almost any trauma. That's why we've succeeded beyond any other species on the planet. We can lose our parents and grandparents in the same car accident and still recover. We can be starved and beaten by foster parents, barely escape sexual molestation by stabbing the sick bastard in his leg with a pencil, have our fingers broken and everything else, and still, a few years later, be back to normal, as fully functioning persons. I believe that to be true.

I also believe that to be bullshit.

There are two things that we Penacooks can tell you about life. The first is that things are simple. The second is that they are not.

Which may explain why at the start of our senior year, with our biggest season ahead of us, Dartmouth's Two Big Chiefs got drunk and went out and enlisted. Slick Willy was prez then, not one of the Bush leaguers. The fall of the Twin Towers was years away, so it was not an excess of patriotic zeal that overtook us, nor had we dreamed since childhood of eventually being one of those Indian vets at the powwow who gets to carry in the 'Merican flag as an Honor Song is played on the big drum. At the time we did it, we might have thought it was funny, a real joke on our school and our coaches and those writers who gushed about us scalping Yale and being on the warpath against Harvard. Ho . . . ho . . . ho. It might have been a result of our shared ironic sense of humor, or—to be honest—a preemptive strike, with us choosing to fail all on our own before anyone else could reject us.

Whatever the case, we turned out to be even better in Special Forces than we'd been on the gridiron. And the brotherhood Dennis and

I shared became that much deeper. We had something we could share with no one else. Total trust.

Don't get me wrong. Despite my hermit existence I liked most people. And I was capable of love, as well. He prayeth best who loveth best, as old Sammy Coleridge once lisped. There were a lot of people I'd loved, even some who would try to kill me on first sight because I was in their country and they felt justified since I was part of an invasion force trying to kill *them*. Trust, though, is a whole other ball game. There was only a handful of people I could trust. Dennis ranked as that hand's thumb.

"Podjo?" Dennis said, his voice soft this time. "You comin'?"

"You know I am."

Click. No *addio*, *nidoba*. No bye-bye. No catch you later, dude. Just our old abrupt Penacook way of ending a phone conversation once all that needed to be said had been said. So abrupt, in fact, that it may have surprised someone listening in on another extension in the tribal offices. Because, just a second later, that click of Dennis's phone line disconnecting had been followed by another click.

What that meant, I had yet to find out. But mentally I filed it away in the Expect Trouble folder as I pressed the off button on my own handset.

Whatever whoever else was up to, I knew what my bro was doing now. He was putting down his whittling, bringing up the commuter airline on his laptop that he had turned on 24–7, checking the arrival time for the earliest flight that would lift me over the intervening mountains to be dropped (gently, I trusted) at the regional airport nearest the island.

I had no doubt that Dennis would be there waiting for me in the airport lot, his beloved old Jeep Renegade even more battered than before, disguising the souped-up engine under its scratched hood, its reinforced bumpers displaying such stickers as

PENACOOK AND PROUD OF IT

IT'S ALWAYS INDIAN TIME

WE SHALL OVERRUN

DEFENDING OUR BORDERS SINCE 1492

The thought of that old jeep and Dennis's broad, smiling face—the sharp intelligence in his brown eyes masked by Coke-bottle prescription sunglasses—brought a smile to my face. I relaxed a little, but I didn't lie back down. Sleep didn't want to be my friend.

I flexed my right leg. The pain in my knee wasn't that bad. No more than an eleven on a scale from one to ten. I massaged it, straightened the leg and bent it a dozen times, hearing the Velcro crackling of tendons as I did so. Gradually it loosened up and the pain lessened. I suppose I could have taken painkillers for it. Sure. But it would have required far too many of those to dull the knife-sharp pangs I'd gotten used to feeling. I'd have ended up as hooked on oxy as I used to be on booze. Thank you very much, but *nda*.

I unlocked my heavy bedroom door, swung it open, and walked out into my combination living room and kitchen. I stood in my fashionable plaid boxer shorts in front of the open window and peered out through the thinning dark, the quiet expanse of tree-clad slopes rolling below the cabin. Two of my jade plants were in bloom and their sweet scent filled the air, making me think, pleasantly for a change, of certain tropic places I'd been.

In the light from Grandmother Moon, I could easily make out the two lines of my blueberry bushes and the rounded shapes of the pears and plums I planted a few years back. I wondered what animals might be looking up at my window or just ignoring me as they went along their way, indifferent to a human being who felt no need to hunt them. Maybe my five grey foxes were out there.

Thinking of them brought a smile to my face. I'd first seen them a few days before from my picture window and observed Mama Fox walking past with the biggest Anjou pear from my tree held firmly in her jaws. I say "Mama" because no sooner had she settled down to start eating that pear than her baby came rollicking out of the woods. Half her size, the reddish tinge on its side and the white on its puffy chest even brighter than hers, the baby looked as cuddly as a stuffed animal. Its tail was bushier, too, and held up like a question mark.

"Kwai, kwai, Q," I whispered, as the baby fox jumped over its mother's back, rolled off onto its side, then picked up a leaf and hightailed back into the pines. To reappear a minute later, but tail straighter, body looking skinnier than before . . . oops, not Q at all, but a sibling. And, yup, with tail like a bushy punctuation mark, out burst Q again, leaf still in its grinning jaws with a third young fox in pursuit. I stayed there without moving, just watching the show. My right knee started spasming from standing still so long, but who cared. It was a small admission fee to pay for that matinee. When, two hours and three of my prize pears later, the four of them finally faded for good back beneath the pines and hemlocks, I felt like applauding. Who needed Net-Fix or whatever it was called?

It felt good to think about them being safe from hunters and trappers here on my property. "My property," as far as the eyes of the law can see. (Admittedly, not that far, law being notoriously near-sighted.) But I never thought of it as my own, even though that deed registered in the county seat claimed that those five hundred acres were owned by one Jacob Jesse Neptune. The twice-yearly property and school taxes I paid reminded me of that legal relationship, though said taxes were a bit less than they would have been if I hadn't placed the land into a conservation easement as soon as I got title.

I didn't feel guilty about the way I'd obtained the money to buy the land. I'd done a better job of earning it than those three former Stasi men had done in the Yucatan when they failed to accomplish the blood work they'd been hired to do. After all, if they'd succeeded, my breath and that of a bunch of Lacandon Mayans would have vanished from the living wind, not theirs. I looked at the long scar on my left forearm, reminder of another story to tell another time.

We own our scars more than we own any soil. Matter of fact, Earth owns us more than we own it. Soil always outlasts individual humans. Hubris may be the applicable word in English. But respect is better. Respect. Just a little bit now, unh-hunh, and a little bit later.

I slipped into my sweatpants. Shrugged my shoulders up and down a few times, circled them. Time for the daily two hundred. Push-ups in series of twenty. Twenty on palms. Twenty with arms out double shoulder width. Twenty on knuckles. Twenty on fingertips, twenty on thumbs. Sit-ups now. Twenty stomach crunches, knees bent. Twenty toward my right knee. Twenty toward my left knee. Twenty with my feet up on the bed. Twenty *V* sit-ups, legs straight.

Paused for stretching. Then the Thousand Strikes. Hammerfist, backfist, tiger, crane, snake, monkey. Block, strike, block again. Front kick, back kick, side kick, round-house, hook kick, spinning back kick, flying side kick. All successfully executed as the flow of blood and the accompanying release of endorphins washed away much of the pain in my knee. Who said I needed total replacement surgery?

Wiping the sweat from my face with one of my extensive set of personalized towels hung by the stainless steel sink, the ones neatly labeled HYATT, RAMADA, MARRIOTT, and HOLIDAY INN, I stood again in front of the picture window. Birds were singing downslope from the pines and cedars. Nanibonsad had gone to her rest. Kisos, the sun, was beginning to redden the horizon before showing his face.

Tai chi then. Embrace Tiger, Return to Mountain. I found myself, as usual, remembering Sifu Huang's words as I moved with him circling, pushing hands. No mind, no force, no guilt. Of course, I heard those words from him back before I went to college, way before my hands ever took the life of another human being. I could still manage the "no guilt" part. But Sifu Huang's teachings had not proven invulnerable against sorrow and regret.

My breathing had slowed enough for me to return to clock time. I picked up my wristwatch from the kitchen table. *Papeezokwazik*. That's the word our old people made up for the clock. The thing that makes much noise but does nothing truly useful. The thing that makes time take time.

My watch told me there was not enough time for the walk I'd planned with my neighbor Tim's dog. Tim was sort of my renter in that he lived on my property half a mile from me in a house just slightly larger than mine that I helped him build. Helped less than you might expect, despite the fact that the explosive device which none of us saw on the road before it lifted our Humvee twenty feet into the air left him paralyzed from the hips down. It took two years of therapy and a will stronger than titanium, but he brought himself back to the point where he could physically get by fine on his own. For the emotional and spiritual part of his healing, he had Pal for company.

Pal was part-wolf, part-husky dog, and I had a special bond with Pal. Admittedly, when we were up running the mountains trails together I no longer called her Pal, which is what Tim named her when I brought her to him as a gangly puppy. Me, I addressed her as Pebon, which means "Winter" in Abenaki. The way she grinned and lolled her tongue out whenever I said that name proved how much she preferred it. But she and I kept up appearances around her erstwhile master. We were a civilized interspecies ménage à trois.

The first flight from Albany would depart at seven. I had just enough time to pack my overnight bag, drop by Tim's, apologize to Pebon for breaking my date with her, and ask my former Special Forces buddy to keep an eye on and water my houseplants. Since I put in the wheelchair ramp to my door, he had no trouble rolling up into my living room. Tim was originally from Georgia and still voted Republican, but he was a member of the same brotherhood of wounded warriors to which

Dennis and I pledged allegiance. Tim was the little finger on that handful of folks in this world I trusted.

However, I did keep my bedroom locked while I was away, and Tim did not know the combination to open the reinforced door. Nor was he aware of the trapdoor beneath my bed and the tunnel that led to a well-concealed exit a hundred feet away in the woods.

Ah, time to go. First, though, I paused for a few heartbeats. Looked out the window. Said a soft farewell to that place of refuge I prayed I'd see again.

Addio nwigwamsis. Goodbye, my little home.

As I whispered those words, I found myself wondering how my dream of pursuit by something dark and Dennis's need for help were linked. In that irrational part of my mind where my dreams came to life, I had no doubt that they were connected—as surely as the night is to the dawn or the darkness to the light.

2

*Clouds still float over
the highest mountain*

A s I drove south on the Adirondack Northway, passing the exits
for Wilton (soon to be the site of yet another sprawl of malls),
Ballston Spa, Round Lake . . . I let my mind travel ahead of
me to the Island. That place where my parents used to send me—
before their accident—to spend a few weeks each summer with Uncle
John and Aunt Mali. I'd always suspected that their main plan was to
give them respite each summer from a kid whose every other sentence
began with "What?" "Where?" "When?" "Why?"

Their stated plan, however, was to keep me from losing that part of my
heritage my father had almost forfeited. It was okay by me, because I
loved almost every minute of it, being on a lake, being around elders who
treated me like a gift from God, fed me the best food I'd ever tasted, and
also let me run wild. In retrospect, you could say that my parents' plan—
even though it was aborted after only four summers—worked. Not only
did I learn to speak a little Abenaki and feel a little less self-conscious
about being a brown-haired, hazel-eyed guy calling himself an Indian,
I formed a life-long attachment to that community. And every day I was
with them I heard another of Uncle John's stories.

The old stories say our island was once a big fish. Maybe all islands
are. When I lived in Manhattan, before seeking semi-anonymity in the
Adirondack foothills, I'd wakened some nights feeling Menahan strain-
ing under the weight of too many human tons of steel, glass, and concrete, trying to shrug it all off into the Harlem and East and Hudson

Rivers, flick its tail, and dive into the mile-deep trough just off the painfully civilized shores.

But there was no island that felt more awake to me than the one my father left behind to go to college and then to take a job as a big city banker. Abenaki Island. I smiled as I remembered the first time I rode the ferry across to it. Six years old then, I was just tall enough to reach up and grab the top rail so I could pull myself up to look. Even back then, when I was a little kid, I was already surprisingly strong. Dad could hold a stick out and I would grab it. Then he would lift it up and I would dangle from it by one hand. He told me that when I was three he boosted me up so I could grab a branch on the maple tree in our suburban yard. His idea was to see how long I could hold on. After fifteen minutes he got bored and pried me off. Otherwise, I might still be hanging there, gently swinging like a baby orangutan, my serious eyes taking it all in from above.

That morning of my sixth year, coming to Abenaki Island for the first time, I could see the fins of that huge stone fish trembling just below the surface. I could tell which end was its head, see how its tail was pushing, holding the island steady against the current. And I heard it saying something to me . . . in breathless words I could not yet understand.

Abenaki Island. It had been too long since I'd been back. It would be good to return to that place as close to being home for me as anywhere on this planet. At least I hoped it would be good, even though some part of me deep behind my cerebral cortex was whispering of danger.

The sun had risen the width of two hands above the horizon to my left as I passed the exit to Clifton Park and saw my first hawk. It was a young goshawk in the top of a maple tree by the roadside. *Accipiter gentilis atricapillu* its Latin name. In Abenaki, *sigwanihla*. I could see that it was waiting for breakfast to be served. Like most big four-lanes, the Northway was one long smorgasbord for raptors, offering up a daily menu of small mammals, amphibians, insects, and the occasional semi-filleted snake. The goshawk swiveled its neck to look at me. I nodded back.

It was always an important thing to see a hawk. A sign, Tom Nicola, my adopted uncle, said. A mile farther down the road, a red-tail—*Buteo jamaicensis*, or *siawmo*—detached itself from another tree and swooped down toward me, almost touching my windshield. So deliberate that it seemed as if it was delivering a message to me.

Oh-oh.

So maybe omens aren't real. Maybe the natural world doesn't give a damn about the things humans do, whether they're ancient Roman seers, Chinese geomancers, or a part-Abenaki private investigator with Medicine in his bloodline and aspirations to publish poetry on the side. I never argued about belief. After all, much of what some people believe is entirely on faith. Virgin births, the afterlife, undying love, honest politicians, peace in our time.

Let's just say this, then. The possibility of an ominous message from something other than an interoffice memo relating to downsizing, the simple chance of it meaning *something* can keep us on our toes. It can make us look out for some menace heading our way that we might otherwise miss. Although it would not miss us. As Charlie Manson—my favorite convicted mass murderer with a cross carved into his forehead—so sensitively expressed it, "Paranoia is the highest form of love."

So I noticed the four bikers who had been tailing me since the Clifton Park exit.

3

The hardest to forget
is memory

The four motorcycles roared past me. Choppers, all four. Not a Japanese name among them. No straight eye contact from any of the riders, but plenty of awareness. The hackles on the back of my neck prickled.

Storm trooper–style helmets worn far back on their heads. One-way window shades over their eyes. The perfect stereotype of the drug-smuggling, wounded-water-buffalo, mean biker gang. I should know, seeing as how that was once me. To prove it, I can show you a photo of what I looked like when I rode my Harley. Black leathers, beard, shoulder-length hair, one earring. Okay, so I still had the long hair and the earring, even if the beard is but a fond memory and the black leathers never replaced after the last time I dumped my hog and skidded fifty yards on my back down a gasoline-soaked, soon-to-be-ignited highway. But the point was that I usually held no inherent prejudice nor ominous expectations when I saw men in leathers astride 1200 or more cc's of engine.

This time, though, there was something brewing. No question about that. Though other questions did remain, some of those childhood "Wh—'s" I'd never outgrown.

I didn't see any more hawks, not with my eyes. But I could feel the wingbeats of that red-tail that had swept down. I felt its wings against my face, felt the answering throb of my heartbeat speeding up.

Softly, Jacob, softly. Wave swallows stone. Un-hunh, Sifu Huang.

The turn for the airport came up on my right. I can't say I had no choice. There were plenty of choices. Drive to Boston instead. Turn around and go back to bed. Change my name and move to Milwaukee.

Instead, I took the turn.

Driving to the Albany Airport is always a little like slipping into a time warp for me. Not because of what is there. The oldest commercial airport in America, it has a new multi-million-dollar terminal, the gateway to the Capital Region. It's because of what little remains of what was there that I share Yogi Berra's feeling of déjà vu all over again. The airport is built over what were once some of the richest farmlands on the ancient floodplain where Hudson and Mohawk meet.

When I was ten and we were living in Albany—the last place the bank sent my father—Dad and I walked those fields one autumn, shotguns over our arms to hunt pheasant. I'll never forget the morning smell of frost among the rows of corn, the sudden flutter of the pheasant's wings as it cackled up into flight. My great-grandfather's old 12-gauge bucked against my shoulder and the bird crumpled in flight and fell. The smell of cordite hung in the air as the retriever's wet mouth nuzzled my hands after dropping the bird at my feet. I remember my father's voice, speaking the old words of thanks to the pheasant for giving us its life, the warm feel of its body in my hands.

As I slowly cruised along the entrance road, a stiff-winged DC-10 roared down to screech along the blacktop runway that buried those fields where my father and I would never walk again.

The illuminated sign at the turn to the lots told me that the garage was full, the closest parking place in long-term a hundred yards from the terminal. That left plenty of space for something to happen—as I knew it would. I could see at the distant end of the lot the four motorcycles waiting, their riders still astride them.

4

Teeth are hard and decay
Tongue is soft and remains

I stopped at the gate. A ticket extruded itself with a bing, sticking out at me like a blue tongue to be pulled. As I drove through the gate, I took note that the biker boys had chosen well. All the empty spaces left in the lot were far in the back where they were waiting.

Strategies filled my mind. The first was to put the ticket into my ash-tray right now. That way when I was in the hospital recuperating from whatever Alphonse, Gaston, Rene, and Pierre (little spur-of-the-minute nicknames for my two-wheeled buddies) were about to do to me, I would not forget where I placed it and have to pay excessive parking fees after getting out of the Emergency Room.

Assuming the anxious, innocent, and slightly predatory look of a driver seeking a parking space, I cruised the lot, gradually coming closer and closer to my would-be ambushers. They were pointedly ignoring me. One was picking at his fingernails with a stiletto that appeared to be just a bit too short to use as a roasting spit for a pig. I cleared my mind of everything but one thought—why is it that no one has ever found a word to rhyme with "orange"?

The spot I chose had two advantages. It was the farthest from the bikers and next to the guardrail fence that encircled the lot, making one avenue of attack impossible to take.

The attacker is always the one at a disadvantage, Sifu Huang's voice was whispering in my memory.

I got out slowly, my bag in my hand, shut my door, and turned to face them.

18

Even though the smallest of them looked to outweigh me by twenty pounds, they moved more quickly than I'd expected. Lazy quick. That bothered me a bit. Nervous quick is more predictable. They stopped a few paces away from me and I stood with my overnight bag in my left hand.

Verbal discouragement is sometimes the best tactic for defense.

I looked Alphonse, the largest of my potential playmates, in the eye. It wasn't all that far to look up. No more than two or three feet.

"Tell the editors of *Poetry Magazine* who hired you that it won't work."

"Huh?" Alphonse said. Perhaps he was not the leader after all. I shifted my gaze to Gaston, he of the long knife now hidden behind the left hand held loosely at his side.

"Even if you break all my typing fingers, I shall still continue to submit my manuscripts."

"Cute," Gaston countered. I was right. He was clearly the brains of the group. Oscar Wilde could not have done much better in terms of witty repartee.

A sound like chalk screeking across a blackboard came from my right, where the one I thought of as Rene had slid next to the front fender of my factory-fresh Explorer. I didn't turn my head because I knew what made that sound. Rene was adding an irregular racing stripe to my fender with the sharp end of a key held so that it thrust out between the middle fingers of his clenched fist. His purpose was to distract me.

It was a smart tactic. Few things are more beloved to the average American than the finish of his new car. I should have turned, face red with anger as I yelled at him. Leaving myself nicely open to be sucker-punched or worse. I didn't turn.

"That won't work, mon ami," I said.

I rolled my shoulders, just to loosen up a little because I really *was* upset about the finish on that fender. Then I dropped my shoulder bag and took a step backward into the space between my truck and the grey Maxima next to it.

On cue, the four of them moved toward me. Just as I'd expected. But Pierre, who had materialized a lead pipe from someplace in his capacious jacket, was the first one to strike. That did surprise me. I'd been betting on Gaston. But it really didn't change anything in the geometry of my response as my shoulder bag on the ground nicely slowed Pierre's attack in that narrow space.

Just before the back of my knee touched the railing behind me, I stumbled and fell sideways. Somehow my hand came up and grasped

Pierre's pipe-wielding arm and pulled him past me. He tumbled, open-mouthed, over the railing, barely managing to break his fall with his teeth as he ate a large chunk of asphalt from the parking lot. I stepped forward and—darn it all!—tripped again, falling forward into a fast roll as Gaston thrust that knife of his like an épée toward the place where my throat had been.

My legs tangled with his and as I tried to straighten up and stand—clumsy me!—Gaston toppled forward like a chain-sawed pine. His knees struck the pavement with a very nasty crack. As I rose—like a drunken monkey confused by the havoc he is causing—it appeared that walking was not in Gaston's immediate future. Dislocated or broken kneecaps are a bitch.

Somehow his stiletto had ended up in my hand. Don't ask how. It happens. I looked at Alphonse and Rene. They were just standing there. That was unfortunate. A part of me really wanted to *do* something to Rene for what he had done to my new car. It being a mere material possession, that was an unworthy thought on my part.

"Want to see an old Indian trick?" I said.

I clapped my hands together and the stiletto disappeared. It went into my pocket, of course, but I wasn't about to tell them that. Why spoil the effect?

I spread my arms. As I did so, Alphonse threw a punch at my stomach that argued for his having been a Golden Gloves heavyweight semi-finalist. I didn't try to block it or step aside.

Remember those sit-ups? Plus a little thing called "*chi*," a way of breathing and concentrating natural energy in such a way that your body is like steel at that point?

Alphonse's fist thudded into the center of my body at the exact second that I shouted, "*Ki-yah!*"

I didn't move, but his fist bounced back fast. Alphonse looked visibly shaken. He edged away, eyes filled with the confused look of a bulldog that has just bitten into an iron bone.

"I know," I said. "I hate it when that happens."

Rene was also backing away. Too bad.

"Wait," I said to him, "aren't you going to give me the phone number of your insurance agent?"

I ran my finger along the six-inch scratch in the fender of my truck and then pointed that finger at Rene. He flinched, grabbed the shoulder of Gaston—who had struggled to his feet and was limping away stiff-legged—and pulled him toward the waiting Harleys. Alphonse and

Pierre, whose face was obscured by the red kerchief he'd shoved into his mouth to staunch the bleeding, were already there.

"Come on," Alphonse was yelling. "Come on."

Somehow I sensed that he didn't mean me, so I didn't move.

They got on the bikes and roared for the exit gate. It was understandable that they were in such a hurry. If they managed to get out of the lot in less than fifteen minutes they wouldn't have to pay any toll.

I lowered my hand. If I'd kept pointing like that much longer, I might have been mistaken for a slightly lighter-skinned version of one of those sculptured African-American jockeys so beloved to the lawns of yesteryear in Saratoga Springs. One had to be careful to avoid stereotypes.

I picked up my shoulder bag and looked at the door of my car, which I'd forgotten to lock. I pressed the lock button on my key chain and enjoyed the satisfying thud of four doors locking simultaneously.

Then I shook my head. Locking my doors was not all I'd forgotten. While getting acquainted with my now-departing buddies, I'd neglected to ask them two simple things. Who? And why?

5

A good explanation
explains nothing

I always try to arrive at airports early. It's not just the capricious threat levels set by Homeland Security that can make what used to take minutes stretch into hours. Somehow, the chaos of a place where all the people you see around will soon be hundreds of miles away from you, allows the opportunity to think. Even before I check in at the gate, I buy copies of the *Albany Times Union* and *USA Today*. Strip out the advertising inserts, the classifieds and the financial sections, and drop them into a trash can with the feeling of having shucked far more than their weight in paper and ink. And with a momentary regret, as usual, because there are no recycling bins.

After that, I go through the metal detector. When I hand my ticket and photo ID to the gate agent, I wait patiently for the latest wording of the questions that will accept nothing but simple, straightforward— usually yes or no—answers. No ad libs, no funny ha-ha's unless you enjoy the intimacy of a strip search or the revocation of your flying privileges.

The necessary preflight protocol completed, I sit down, my bag under my feet. I read the sports section of both newspapers and place them on the floor or an empty seat for some other traveler to pick up. I do the same with the first sections. It's like scaling and boning a fish until nothing is left but the fine filet—the crossword puzzles.

The world of crosswords is a small and secure one. It's a place where there always are answers and seldom, if ever, mistakes. You can count on certain things. For example, "A Guthrie" (four letters) will always be "Arlo." And as my pencil point fills in the empty spaces, my mind is free to pursue other paths, to think beneath the surface. It isn't conscious thinking, but I often find that after completing a crossword—Bingo!—the answer to some larger, more open-ended conundrum of my everyday life will appear.

So it was that morning. I filled in both of the crosswords in the *Times Union*, located as always on the comic pages. Thanks be to the gods of syndication for granting us the left-brained dementia of "Bizarro." One consolation for the deeply mourned departure of "The Far Side." Then, even faster than usual, I whipped through the *USA Today* puzzle. Arlo was there. So was Fred Astaire's sister with a sea eagle hovering over her head.

I looked up. It was not yet time for my flight to Boston and no answers had come to me. No little light bulb over my head. No need to leap up from my bath and run naked through the Greek streets. I sighed. Time for conscious consideration.

I took out the pad that I used to solve really big crimes and write my first drafts of really bad poems. Purely by accident, I have been published a few times in literary magazines with names that may give you a clue to the size of their readership. Ever heard of *Big Swamp Quarterly*? But more often than not, almost more often than always, my submissions have been rewarded with polite, impolite, or excessively offensive rejection slips. I gratefully reward the rejecting editors with a plethora of further opportunities to make up more insults such as "Give up poetry and spend your time in something more fruitful like coaching Little League." I've always been a fan of good sarcasm.

That morning, my pad had two drafts of a new poem on it and not a single page devoted to a really big crime. I flipped to a clean sheet.

Starting off with a list is my first rule. Just writing it all down is a beginning, if nothing else. So I wrote as follows:

1. Bad dream.
2. Phone call from Dennis (overheard by ?).
3. Hovering hawks.
4. Ambush by 4 bad guys.

I drew a line connecting point 2 to point 4. The bruised bikers had appeared too quickly for them not to have been tipped off that I would be on my way to the airport. Possibly they were an immediate result of Dennis's overheard call—maybe too immediate.

I've learned that real life doesn't move with the neat mechanical precision of a *Mission Impossible* plot. It's more ragged and uncertain around the edges. Gears don't mesh, wooden shoes fall into the machinery. The hit man that the villain hires gets lost in traffic or decides to just take the advance given him and get drunk. Your own surveillance expert turns out to be unavailable at the drop of a hat because his kid has an ear infection. And your first logical assumption about anything may turn out to be wrong.

Was there enough time for their appearance to be connected to my summons to Abenaki Island? Were Alphonse, Gaston, Rene, and Pierre brought together at the drop of a hat or helmet because of overhearing that request for help from my oldest friend—or had they been after me well before that morning?

I looked at my list again and added to it.

5. My colorful past.

That also made some sense. The four heavies could have been hired a month ago to beat me up at the first possible opportunity (after being given my approximate location, physical description, and license number). They could have acted because of something I'd done at some point between taking up my current profession and going to bed last night.

If, for example, you have rescued a teenager from a new religious group more unforgiving than a Scientologist miffed by a scathing review of L. Ron Hubbard's last sci-fi novel, you may find some heavy payback heading your way.

I lifted up the pencil, paused, shook my head. Not enough pages to list all those who might have varying degrees of retribution in mind. Nor enough lead in the pencil.

I looked back at my list and drew another line. Between point 1 and point 2. And could think of nothing logical to add.

6

Expect nothing
Be glad when you get it

That mental blankness stayed with me as I ambled through the gate. Down the jet bridge, across the nose bridge. Nodded to the nice flight attendants. Good morning, sir. We sincerely hope that we will not all perish today in a twisted and burning mass of molten metal and plastic. Good morning. Good morning.

Seat 13 C. Shoulder bag under the seat in front of me. Buckled the seat belt. No crossword puzzles left, so I constructed my cone of silence to discourage conversation from the nervous businessman to my left. *I am deaf,* I thought. *I cannot speak.*

It didn't work.

He leaned over so that I could better smell his cologne, his breath mint, and the faint smell of fear sweat that betrayed the uncertain traveler.

"So," he said, his voice a good one for selling you that insurance policy you have *always* wanted, "where to?"

I didn't answer. I opened my pad to an empty page that was destined to be filled with a really good poem this time. And why not? I was off to an excellent start. After all, every great poem always used to begin with an empty page of paper—before the inventions of computer screens, spray paint, and refrigerator magnets.

He leaned closer, his shoulder firmly against mine. "I mean," he said, in that voice used for slow children and fast-food workers, "where are you going, buddy?"

No use anymore pretending I was deaf because I recalled that he had been right in line behind me when I bought my ticket from the gate agent.

I lifted the index finger of my left hand.

"Up," I said, "and then down. Gradually, I hope."

His eyes focused on my bear paw earring, my long hair, my less than Brooks Brothers attire. He swallowed once and then swiveled his head toward the window passenger to his left. In no time at all they had struck up a merry conversation about equity and bearer bonds and I had closed my eyes contemplating the first line of my poem.

When I opened them again, an hour had passed. The only line on the page was the drool from my gaping mouth. The seat belt light was on and we were descending—much less gradually than I preferred.

Lest you get me wrong, I am not afraid of flying in the same way that I am not afraid of guns. It all depends on whose hands are on the controls or the trigger. But having been through flight school myself, I may be a bit too aware of the various margins of error that exist. That's why I always take an aisle seat. I don't want to watch what is happening outside the window. Even so, I can always see in my mind's eye the airport floating into view, dauntingly tiny from our distance and height.

I envision the threshold lights, the chevrons of the overrun area and the nonprecision approach markings as we reach the landing threshold. Visual approach indicator lights are blinking, runway edge markings now clearly in sight. There is the centerline stripe. Then comes the shudder of the jet engine, its apocalyptic roar increasing, air inlets and compressor fans working overtime while the compression chamber gulps air and fuel as we are about to touch down—one way or another!

Thump, a slight bounce, the screech of wheels and brakes and we were taxiing toward the terminal. Noooo problem. It had not bothered me one whit. Though I was holding a splintered pencil in my right hand.

Welcome to Boston. Right!

A short, wobbly-legged walk later and I was at the commuter air link gate where I would board the dragonfly that would flutter me to my final destination. *Final destination.* Yes, George Carlin, not the most encouraging choice of words.

But I was no longer as filled with foreboding about the next flight. Smaller planes had always bothered me less than big jets. Somehow, feeling the wind move the plane around as it bobbed and weaved and skirted the mountain slopes had always made me feel more secure. There were few flights I'd enjoyed more than one I'd taken four years ago into the brunt of a wolf-toothed Alaskan wind with a bush pilot buddy.

I relaxed, watching the airport grow small beneath us as we took off. On that pencil-thin plane every seat was a window one. We left behind the bay and the brick building blocks of that city where Brahmin transcendentalists flirted with Buddhism more than a century before the birth of the Maharishi. The suburbs melted back into the land. Then the square, planted fields were left behind as we floated over hills and more hills.

Linguists wrote that Massachussetts, an intelligible word to my native ancestors before it was re-spelled by tin-eared Europeans, meant "to the great and small hills." Maybe.

The plane banked, headed northeast toward even greater hills and some of the tallest mountains in our Land of the Dawn. High living summits now named for dead presidents. Ancestors wiser than I will probably ever be said they could hear our mountains sing. I believe that.

> If I could write down
> the song of the mountains,
> that song would be
> a deathless poem.
>
> But if I could
> write down that song,
> if I knew enough
> to hear the words of mountains
> and put them into human speech,
> I would also know enough
> not to write it down.

I looked at the words I'd written on my pad. Sometimes even not saying something is saying too much. I shook my head, tore off the page, crumpled it up . . . and then stuck it into my vest pocket.

7

*The eyes see more
or less than the mirror*

Dennis Mitchell was at the airport that was built on a slightly larger scale than Dennis himself. To say he stands out in a crowd is like saying a pine tree is bigger than a petunia. Everything about Dennis is big, his broad shoulders and chest that strain the fabric of a 3XL sweatshirt, his bear paw hands, his snowshoe-sized feet, everything except those little pieces of shrapnel still inside him, including the one near his heart—the one he stubbornly refused to allow them to remove by surgery, even though they told him it was likely to migrate into the aorta and kill him one day.

Then we had swept past the terminal and my thoughts turned away from my best friend's death wish to concern for my own mortality as the little plane dropped like a string-cut puppet to trampoline the runway in bounces that jolted my liver up past my tonsils.

A-boing, urrrk, a-boing, urrrk, a-boing, urrrk . . . and so on.

Dennis was at the arrival doorway by the time I got out of the plane. The passengers ahead of me still had to turn sideways to get past him, even after he had politely stepped aside.

"Podjo," he roared, a broad smile on his face crinkling the laugh lines around his eyes. "Better landing than usual today?"

I threw my shoulder bag at him.

It was a two-hour drive to the Island. There was plenty of time to talk. I had my pad in my lap and my pencil in hand to take notes and look for clues.

But for the first half-hour, what I listened to was devoid of any clues other than those about my big buddy's musical tastes. There was a CD player in the jeep and Dennis had loaded it with a new mix tape. First, the rock band Big Head Todd and the Monsters. That little Navajo boy could sing. Then it was "Against the Wind," followed by "I Won't Back Down," "Dancing with Myself," and "Born in the USA." As the last of the Boss's beats faded, Dennis delicately reached out a sausage-sized finger to flick off the sound system.

"It's that bad?" I said. Dennis's song mix had sent a clear message of defiance.

Dennis sighed. "You know what's been going on?"

I thought I knew. Although it would take volumes with exceedingly small type to explain it all, it was basically about us and them. Us and Them and the Land.

"Us" being the Indians who are still here.

"Them" being the current owners, private and governmental, of the land that owned our ancestors. The same "them" who have kept up the twin legalized fictions that the land our ancestors owned was legally appropriated and/or that we are not really the descendants of our own ancestors from whom said land was taken.

The land being that same land which had indeed been fraudulently conveyed, coerced, and stolen from our ancestors. In the late twentieth century, there had been some redress. Like the sacred Blue Lake being returned to one of the Pueblo nations. In Maine and in Alaska, huge Native land claims had been successfully pursued. Especially by the lawyers who made out like bandits. Though, now that I think of it, the simile is oxymoronic. Still, those could all be counted as wins for the "us" side.

But there was yet another element in the "us" part of the equation, namely doubt about us really being us.

Although we knew who we were and had enjoyed (more or less) an organized tribal government for a decade, our particular branch of the Abenaki people was unrecognized. Belonging to an unrecognized tribe is like being a squatter on your own land, like being evicted from the place where you have always lived. Though it is not even that simple. It involves being told that you're not a real Abenaki because everyone knows Abenakis died out a century ago—and at the same time being looked down on by your surrounding non-Native neighbors because of your Indian blood.

If you've got a drinking problem, everyone knows it's because "you Indians can't handle alcohol." But try to claim any aboriginal rights and the rapid reply is "we all know you people are just fake Indians."

It can lead past resentment to terminal cases of confusion, or self-loathing, or to what Dennis and I developed by the time we were in our teens—an ironic sense of humor that few people appreciated as much as we did.

Imagine us in the line at the Dartmouth student cafeteria as we observed one of the items being offered was rooted in our cultural traditions.

Dennis saying, "Look, Powhatan, it is Corn."

Me replying, "No, Squanto, *they* call it Corn."

Then the two of us chanting together, "*We* call it Maize!"

And no one laughing but us.

Now, though, it seemed it might all be about to change. With the help of several Harvard lawyers endeavoring to assist us (and their own investment portfolios), we were in the midst of petitioning for recognition. Their hope was that our fate would not be the same as the Wampanoags of Mashpee, who were told that they were no longer a tribe, although they had been a tribe once . . . no, actually three times. Apparently, they spent decades flickering into and out of existence like one of those trick birthday candles that rekindles after it is extinguished. The takeover of the Mountain, if not planned by those lawyers, was playing into their hands. Get enough public attention to get it into court with a case based on Aboriginal title.

So all we had to do was keep up the takeover long enough to go to court, win the case, and then get federal recognition for our tribal government. Except that there were now some Penacooks no longer backing the current tribal government. The most vocal ones had actually talked about breaking away and forming a new tribe. That bickering alone should have been enough to prove to anyone that we really were Indians.

Look, Grey Elk, we are about to win.

Ah, in that case let us begin to divide and fight among ourselves.

Then there was the issue of gaming. Ever hear of that? If not, then you are neither a Pequot, a high roller, nor an offshore investor from Indonesia. If we could get recognition, then we would have the right to set up gambling. Build a little Las Vegas among our sacred hills.

Indian gambling has been called by some, for example Russell Means (aka Pocahontas's Disneyfied Papa Powhatan), the "new buffalo." It has meant money and jobs—and not just for the Indians whose land hosts the casinos. Indian nations whose people were among the poorest and most chronically unemployed of all Americans have been given some hope. Not all. Less than 25 percent of Indian reservations have gaming. And on places like Pine Ridge in South Dakota, which does not have a casino, the life expectancy is shorter than anywhere else in the United States.

So I'm not opposed to Indian gambling, especially if the money from it actually goes to the Indians and that money is used for the right things. Like the Pequots building new homes for their people who lived in shacks and rundown trailers before. Putting together a museum and giving away big grants to other worthy Indian causes. All right, red brothers.

Except the thought of a mini Lost Wages here, on the Island, or on the Mountain, troubled me. I felt a little sick thinking about it, sort of the way you feel after you've been hungry a long time and then you're given all the rich food you can eat.

Some said that the governor of our fair state was on the side of the gaming faction. He was just waiting for the right time to step in and lend a hand. Once the right deal was cut, he would make sure that plenty of the gambling revenues went into the state coffers. After all, he was a Republican, not one of them Democratic commies like Governor Howard Dean in Vermont who opposed the introduction of casinos so vehemently after spending millions of dollars fighting the St. Francis Abenakis' bid for the state recognition they had briefly enjoyed before it was snatched away from them.

But months and then two years had passed without any tangible support from the state government. Our people (and, to repeat, our lawyers) had grown impatient and that had led to Mikwe's decision to occupy peacefully the abandoned state park.

Violence, they say, solves nothing. Does that mean that nonviolence solves everything? In ten words or less, explain how Mahatma Gandhi won back India from the British. What were the goals of Martin Luther King?

I know, these are questions that stump most college students these days. Gandhi? King? Who they? But then again maybe you've seen the eponymous movies and so you know that long before film producer and actor Steven Segal ever opened a bully's third eye with a corkscrew there were people who believed that risking their lives while doing no harm to others could produce a greater good.

Being philosophically between the venerable Segal (now revealed as the incarnation of a Tibetan monkey, oops, monk) and MLK (whose indiscreet tastes in private suites left him exposed) I had my doubts about the takeover. But it had begun in early spring and now, in mid-summer, was still going on with a lot of support from our tribe—many of whom had turned out to place their bodies in peril by doing such things as linking arms to block the road when the state police first tried to end the takeover. Said staties were deterred not so much by those Native protesters as by the fact that the news crews had gotten there first. With reelection coming up and the possibility of even higher office in his future, the governor had given the order to pull back rather than have images of Indians being clubbed by cops on his watch.

Not that all of our people supported the takeover of the Mountain. Some opposed it on traditional grounds. A sacred place should not be the site of conflict. I could respect that. Others, though against the creation of a separate Pencook tribe, a sort of Penacook 2.0, eyed the tribal council and the chieftaincy as their own destinies and wanted nothing more than the takeover to fail so that they could ascend to power. Then there was the pro-gaming faction, gambling on the hope that with recognition they could attract offshore backers to bankroll another Foxwoods-style resort in our woods. They were sort of supporters and sort of not—having been upset by Mikwe's frequent assertions that we wanted land and recognition, not casinos. Of those three groups, it was the gamblers that I saw as the most likely to have hired the bikers sent to either discourage or disembowel me.

There were so many players, so many historical and hysterical ins and outs in our current case, that feeling merely dizzy when considering the issues meant that one was in relative equilibrium.

Things were not in balance.

Now, from the serious tone in my best friend's voice, it seemed as if that balance might have been tipped even further toward chaos.

"You know what's been going on," Dennis said again. "But you don't know what's just happened."

As he spoke, he was carefully cleaning his glasses with the large red handkerchief he always carried, holding the steering wheel steady with his knees. Don't you just love people who drive like that at eighty miles an hour? But at least he wasn't reading a book while he drove. I had taken *Playing Indian* away from him and tossed it into the backseat half an hour ago.

"I thought I knew what was going on," I said. "But now I guess I don't. What's happened now?"

"Somebody got killed," he said. "That's why the Children of the Mountain asked for you."

8

To see the mountain,
be the mountain

The Children of the Mountain.

The name sent a tingle down my back, even though I knew it just referred this time to what Mikwe and the other Indian occupiers called their group that had taken over the campsite. Somewhere within the walls of my memory I heard again Aunt Mali's voice begin the telling as I leaned closer to catch every word, every inflection, every breath.

Long ago a girl was out picking blueberries. She was strong and good-looking, this girl. But she had not yet been able to choose a husband. So, as she picked the berries, stripping them from the bushes, like so, like so, she was thinking. It would be good to find a fine man, she was thinking. As she thought this, she lifted her eyes up to the top of Wonbi Wadzoak, the big white mountain. It rose there above her.

I would like to find a man, she thought, as tall and strong as the mountain.

Then, as suddenly as if he had come out of the earth, a man was there in front of her. He was taller than any man this girl had ever seen. He was handsome and looked strong. The only thing strange about him were his eyebrows. They were gray and looked to be made of stone.

"If you wish it," he said, "I will be your husband."

The girl could hardly speak. Finally she managed to draw a breath. "I wish it," she said.

The tall man took her hand. "Come with me to my place in the mountain."

"That is too far to walk," the young woman said.

"You do not have to walk," the tall man said. He bent and picked her up. He took one step and they had traveled halfway to the mountain. Another step and they were at the bottom of the mountain. A third step and they were halfway up the mountain. A fourth step and they were within the mountain's heart.

The young woman lived with her husband inside the mountain. He was a mighty hunter and provided plenty of food for them and skins to make clothing. He was kind to her. Their life was good together. One day, she gave birth to twins, a boy and a girl. They were just like ordinary children except for one thing. Like their father, their eyebrows were gray stone. They had special power. They were the Children of the Mountain.

"They got in touch with me," Dennis said. "Just before I called you last night. Lines in to the camp been cut by the state police. Mikwe made a rule against cell phones right from the start, since he figured that the police could just pick up the frequency and listen in. Nearest landline is at the county store a quarter-mile away. Anyone can leave anytime they want, walk right past the roadblock. But no one is allowed to go back in. So that pay phone just past the state police barricade is supposed to be like a lure to draw them out. That and Coca-Cola, pork rinds, and Twinkies in the store. Except there's another pay phone five miles farther down the main road. All anyone has to do is sneak through the forest to get to it." He smiled. "The staties may be hell on wheels, but when it comes to going into the woods, forget about it."

Dennis tapped the steering wheel with his hand. The double beat of the heart and the drum. His chin nodded up and down. I thought he was about to start singing a greeting song. Then he nodded.

"It was Mikwe himself who called me at the Tribal Office. Said he didn't trust anyone else, like he didn't trust anybody else but me and you to come in and help."

That surprised me. I had some history with Mikwe.

Dennis saw it in my eyes. "Yup, I know. But Mikwe's not exactly the same as he was before, partner. And despite it all, he always respected you."

That I found harder to swallow than one of the frozen Meals Ready to Eat (MREs) that were all we had in the hilltop outpost near the Khyber Pass, where one weekend Dennis and I spent what seemed like a month holding off the Taliban. But I let it go because I had a question.

"So why were you at the Tribal Office that late at night to begin with?"

"We'd agreed I'd be there two nights a week—at a time when no one else was likely to be around. Mikwe figured it was important for him to be able to check in like that after the first death."

The first death?

"Whoa! You mean there's been another? Who was the first to get killed?"

Dennis elaborated. "Just a week ago. The poor guy was chewed up so bad everyone thought it was an animal. Passamaquoddy named Jock Sockabasin. They figured maybe he got between a mother bear and her cubs. You know there's no wild animal left in the whole state that would attack a human being for no reason. Even though the wolves are sneaking back in, we know they wouldn't never hurt no one."

"Nothing in the papers or on the news about it."

"No. Guess why?" Dennis cleared his throat and spat out the window.

"Reason for the medical examiners and the state police to move in?"

"Unh-hunh. So they sneaked the body out through the woods. Drove all the way over to Pleasant Point. Explained to his family that Sockabasin died for the cause and how it would be bad if it got out that anyone got killed, even by accident, at Camp Freedom. His family agreed to say it happened to him while he was out hunting and that a pack of wild dogs got him."

"Shit."

"Unh-hunh."

"But the second death was different?"

"Micmac woman name of Louise Brooks. Went out to gather herbs late in the afternoon and didn't come back. By the way, you know there's Micmacs and Penobscots and Passamaquoddies there. Almost more of them than our own people. Showing solidarity for the cause. Even a few Mohawk warriors who are veterans of the Oka standoff."

Dennis paused for a moment, looking down at his hands as if he wished he were holding a knife and a piece of wood to carve instead of a steering wheel.

"Louise Brooks was an older woman. Quiet, respected. She really knew tradition and she even thought she had an idea about what had happened to Sockabasin—though she wouldn't tell anyone what that idea was. She went out, looking for herbs and mushrooms, she said. Said she'd be back before dark, but she wasn't. Next day, soon as it was light, they found her trail. She'd marked it by bending branches into little circles as she went. It led up the mountain and then . . . there was a lot of blood. It was easy to follow the blood trail. It led straight down the mountain and right up to where one of the state police roadblocks was set up. The staties already found her body by the time any of the Children of the Mountain got there. It wasn't hard, seeing as how what was left of her was dragged right into the middle of the road."

"What was left of her?"

"She'd been killed like Sockabasin." Dennis pressed his foot down harder on the gas pedal and the jeep picked up speed. "Except this time the body'd been partially eaten."

Eaten, I thought. A strange thought was coming into my head, but I didn't say anything.

"The state police didn't see the tracks. Mikwe did, even though he never pointed them out to the police. He never listened as closely to Tom as you and I did, but you know he's a pretty decent tracker. He said those prints started on some soft earth far enough back from the roadblock that they weren't visible from the paved road. Those tracks led down and then back up toward the Mountain. Big prints, real big. Not the tracks of a bear or a wolf or a lynx or anything else that walks on four legs. What Mikwe told me was that they looked like the footprints of a barefooted human being."

9

*Every road
goes nowhere*

Ilooked at the pad in my lap. I know that all Indians are supposed to have perfect, photographic memories. In my case, the prints of them get lost far too often. I write things down. Not much, just enough to give me the sort of cue into deeper memory the way that the designs on our wampum belts kept our histories alive long before we were invaded by alphabets.

All that I had jotted down thus far was a list of names.

1. Mikwe
2. Jock Sockabasin
3. Louise Brooks
4. Mikwe
5. Barefoot Giant

Item 5 presented a problem for me. The first four were identifiable, Mikwe's name appearing twice, as it had in Dennis's narrative. The fifth name, though, was a mystery. True, I might have listed it by another name, but that name was mere conjecture, as well as something that I didn't want to record or say out loud yet.

It is like talking about snakes at night in Africa. In Ghana, for example, you don't say the name "snake" after dark. It is like inviting a snake to visit you. Instead, you say "the stick that moves."

Or like talking about bears when you are in bear country. Our old people said that bears don't like you to talk about them. Just mention

38

their name and they might carry you off with them or take revenge in some other way. If you want to be safe, if you want to show respect, you must say "the one who walks like us," or "the black one."

So it was that I chose the less obvious, and less evocative, in listing item number 5.

"Which way, Boss?"

Dennis was lifting his foot off the gas pedal. We had reached the crossroads.

Any one of the three choices ahead of us could lead to Indian Island. As would the two or three forks in the twenty or so miles of road yet ahead of us, whichever way we went. The choice was ours. There was a stop sign ahead of us. No traffic in sight coming from either direction to right or left. No one behind us on the road.

There's this Indian joke. What does a Mormon do when he comes to a stop sign in the middle of the desert with no one else around for miles? Answer: he stops. What does a Catholic do? It really doesn't matter. Whatever he does, he'll feel guilty about it.

Dennis, of course, was starting to speed up again. I raised my hand slightly.

"Wait," I said. "Pull over."

Dennis did as I asked without asking why. He scratched his chin and then pointed at the key.

"Yeah," I said.

Dennis turned off the ignition. Then he took off his glasses and started to clean them.

I put the pad down and got out of the jeep. I walked once around the jeep, just looking at it. Nothing suspicious in plain sight. I eliminated both bumpers. On the verge of falling off, they wouldn't be a logical choice. Look to the least unrusted place. Easily accessible, chillingly out of sight. I reached in under the back wheel well on the passenger side. Bingo!

It was no more difficult to pry off than a refrigerator magnet and not much larger. The wonders of microtechnology. I held it up so that Dennis could see it. He raised an eyebrow. Oh my!

Oh my, indeed.

Less than twenty-four hours had passed since I had lain me down to sleep. I had already been pursued by dread in my dreams, summoned on a mysterious mission, bruised by bikers (well, there was a nasty little purple mark on my right shin from Gaston's boot buckle when I swept his legs out from under him), confronted with a cannibalistic conundrum. And now tracked by a transmitter. It was all alarmingly ambiguous.

I looked at the deceptively innocent piece of microcircuitry glittering in my palm. Dennis pointed to his mouth.

"No," I said. "It can't hear us. It just sends off a tracking signal."

"Isn't it nice to be wanted?" Dennis said. Nothing ever made him nervous.

This made *me* nervous. Especially since seeing the why of it suggested the eventual what. Simple logic. Process of elimination. If they knew who we were—and of course they did or else why bug us, then they knew where we were going. It wasn't our planned destination that interested them then. It was the route we were taking through the maze of roads that spider-webbed their way to Indian Island.

It meant there has to be two teams. One behind us with the receiver, plotting the course we were taking, and the other ahead of us. Tracker team. Clean-up crew. The two in contact by mobile phone. Team Two only moving to intercept when we had committed ourselves to a stretch of road long enough and lonely enough for them to set up an ambush.

"Houston," I said, "We have a problem. And us without any guns."

A smile illuminated the brown balloon that passed for my friend Dennis's face.

"Guns?" he said.

He liked saying that so much he repeated it as he pulled out a Ruger .22 with a banana clip from beneath the blanket on the back seat.

"Guns."

Then a Winchester 30.06, semi-automatic with a 12-power scope.

"Guns!"

Followed by a 12-gauge Remington pump, full choke. I was smiling now myself. I held my hand up before Dennis could dig any further to disclose an AK-47, a Browning Automatic Rifle, or a Gatling Gun. Or continue his extemporaneous ode to firearms that was beginning to match Poe's obsession with bells.

"Okay," I said.

Dennis then pressed the button on the glove compartment with his little finger. The door fell open to disclose enough boxes of cartridges for us to lay siege to Fort Number Four.

"And ammunition," he added unnecessarily.

10

*Lines on maps—
less than tracks on the earth*

As I drove, Dennis studied the topo. My guess was that we had no more than ten minutes to unsettle whatever was being set up for us.

"Next right, Podjo."

Anyone who hadn't grown up around here as we did might not have seen anything more than birch trees and maples, rocks and hills. But there it was, just as I remembered it, a barely visible ribbon of brown earth where trail bikes had kept the center of the old logging road clear.

I slowed, dropped the jeep into four-wheel. The treads thumped over the rough shoulder, caught in the leaf litter and spun us up the slope, past a huge beech and then out of sight of the main road.

Dennis held the map over so I could see it. He tapped on the concentric circles indicating a rise in elevation. I smiled because I knew that spot well. I'd walked this same road some two decades ago before when I was a thirteen-year-old kid tagging along behind Uncle Tom Nicola.

Tom was my "Uncle" in the Indian way, not a "blood" relation in the shallow way that majority culture measures kinship, but a trusted uncle, indeed. One who took seriously the job of guiding a spirit-wounded boy to manhood. It was autumn. Together we'd been following the tracks of a big deer. We'd seen the small maple where it had scraped the velvet from its horns and we knew it was a buck.

But we knew more about that particular deer. Tom had been watching that same buck all summer and into the early autumn. He had sung to it. He had told it what we intended to do. He had asked it to give its life to his nephew.

The jeep rocked from side to side over the hidden stones in the trail. Those would not be fun for anyone following us in a vehicle lower to the ground than ours. We bounced past a pine tree whose split top I remembered, even though it was larger now by two decades. Lower branches which had been green with needles back then were now dry stubs. But the roots were still living.

That was where Tom had knelt. He'd swept away dry pine needles with the side of his hand. Then he'd traced the shapes in the earth. A straight line for trail we followed. Then a curving shape like a uncoiled fern.

"This is how our old brother, that deer, is gonna go. He knows we are following him. So he is gonna swing back, watch this trail from a high place."

I nodded. I had learned not to ask questions with words when Tom was teaching me. He'd tell me what I needed to know.

"So what do we do?" Tom said.

I shifted the unscoped .308 to my other arm, reached out and drew a second line off the trail, a line that curved above the track followed by the buck.

"Wligen," Tom said. "Good."

By cutting up and back, we'd be looking down on the buck as it waited for us to come up the trail we'd left.

The trail was more stone than earth now. Even the heavy treads of the jeep were not leaving much of a track that would be discernable to the untrained eye. I stopped the jeep by a large flat-topped boulder, took the transmitter out of my pocket, and put it on the big stone. Then I placed the page I'd taken from my pad next to the transmitter and put a rock on top of the page, arranged it so that it would not obscure my neatly printed words. Spur of the minute, but apropos. The last words, some graveyard humorists have said, of Joyce Kilmer, a poet killed in World War I.

> I think that I shall never see
> A sniper hiding in a tree . . .

I backed the jeep up a hundred yards, then pulled it off the road, Dennis walking backward behind me, strewing sticks and leaf litter over the wheel marks where we'd left the old logging road.

With the jeep well concealed behind a jumble of rocks, we chose our weapons. Dennis took the scoped 30.06. I shouldered the .22. Then we began to climb.

It had been a good spring for the grouse people. We jumped three different flocks. Each one with a mother who tried to decoy us with a feigned broken wing while her little brown offspring fluttered into the underbrush and hunkered down to wait. By the time we were halfway to the vantage point I'd picked out, we could hear the roar of an engine. Dumber than I'd thought. Our trackers hadn't even considered waiting to see if we were coming back out.

Their progress through the woods was marked not merely by the revving of the engine but by other sounds: the painful screech of an undercarriage hanging up on granite, the thud and clank of a muffler as it bid its final farewell to the exhaust system from whence it came.

These guys were either really dumb or really determined.

I looked over at Dennis. He was sitting with his back against the tree next to me, facing behind us. The barrel of the 30.06 lay in the curve between right bicep and brachioradialis, the trigger guard in his lap, the recoil pad just touching the earth. He'd remembered to bring a piece of wood he'd been carving with him. He wasn't looking at the piece of wood as he worked it. But a shape was appearing as small shavings thwicked off to rejoin the mull and mor of the forest. I could already see the four legs, the slope of the back, the uplifted head of a doe.

It was a doe that came first into that clearing by the rock. I didn't raise my gun, but my breathing deepened. I knew that the doe would always come out first. The buck would follow. In the cold autumn air I could feel the warmth of Tom's breath beside me. I could hear the very soft song that he was singing. It was barely loud enough for the wind to hear, but loud enough for the deer.

Rustle of fallen golden leaves, sound of hooves. Hop hornbeam saplings rattle and part. Head down, slow steps, then quick. Slow steps. Pause. Raise its head.

The buck stood in full view and looked up toward us.

I pressed my thumb against the safety inside the trigger guard, filled the open sights with the buck's shoulder.

Thank you, *my thirteen-year-old voice whispered hoarsely. Then I squeezed the trigger.*

Dennis nudged my elbow. My eyes from another decade came back into focus. He was pointing downslope with his lips. Then his mouth moved to shape a silent word. *Company.*

11

*The hilltops see
in all directions*

The vehicle rumbled and scraped its way up to the big rock. A Toyota Camry. Canary yellow. Then the engine either stalled or the occupants of the mufflerless car decided they had done enough damage to the delicate bones of their middle ears.

Three doors opened and three men got out. One held what looked like an Uzi. The other two were armed with short-barreled Berettas. No real range to those handguns, but highly recommended for use within six inches of the nape of the neck.

None of them were dressed for off-road exercise. Nice shiny black city shoes. Almost like cop shoes. Two wore off-the-rack gray suits with turtle necks. The rifleman had on a Hard Rock Cafe T-shirt. Maybe a sign of lower social status. We detectives learn to interpret such sartorial clues.

Gray Suit One walked up to the rock and stared at my note. A true fan of poetry, he couldn't pry his eyes off it. Perhaps if I revealed myself now, he would ask me to autograph it. Or perhaps not—as he uttered a postmodernist expletive, grabbed my carefully printed note, and tore it in half.

At that point, sensitive as I am about poetry, I let go with the Ruger. Crackety-crack-crack-crack-crack-crack.

I didn't shoot all *that* fast. A banana clip in a .22 Ruger tends to jam when one empties the clip too quickly. The right front tire sensed that its mission on the earth was over and collapsed in despair as a neat little pattern of holes stitched its way through its sidewall, up across the fender and then into the Toyota's windshield, which deconstructed itself into shiny popcorn-sized pellets of plexiglass. Those .22 slugs may be little, but they are hot and mean at the rippling point of impact.

BWAM! The .306 bucked against Dennis's shoulder and the right back tire exploded.

The three men reacted quickly. Trained professionals. The T-shirted driver promptly shot a hole into his own foot with his rifle at the exact moment when the windshield became one with the larger cosmos.

The looks on the faces of Gray Suit One and Gray Suit Two hardened. Ducking down into two-handed marksman crouches they swung their guns right in our direction.

By then, both Dennis and I had ducked down below the protective brow of the hill. Bullets whizzed overhead into the low overhead branches of the pines. A single beech leaf was clipped from its stem and came floating down to land on my chest.

POP! POP! POP!

POP! POP!

POP! POP! POP!

POP! POP!

Then the shooting stopped.

I rolled to my right to peer out from a different vantage point. The car was still there, but the three men were gone. I cupped my hands over my ears and listened. I heard the faint sound of running feet—limping feet—moving away from us down the logging road toward the highway.

I looked at Dennis. He was removing twigs from his hair and pine needles from his lower lip.

"Just when we were starting to have fun," I said.

Dennis raised an eyebrow and shrugged. He took off his glasses and cleaned them. Then he motioned with his chin down the trail.

Why not? Just because trouble was running away from me didn't mean I had to let it get away.

"Got a date," I said. "Bring the jeep."

I handed Dennis the .22. Extra weight can slow a man down. Then I ran down the slope.

There is a way of running in the woods. I try to run that way. Sometimes I think I almost succeed. Maybe you can learn it by watching the deer. Or maybe not. The only way to know is to try for a very long time. Watching the deer. Running.

And as I ran, even though I was off the trail, I didn't make much noise. Not half as much as those who were ahead of me and moving less than half as fast.

I caught the limping man first. His friends weren't waiting for him. Who waits for a driver? In his mingled pain and despair, he'd already lost the gun. A gentle shove from behind and he went sprawling down face first with a moan.

I didn't try to knock him out. People only do that in the movies or in books whose authors don't realize the delicacy, as well as the toughness, of the human skull and its carefully cushioned pink-packed sponge of a brain. Some people never wake up from a serious concussion.

My knee in the moaning man's back, I pulled the lock-bladed buck knife from the sheath on my belt and cut his t-shirt into strips. Then I tied his hands behind his back.

As I did so, it dawned on me that there was a pattern to his moaning. Words. Words I could not understand. Maybe what? A little voice in my memory chose a language. Romanian. I rolled him over, sat him up. He opened his mouth to disclose a set of bad teeth that definitely suggested Eastern Bloc dentistry.

"Who sent you?"

He shook his head. Not in disagreement, though. Just no understanding. His was the look of the recent and more than likely illegal immigrant.

He groaned as I levered off the shoe that was leaking blood. The wound wasn't bad. The small-caliber bullet had punched its way between the large metatarsals. I wrapped another piece of T-shirt around his foot as he whispered a few more unintelligible words to me.

Either thanks in Romanian or recognition that he was in an HMO that didn't cover any medical problems below the waist.

I stood up and started running again. Ministering to the T-shirt man from Transylvania hadn't taken long. It was still two miles to the road by the logging trail. Half that distance as the crow flies or the Abenaki runs. Men who wear black loafers in the woods do not leave the trails. Even when attempting to exit pursued by a bear. There was still time to angle through the woods and get ahead of them. Cut across Shorty. That's what Miss Lucy said in the song.

So I did just that.

12

Appearances are deceiving
Disappearances are worse

Two jogging men with slippery street shoes make an interesting spectacle on the uncertain footing of an abandoned logging road slick with leaves and strewn with sticks. I had no doubt that they had, at first, tried to look behind them and to the sides as they ran. Not a wise idea for one unused to such trails. The mud smears on Gray Suit One's shoulder and face showed the inevitable results of such inattention. The torn knees of Gray Suit Two's polyester slacks also bore witness to a similar pratfall or two. So they were jogging now, their eyes straight ahead on the path.

They both still had their guns. I could see now that both of them were bigger than I, taller and broader. And their faces looked to be more pissed than panicked. It appeared they were trying to stay together as they jogged, but Gray Suit Two, the heavier one, was breathing harder and falling back.

As luck would have it, a space of about fifty feet had opened between them by the time they passed my place of concealment. Just enough space for Gray Suit One to round a bend in the trail and go out of sight of his buddy. All of the animals have lessons to teach us. From *bihtahlo*, the long-tail one that is called the mountain lion in English, we have learned that the last one in line, the one who falls back, is the most vulnerable.

To his credit, Gray Suit One heard the thud that knocked the wind out of his partner and kept him from crying out. There are some powerful throws you can use on a big man while also disarming him of his weapon. It takes about the length of an average breath, then another breath and a half to heave him off the trail behind the large fallen pine that had been my hiding place.

Gray Suit One reappeared, looking back up the trail. "Greg?" he called, his voice hesitant, "Where you gone?"

His accent, unlike that of our T-shirted friend, was as far from Eastern European as Boston is from Bratislava.

Greg, née Gray Suit Two, did not answer. It was not because he was the strong silent type. The gun muzzle stuck in his mouth like a dental probe was a serious deterrent to conversation.

Gray Suit One looked so concerned that my heart went out to him. Rather than leave him in suspense, I decided that it was best to let him know he was not alone.

Ever hear the cry of the wild turkey, the long, ululating call that pierces the air like the feathered flight of an arrow? Back in the good old days when so-called settlers were moving north into our already settled land, we used to visit their camps before dawn, wait until the right moment and then . . . a hundred Abenaki throats would make that eerie wild turkey call. More often than not, that was all we had to do. Before the sun set, those people would have packed up their portables and headed back south.

As did Gray Suit One. He turned and fled, really trucking this time, smooth-soled brogans and all.

"Greg," I said, "looks like it's just you and me, kid."

I slipped the gun from his mouth—the polite thing to do when wanting a response. Greg's response was monosyllabic Anglo-Saxon and anatomically impossible. I tapped his nose with the gun and he again grew silent.

My other hand held out the interesting things I had just unhooked from the back of his belt. Handcuffs, standard police issue. I dangled them in front of Greg's eyes and made a motion for him to turn around.

After fastening his hands behind his back, I reached into his jacket, pulled out his wallet, flipped it open with one hand. This time it was my turn to utter an expletive.

The photo ID and badge in Greg's wallet identified him as a member of a certain city's PD. In another state.

"Out of your jurisdiction, Greg? Moonlighting?"

"Eat me, asshole," Greg said.

I shook my head. "Greg, Greg, the reports of indigenous anthropoph-agy are highly exaggerated. I, on the other hand, would hesitate to cross the Sierra Nevada in winter with a wagonload of your ancestors."

The sound of a jeep's approach ended my attempt at male bonding. It was, of course, Dennis with the Trussed-up Transylvanian T-shirt man in the back seat.

I pulled Greg up by his lapels, shrugged him up on my shoulder in a fireman's carry, and deposited him in the back next to T3.

Dennis raised an eloquent eyebrow asking what now?

"Turn this wagon train around," I said. "We're heading back into the wilderness."

13

*The river washes away
everything except itself*

I t took us a couple of hours, but we came out on another paved road. We were ten miles farther from our eventual destination, true, but also well beyond whatever activities our erstwhile ambushers had planned for us.

We emerged from the forest primeval without Gary or T3, or, for that matter, Longfellow's Hiawatha. We'd left the moonlighting flatfoot and the wounded ex-communist in that yellow Toyota, which had lost a good bit of its resale value. Since that magnetic transmitter was now firmly attached to its perforated fender, their friends would find them soon enough.

Why not turn them in to the local authorities? We had more than one reason not to do that.

First of all, which local authorities would we go to? The sheriff, who was rumored to be in the pocket of certain real-estate developers who had other plans for the lands the Children of the Mountain sought to reclaim? The state police, who were being required to work over-time and were not likely to be sympathetic to us red brothers of those on the other side of their roadblocks?

Secondly, how could we prove who opened fire first? It was only our word against theirs. Who do you suppose would end up charged with assault with a deadly weapon? Two trigger-happy Abenakis or a vaca-tioning brother in blue and his exchange-student buddy whose only sin was failing to realize it was not yet hunting season?

Thirdly, we were in a hurry to get where we were going as inconspicuously as possible. So, unhampered by excess electronic baggage, multinational hostages, or charges of unlawful imprisonment, we chugged along on our way and got to the Island just after dark.

It was too late to go by the tribal office and pay our respects to Chief Polis. He would have gone home long ago. We passed the Polis house on the way to Dennis's place. Only one light burning.

"Mary," Dennis said. "She stays up late."

But we did not stop. Even I, who had long been away, still knew enough not to go this late to our chief's home. It was not for fear of lack of hospitality. Ill as he was, Chief Harold Polis never turned away any visitor from his door. He would have insisted on getting out of bed. After all, it wasn't that late, just a little after ten. There would have been firm handshakes, coffee poured, bowls of stew on the table. Just like the old days.

Except Dennis and I would have noticed the weariness around his eyes, the loose skin under his jaw, and the way his hands shook. And we would have seen how hard it was for his wife, Mary, and his daughters to keep up that tradition of hospitality, knowing that every lost hour of sleep might be too much for the man they loved. That man who had seemed once to be carved out of hard cedar, as tough to uproot as an old tree, now looked as if the first strong wind would blow him away from them forever.

We could wait until tomorrow.

We continued on down Nolka Way, passing the Boulet family home, the biggest, newest house on the street and the one built in the poorest taste. The Boulets were the mirror opposites of Chief Polis and hated him for just about everything from the past, when their families had been antagonists in war, to the present, when his family held the chieftaincy and theirs didn't. Molly Ann, the matriarch of the family, had long been counting on a future in which her son Paul would take over the office after Harold passed on. They were the most vocally pro-casino voices among the Penacooks and it was whispered that the money for their new home had come from offshore investors hedging their bets on getting the contract to build an eventual casino. It went without saying that neither Paul Boulet nor any of his relatives were supporters of the Children of the Mountain and Mikwe.

We turned off Nolka Lane onto Awasos Way, the little street that ended at the boat landing, and there was Dennis's kit-built log house.

There were more lights on in the Mitchell home, as many as possible, in fact. The later Dennis got home, the more lights Patty Jean turned on, until by 2 A.M. you could see his place from the International Space Station.

Patty Jean was smiling as she stood in the door. She had never been beautiful, but was always one of the best-looking women I'd ever seen, and the years since I last laid eyes on her had only made her look better. The line of gray in her shoulder-length black hair was designed to accent the angles of her memorable face. Patty Jean was a former volleyball star and was as tall as I, with broad shoulders and long-muscled arms. She didn't ask why we were so late. She'd do that later when she and Dennis were alone and talking late into the night since he shared everything with her as he'd always done. Everything except one thing.

But even before that long talk with their arms around each other and expressing the griefs of the ages, Patty Ann sensed something dramatic had happened. She looked both of us up and down as if making sure we'd arrived with all our limbs intact. Then she grabbed me, pulled me in, and gave me one of her famous rib-cracking hugs.

"We've missed you, Podjo," she said.

"Unngggh," I replied, wondering how well I'd function with my one lung. Then, as soon as she let go, the kids and the dogs hit us.

Whenever they've stood still long enough for me to count them, I've always figured that the Mitchell household is home to six kids and sixteen dogs. Although it might be the other way around. Next time I'll try counting tails instead of noses.

And it was not just dogs and little Mitchells that filled Dennis and Patty Ann's large two-story cabin. Dennis had been working steadily—whenever he was not volunteering or doing tribal council business—as a contractor for the last seven years. More income meant more to share. Extra rooms added on meant more room for extra relatives. In addition to Dennis and Patty Jean and their own children, the daily census included Patty Jean's sister, her uncle, two teenage cousins, and five foster kids. Cozy.

Like Patty Jean, all of them were huggers. I was quickly engulfed in Mitchells from tibia to scapula, never to be in need of a chiropractor again.

By midnight, everyone was in bed except for Dennis and me. We sat at the kitchen table. My notepad was in front of me, but I'd stopped scribbling on it a while ago. Now, a fresh cup of coffee between my palms, I was looking out through the open, unscreened window that I'd helped Dennis put in two summers ago. The trim that Dennis added had covered over my bent nails and hammer marks.

Through that window the leaves of a mountain ash tree framed the wide river. For a moment, it seemed as if I could see a birchbark canoe on its surface, bobbing with the current—a canoe like the one that Uncle John took me fishing in. Then it was gone, only a wave reflecting back the light of the moon.

An old clock ticked on the wall behind us. It was flanked on one side by a Plains-style eagle feather headdress in a clear plastic case and on the other by a crucifix. Two sprays of sweetgrass arched over the crucifix—which was one of Dennis's own carvings, its Abenaki eyes of Christ turned toward the window, watching the ever-changing, ancient vista of the river.

I sighed. Despite the crazed events of this day that was almost done, I felt at peace. This was my second home, a sanctuary even if, like everything else in life, it was never truly safe from the future—or the past. I looked over at Dennis, focusing my eyes in a certain way, and I could see it, that faint aura of darkness within him that he strove to never allow anyone else to notice.

"You ever going to tell her?" I asked.

He didn't look up from the carving that was again in his hands. He knew what I was talking about, the shrapnel he'd absorbed when he threw his body over mine, busting up my knee but saving my life, that one small piece in particular circling his heart like a planet-killing satellite.

"Nope," he said.

I removed my right hand from my coffee cup and looked at my palm. Across the table from me, like a considerably larger, darker mirror image, Dennis put down his carving and did the exact same thing.

At this same table, two small, serious teenage boys had pledged friendship forever. On the TV that morning we'd seen an old movie in which a white man and an Apache chief went through the ancient ritual. We had done the same thing. Each of us sliced a wavery line across our palms—using a tile knife Dennis's mom had been cutting linoleum with. We'd clasped the other's hot, slippery hand for a long time. Finally, we figured it had been long enough for the blood to mingle.

The infection I got put me in bed with a fever. Wiggly images of Cochise and the Lone Ranger, both of them wearing boxing gloves for some reason I have never fully understood, danced about my head. The first thing of the more rational world that I saw when I opened my eyes was the round solemn face of my friend.

"Luke," he said in a deep voice, "I am your father."

Then he held up his right hand and showed me his scar.

> Those scars we still could see as grown men,
> Connected us to the kids we were then.
> Carved into lines of life and love,
> Obscuring . . . or extending them.

I flipped the page on my pad from semi-rhymed quatrain to a clean sheet.

Dennis cleared his throat. Two of the dogs on the couch growled back in response while a third one burrowed its head under the sofa pillows. I was supposed to sleep on that sofa.

"Podjo, you remember how your Uncle John used to go fishing?"

I nodded.

"When I was a kid he took me along sometimes when he was guiding some sport up from Boston. They loved to hire him because he always knew where the fish were. He would do that 'tasting the water' trick. You know the one—when he'd show the sport our Old Indian Way of finding fish. He'd cup a little water from the river with his hand, taste it. Nope, no big fish here. Then go a little farther, taste again. No, not this spot either, just little fish here. Next spot. Nope. Fish are bigger, but not big enough. Finally he'd get to the place he'd been heading all along, where he'd maybe seen a big fish the day before. Cup the water, taste it, look thoughtful. Taste it again. Yup, big fish here all right. By now the sport was about going crazy. He'd been tasting the water, too, and declaring it didn't taste any different to him. Toss your line right in here, Uncle John would say. And as soon as the sport did it—WHAM! that big fish was just waiting to be caught."

"Well, I must have seen him do that trick a dozen times over the years. He never failed to get those city clickers all awed and stupefied over the way he could find a fish by tasting the water. They'd give him big tips, real big tips. And all the while I was about peeing my pants trying to keep from laughing out loud about the way he was fooling them.

"But, you know what? The year before he passed on, him and me went fishing together in that old bark canoe of his. What did he do but start tasting the water? Well, I went right along with it. I tasted it every time he did, chuckling as I did it. I chuckled right up until the time when he cupped a handful, just sniffed it and then nodded to me. 'Really Big Fish here,' he said. I took a taste of it—and I almost choked. I actually *could* taste fish in that water. Something in my brain just clicked. *Big Trout*, it said. And that is what I caught as soon as my worm hit the water—the biggest trout I ever pulled out of our river!

"While we were paddling back, I kept quiet as I could, even though it was about killing me. Finally, just as we were pulling in to shore, I had to say something.

" 'I really could taste that fish,' I said. And Uncle John just looked at me real slow and smiled.

" 'Well,' he said, 'You and I are the only ones who can taste the really big ones.' "

I shook my head and smiled with Dennis. "He did that same thing to me," I said. "All I could taste was the big ones, too."

Dennis poured our third cups of coffee, then picked up the piece of wood he had been whittling on. For a time the rhythm of his blade kept time with the ticking of the clock. Then he stopped and looked over at me.

"Podjo," he said, "I am tasting a really big fish in the water now."

14

*A straight line
can be bent into a circle*

Everyone else was in bed. From upstairs I could hear a soft rumble like thunder on the other side of a mountain that was Dennis's voice as he went through the events of the day with Patty Jean, punctuated every now and then by the exclamation points of her lightning-quick laughter. Maybe someday I'd find someone like Patty Jean, have a house like that, not have to borrow someone else's dog when the need for interspecies excursions struck me. And maybe not.

Meanwhile, I had more than enough canine companions. I looked over at the couch where I was supposed to sleep. It was barely visible under the mingled furs of a white Labrador, a spotted Great Dane, and two mammoth mutts that looked to have equal proportions of malamute and mastodon in their genes. One lifted its muzzle from what was supposed to be my pillow to look at me and then curled its upper lip to bare a pair of canines each as long as my index finger.

Wrestling the dogs for my requisite two and a half yards of stretching-out space could come later. I was in no hurry to sleep and I was pretty certain that sleep was in no hurry to arrive. Probably in a holding pattern over O'Hare Airport about now.

I tapped my pencil on the pad. Write it all down. Something might become obvious. I made a new list.

1. Doom-laden Dream.
2. Phone call from Friend.
3. Murders on Mountain.

4. Boisterous Bikers.
5. Crooked Cops.

Or perhaps point 4 should be "Hostile Harley Heads." I was getting punchy. I stood up and rolled my shoulders, moved my arms through the circles of Offering the Master Tea. Then I did Embrace the Tiger. Return to Mountain, pumping oxygen through my system, especially into a brain that was perilously close to running on empty.

I sat back down, eraser poised over the pad. Then I remembered a Haitian proverb that I first heard in the hills above Port-au-Prince: the pencil of God has no eraser. I flipped the sheet over to start again on a new one. As soon as I did that, something immediately became obvious.

There was only one clean sheet left. I was going to need another pad of paper.

I decided to make another list, simpler, more basic, no playing with words. Well, not much. It is hard to recover from three semesters of Creative Writing in college. I would recapitulate. From "capitulare," to count heads. In any event, this time I'd try putting things in a format.

A line drawn down the middle made two columns. Then I wrote down a heading for column A: PEOPLE.

1. Chief Polis
2. Dennis
3. Me
4. Mikwe
5. Bikers
6. Hit? Men
7. Big Fish
8. Unidentified animal/human murderer

The first three were linked together, of course. People knew that this time Chief Polis would not recover. The chieftaincy would soon be open and a new tribal election would take place. The two leading candidates would probably be Dennis and Mikwe. Dennis had stated publicly so many times that he never wanted to be chief that everyone assumed he was already running for the position. But knowing Dennis as I did, I was sure he was serious about his lack of ambition and would refuse to run for anything other than another term on the Council. As for Mikwe, even though he was leading what some were calling a breakaway from

the tribe, few doubted that he would come back when the real chieftaincy was up for grabs.

There were others, of course. So many that before Chief Polis took
office ten years ago, the joke was that our main problem was not a lack of
recognition but that we had too many chiefs and not enough plain old
Indians.

Chief among those who were not but longed to be leaders was Molly
Ann Boulet's forty-year-old son, Phil. Phil was a professional blackjack
dealer now living in Connecticut after a decade of drifting from one
reservation casino to another all across America. To say he had connections to gaming was like saying trains traveled on tracks.

If all of the violent happenings of recent weeks were connected, that
violence most likely had its roots in the impending struggle for control
of our tribe. Eliminate all the pieces that didn't fit and you'd find the
piece that did. Assuming, of course, that piece was actually part of the
puzzle.

I drew a line from Number 1 to Number 2 to Number 3. After all,
Dennis called me in at the request of the Chief.

How about connections between the three of us and Mikwe—not
counting the old unpleasant intersection between him and me? I added
two question marks after his name.

Which brought me to Numbers 5 and 6. A line from 5 to me, that
was clear. But how about the two cops and their rifle-toting pal? Maybe
those guys were actually after Dennis and not me, an innocent passenger who had been caught in a web of intrigue. Maybe pigs have wings.
More lines drawn.

Number 7, our Big Fish just might be the missing link, the master-
mind behind it all—or the will-o'-the-wisp.

Number 8, the mysterious, murderous, maybe human monster.
I studied it, tapped my pencil.

I suddenly felt hot, carnivorous breath on the back of my neck. I
turned around and removed the white Labrador's paws from the back
of my chair.

"Need out?" I said.

He woofed, crouched, and wagged his tail in doggy agreement. Me,
too, after six cups of coffee.

When the dog and I came back in, each of us some fluid ounces
lighter, my head was clearer from the cool night air coming off the river.
I'd listened to the flowing water's nightly monologue. It's been said that
the wisest of our *mteowlins*, those who could see where others were blind,

could understand the voice of the river. But because they were the wisest of the mteowlins, they never told anyone else what the river said to them.

Wide awake again, I started Column B on the other side of the sheet with the heading:

LARGER EVENTS.

1. Land Claims and recognition.
2. Occupation at mountain.
3. Unsolved killings.
4. Potential struggle for chieftaincy.
5. Possible casino.

Did I say I was wide awake? My eyelids felt like lead weights.

I put down the pencil, kicked off my shoes and eased my way in among the warm, sighing canine bodies. A tongue slapped across my face as I pried the pillow out from under the Great Dane's jowls, flipped it slobber side down, dropped my head, fell into a sudden deep sleep . . .

And I was running.

15

Sunrise and then sunset
sunset and then sunrise

And how was your night? The less said about mine, the better. I rose, as refreshed as a well-squeezed sponge. Despite my late night shut-eyed aerobics, I'd stayed abed longer than anyone else in the household. Even the dogs were sitting and looking at me in scorn.

Don't you have better things to do than sleeping your two-legged life away?

Dennis was waiting for me at the table, a cup of coffee already poured. I drank it without a word.

"You needed that," Dennis said.

No comment.

The sun was two hands high over the river when we went to Chief Polis's house. He was standing on his front stoop, his arms by his side, a Red Sox ball cap on his head. Until I got within thirty feet of him, he looked good. Then he didn't.

He took my right hand gently in his, gripped my elbow with his other hand.

"Thank you," he said. His quiet voice was perfectly sincere. And, as always, I felt myself wanting to say that I was the one who should be giving thanks. I was the one who had been made welcome here, here in this place which held half of my blood heritage and most of my spirit.

Instead, as always, I just nodded and said, "It's good to be back."

Chief Polis smiled. With that smile he didn't look as sick as before. "We're so glad to have you back that we're sending you out of here just as fast as we can."

"Something else has happened?" Dennis said.

"At the Mountain. And rather than my telling you about it . . ."

"We need to see it for ourselves?"

Chief Polis nodded.

❧

A kingfisher flew down out of an alder that leaned over the river. It hovered, head-down, dark eyes seeing beneath a surface that was no more than a play of light and shadows to human eyes. Then it dove, a small blue arrow seeking life.

We were well along our way, following a road that led north, a road I hadn't been on in years, a road that led along our river. It felt good to be able to see its old, familiar flow. We Neptunes feel best when we're near water. I ran my index finger along the carving that I'd found tucked into the top of my bag this morning.

There's this way of gifting that our people practice. It doesn't involve wrapping up something in a pretty package and presenting the gift in a way that calls attention to the giver. Giving without ceremony, without calling attention to the giver's generosity, there's a clean feeling to that kind of giving.

I doubted it had taken Dennis long to do that carving, but it was as beautifully made and as familiar to me as the river we were following. It was a water creature, neither fish nor otter, a being with no name in the English language, one at home in two worlds, able to dive beneath the surface or walk on the seemingly firm land.

Someone asked me once if I didn't feel schizophrenic, being half Indian and half white, identifying so much with my Native roots and yet living in the midst of white culture.

"Schizophrenic?" I'd said, "Man, I need more than two personalities just to be able to get up in the morning."

❧

Long ago, the story goes, our people lived by this river. We fished in it. We drank its water. Our lives depended upon it. Then, one day, the river went dry. No one could understand what had happened. Scouts went upstream to see what was wrong. They found that a great dam had been built across the river. A huge monster made that dam. His name was Aglebemu, "Guards Water."

They asked him for water.

"I will give you none," Aglebemu said. Then he drove the scouts away.

The people began to die of thirst. They prayed to the Maker of All Life for help.

The next day, a stranger walked into the village. He was taller than any other man they had ever seen before.

"What is wrong?" asked the stranger.

The people told him.

"Ah," the stranger said, "would you like me to go and speak to Aglebemu?"

"Yes," the people said.

So the tall stranger walked upstream.

As soon as he was gone, the people of the village began to talk.

"I think that one is Gluskonba, the Changer," one man said. "The Maker of All Life has sent him to help us. No one can defeat Gluskonba. He will bring the water back to us."

"When the water comes back," said another man, "I will jump into that water and swim around and never come out again."

"When the water comes back," a woman said, "I will dive in that water and come up and then dive again."

"When the water comes back," said yet another person, "I will drink and drink and drink and never stop drinking."

So the people of the village spoke about what they would do when the water was returned to them.

Meanwhile, that tall man, who was indeed Gluskonba, kept walking upstream. When he came to the dam, he found it guarded by Aglebemu's people.

"Give me water," Gluskonba said.

"Our Chief says that water is his alone. He will share it with no one. Go away."

Gluskonba asked a second time. Again he was refused.

"Give me water," said Gluskonba a third time. This time he was given a handful of mud.

Gluskonba asked a fourth time. The one he asked went to Aglebemu. He came back with a bark cup filled with urine.

Gluskonba became angry. His eyes flashed like the lightning. He began to walk toward Aglebemu's dam. With each step he grew bigger until he was taller than the tallest pine.

Aglebemu's helpers ran away as Gluskonba came closer. Now Aglebemu was a giant himself. He had a big mouth, great staring eyes, a huge belly, long yellow fingers and toes like the roots of a willow tree. But Gluskonba grew even larger. He reached down and picked up Aglebemu with one hand. He grabbed him so hard that Aglebemu's back was bent crooked. He squeezed him so tightly that Aglebemu's eyes bulged out and his mouth grew wide from gasping for breath.

And as Gluskonba squeezed, Aglebemu grew smaller and smaller. He grew so small that he was a monster no longer. All that was big about him now was his voice.

"You wanted all this for yourself," Gluskonba said as he threw Aglebemu into the water. "Now you will live in that water always."

To this day, that is where he lives. With his big voice he still tries to frighten people away from the water, but when you see him, you will not run away. For that Aglebemu is now a bullfrog.

Then Gluskonba broke the dam. The water rushed downstream in a great torrent.

When that rushing water reached the village, the people were so excited! Those who said they would swim and swim, those who said they would dive and not come up, those who said they would drink and keep on drinking—all of those people jumped into the river. Some of them became frogs, some became fish. Their descendants remain in that river, sharing its water to this day.

They are our relatives.

That is how Aunt Mali ended the story.

"That Aglebemu must of been a European," Uncle John had added with a chuckle after Aunt Mali finished.

Not that it was really anything to chuckle about.

Because about four hundred years ago, Aglebemu came back. Once again, he began owning things all for himself. Our old people knew who he really was, even if he used different names. Government was one of Aglebemu's new names. And all of a sudden our people found themselves living downstream from his dams that held back everything we needed to live. Many of us tried to fight him, but he was too big.

He still is, and even though some of us are waiting, Gluskonba has yet to return to help our people.

16

*Rain does not
just fall from the sky*

The Mountain was visible a long time before we got to it. Even though at first it had seemed to be trying to hide, like a bashful giant in a crowd, when we got within ten miles we saw its shoulders rising up above the hills and the lesser peaks around it. On top of that mountain, the eagle Wuchowsen used to stand. From the flapping of its wings came the wind.

Unless they had good reason, no one who used to climb to the Wind Eagle's summit stayed there—until white people finally conquered the Mountain because it was there.

"You see," those intrepid white guys said to their Abenaki guides. "There's no wind eagle here."

They said that even though the highest wind gusts on this planet have been measured up there.

What did those hired "savages" from whom I am descended say in reply to those flatlanders after guiding them to the mountain top, cooking lunch for them halfway up, and lugging all their gear without complaint, only to be repaid with disrespect?

They might have said, "Of course there's no wind eagle here now that you're here."

But they didn't, at least not in English.

While I was still musing about the impact of Western civilization on the nesting habits of enormous aviaforms, just as we crested a hilly bend in the road and began to descend, Dennis spun the wheel to the right, bouncing us over the shoulder, straight toward a large tamarack. At the last minute, Dennis adjusted our trajectory and we whipped beneath the big tree's boughs, through the brush onto a hidden jeep trail.

"Short cut," Dennis said.

"Right," I answered through my confidently clenched teeth.

We stopped fifty yards down the trail and then crept back to the road, keeping low, moving slow. From the cover of the moosewood saplings, waist-high alders, and hop hornbeam that had bounced back up after the jeep passed through them, we could see the road and the faint tracks in the gravel where our vehicle came bouncing off the blacktop. That one sign of our departure from the main road was too faint to be noticed by the cop in the state car that had been hanging back half a mile behind us.

Dennis looked over at me and nodded.

I nodded back. We'd both noted the state police cruiser parked back from the road ten miles ago. We'd been going under the speed limit, but we'd seen the police car pull out and start following us. It had been keeping way back so we wouldn't catch on, so far back that the curving dip in the road had given us enough time to get off without being noticed.

We walked back to the jeep. The trail hadn't been used by loggers for at least a few years, but after the first fifty yards the saplings that should have been growing up in the middle of the road weren't there. Small round stubs marked where they had been clipped off a finger's width above the leaf litter and duff of the forest floor.

"The back way in to the Mountain?" I said.

"One of 'em." Dennis chuckled.

I had to admit, it was funny. The idea of manning checkpoints and roadblocks on main highways to keep our people out of the woods was amusing. Especially when they were men who had gone into these woods as loggers and hunters for most of their lives, women no less familiar with the forest from generations of gathering food and medicine plants.

But such regulation was typical of bureaucratic thinking. Draw a couple of lines on a map and then you can pretend those lines on a piece of paper actually keep in—or keep out—real human beings whose feet know the living land. I'm not saying that those lines on maps marking out counties, states, and countries haven't made a difference. If anything, they've made too much of a difference.

Dennis looked up at the cloudless sky. The sun was a double hand's width above the hills. We'd taken a slow, circuitous route to reach this point. Stopped at lookouts to admire the views, paused for lunch at a roadside place, purchased soda pop and pork rinds at a country store, pretending to be tourists out for a drive. It was a wonderful plan that had clearly deceived everyone—aside from the state police and local cops who passed us on from one cruiser to the next.

Being a detective, I had figured out that we were being tailed. My vast deductive abilities were abetted by Dennis's police band radio that he'd kept tuned to their discussions of our progress.

Dennis pointed with his chin down the trail as he drove. "We could make it before dark," he said.

I shook my head. "No," I said. "I need some more time to think." I tapped my forehead. "Too much going on up here."

"Dennis reached out a huge hand to tap my chest. "How about in here? I saw the look on your face when I told you Katlin was with the Children of the Mountain."

I answered by rolling my shoulders. "Man, I am tight. How about up there? Looks like a good place to set up."

"Good enough," Dennis said, dropping the subject as a good friend should.

A hundred feet uphill there was a rock face with two outcroppings beneath it that looked like arms extended to cradle a giant child. Between those protective limbs of stone, the moss was thick and dry on the level ground, making natural mattress. From this high spot we could see to the south and the east. The warm breeze and the first light would reach us easily here. It was a good place. It felt like one of those old camping places used by our people for the thousands of years our feet massaged the trails of our land after the glaciers left. That was long before the new white ones came with almost as much cold force as those mountains of ice.

I placed my cheek against the smooth stone and ran my hands along the seams in the ancient rock the way Tom Nicola taught me to do when greeting a place that might offer protection for the night. Tom knew a lot about such places, as well as about the caves that might run deep under seemingly solid earth and stone. He'd often trusted the land to protect him during two tours as a U.S. Special Forces sergeant in southeast Asia in the early '70s.

While Dennis spread out the ground cloth and unrolled our sleeping bags, I did my end-of-day exercises on a flat spot a few yards away from the stone face. It was completely dark and he was snoring like a hibernating bear by the time I'd finished working my way through Tiger, Crane, and the basic two hundred, loosening my muscles and emptying my thoughts, trying to allow "nothing" to take the place of my memories of the girl I'd grown up with.

But, despite the fact that my body felt like a torch when I was done, nothing had taken the place of her face glowing in my mind.

I sat down on my sleeping bag next to Dennis. An empty pork rind bag still clutched in his hand, he was already asleep. I reached over to pull the bag from his grasp, folded it several times and stuck it into my pack. Carry it in, carry it out again.

I sighed and leaned back beneath the old stone.

Time to sleep.

17

Follow the tracks
of dreams in dreams

But Sleep-maker didn't want to visit me just yet. So I sat and thought. I thought about the Little Ones, those who watch over the forest and live in places just like this one where we were camping. I thought about the stories Tom told me about tunnels and caves. I thought about finding things. I've always been able to find things. I've sometimes even been able to find myself—for brief periods of time, at least.

It wasn't going to rain. I could tell that by the taste of the wind, the color of the darkening sky. From our little rise in the forest I could see a dark silhouette on the hill across from us, lifting up above the second growth. It was a single big white pine standing tall. The weevil that had bored into its leader branch eight decades ago and created two twisted trunks had saved its life. The other straight trees had been taken for sawlogs. This one remained, ignored as its roots spread out to hold the soil.

We didn't have a campfire. It was warm enough without one and the fire might give us away.

The moon over my shoulder made shadows on white paper. The blocky shadow of my hand, the sharp line of the pencil as I wrote. It was bright enough to read Milton by starlight or dance like the Chinese poet old Li Bai, who wrote about drinking wine and then romping with two faithful companions: his shadow and the moon. But I'd given up the wine several years ago. I almost didn't miss it. However, that "almost" was too big to think about too much.

I thought more about Li Bai, Master White, one of the big three of the T'ang Dynasty of China. Twelve hundred years ago. Not that long ago in Indian time. Poet, Taoist, alchemist. Maybe he was a detective, too. Poets are supposed to be good at putting things together. And Li Bai was also described as one of the greatest swordsmen of his time. A guy who was poet and a sort of knight errant, man of action and a man of dreams, might be a detective.

I read out loud what I'd printed in large letters on the page. My own translation of a few lines I remembered from a long poem the White Master wrote.

> I flew on through the night,
> High above the mirror lake.
> The moon cast my shadow on the waves,
> Traveling with me . . .

I closed the notepad. Really time to sleep, even though a bear kept growling nearby. I leaned over and gave Dennis a gentle shove with my fingertips. It didn't wake him, but he rolled onto his side and stopped snoring, just as he used to do when we were kids sleeping out in the tree fort we'd built behind Tom Nicola's house.

I closed my eyes. Tomorrow we'd go into the camp of the Children of the Mountain. I would start the process of connecting those seemingly disparate parts into a whole, trying to complete an image that I could understand. I already had hints of its shape, some logical, some with no logic at all. My thoughts drifted, but I was no closer to slumber.

I opened my eyes to look up at the grandmother's face of Nanibonsad, the Night Traveler. And Grandmother Moon looked back at me.

I remembered a story that Tom Nicola told me. Back when the American astronauts started to come back from their voyages across that wide sea of interplanetary space. I was a very little kid and I'm not sure why Tom told us the story. But that was typical with Tom. People trusted him, but no one could ever say for sure why he did anything.

We were sitting on a rock beside the river as he told the story to a group of us kids. Me, Dennis, Katlin, Mikwe who wasn't Mikwe yet, one or two others. Tom could always attract an audience by just sitting down and raising his hand up to his chin. That always meant a story was on its way.

"Right after those astronauts made that one trip," Tom said, "they did a tour of America. They had parades and made speeches. People came out to see them."

"So what?" Mikwe said.

Tom looked at him and Mikwe shut his mouth without saying anything else.

"At this one speech," Tom continued, "in Boston it was, this old Indian man raised his hand to the astronaut who had been talking. That astronaut was one of those moon-walkers, the one who took with him golf balls that he had signed his name on and then hit way far away with a golf club. The old man had a question. 'How come you spend so much to go to the moon?' The astronaut went into a long thing about how it was important strategically to be first to the moon, how it had great scientific meaning, all that. When that astronaut was through talking, the old man raised his hand again. 'No,' the old Indian man said. 'You didn't understand me. It is fine that you go to the moon. I just wonder why you do it the hard way, spend so much money.' That astronaut, he looked confused then. 'Is there a cheaper way?' he asked. That old Indian man, he smiled then. 'Yes,' he said. 'You do it like I do it. You go there in your dreams.'"

Tom looked around at us. We were all nodding and smiling—except for Mikwe, who looked confused.

"But that is not the end of the story," Tom said. "As the astronaut was leaving the room, that old Indian man was waiting for him by the exit. It was a really big room and that astronaut was surprised the old man had gotten ahead of him like that. When the old man held out his hand, the astronaut went to shake it. Instead, the old man put something small and round into that astronaut's hand. 'You left this behind,' the old man said. Then he slipped away into the crowd. That astronaut looked at what the old man had given him. It was a golf ball with his name written on it."

There's always more than one level to everything. There's that which we see and that which we cannot see until we close our eyes and look deeper within. Ever since I was a little kid, things have come to me in my dreams. Tom Nicola encouraged me to pay attention to my dreams and always remember them.

So, in my dreams I've found myself flying over mountains, wrestling with monsters, seeing things that I've never seen before. And then, the next day when I've re-entered the waking world, I've run into those things again. Not always exactly the same, but usually close enough. In high school, the mountain that I flew over in my dreams the night before became the bar that I cleared when I set a school record in the high jump.

I suppose it's easy enough to explain that. It's the way the mind works, choosing symbolic challenges to stand for the real things yet to be faced. Except my dreams become more than merely symbolic from time to time. I see the faces of people I haven't yet met, observe exact details of rooms I later enter for the first time. I've seen where things were lost or hidden and then been able to find them in places I visited in my sleep.

That, too, I suppose, could be explained in terms of intuition, or false memory. Explaining it, though, is the last thing I want to do. Bumble-bees don't know how they fly—and neither do the scientists who once proved that it was physically impossible, based on the bee's body mass, wing size, and so on. Bumblebees just fly. And I just dream.

I closed my eyes.

18

When I see through the eyes
of my enemy, I see myself

I opened my eyes. Not wide. Just a slit so that if anyone was standing above me, looking down into my face, they would not know I was awake.

Because if anyone was standing above me in the night, peering down into my face, it would probably be an enemy.

In the old days, it would have been a Mohawk. By the old days I don't mean that long ago. Only two or three hundred years, back when the multinational corporations we called colonies and their warring home offices—England and France—had exported a little number called the Hundred Years' War to our fortunate shores. It had taken some time and it wasn't completely successful, but it had succeeded in setting most of longhouse nations against us wigwam peoples. We Wabanakis allied with the French, while the Haudenosaunee nations to our west largely sided with the British and their colonists. In case the name Haudenosaunee doesn't mean anything to you, try Iroquois, the name our French allies called them. It's from a Wabanaki word that we pronounced *Ireokwa*, which means "the little animal that runs away." We also called them Maguak—those afraid to fight us—and that became Mohawk.

Of course, such taunting names are seldom really true. They're like wishful thinking or pumping yourself up before the big game by saying your opponents have got nothing. Iroquois people, especially that east-ernmost nation of theirs that became known as Mohawks, really were not afraid to fight. They excelled in battle and led their war parties deep

into the heart of our Penacook lands. We admired them for their brav-
ery. We also tried to kill the bastards.

Back then, when we were on the trail and laid ourselves down to
sleep, we did so knowing that we might wake up dead with Mohawk
tomahawks stuck in our foreheads. We weren't so worried about the
English. Aside from Rogers's Rangers, most white men were too clumsy
in the woods to sneak up on us without our hearing them. The joke
was that the English couldn't find the buttons on their pants without
help.

But a Mohawk? Wah-ah! A Mohawk could slip up on you before you
knew it. For two hundred years we frightened our children into being
quiet at night by telling them that if they made too much noise a Mohawk would hear and come and get them. I heard that more than once
from my aunt and it used to shut me up good! I would lie there in my
bed and listen for the sound of the cat owl in the cedar tree outside the
window. The cat owl was the village's friend. Its call in the night was
soft and soothing, but when an enemy came close, its call changed.

Did I hear the cat owl speak of danger? Or was it another sense beyond
hearing that told me to wake up now? Whatever it was, I remembered to wake in the old way. I opened my eyes just a crack, looked
up, and—Jeezum Cripes!—saw a Mohawk standing over me. In the
space between one breath and the next, I took in his face painted black
for death, the tattoos snaking across his cheeks and brow, and the stone-
headed war club being lifted up by his right hand!

I rolled to the side as that war club came whistling down. It thudded
into the earth where my head had been, where my skull would have
cracked like an egg. With the quickness of a big cat, he followed me as
I leapt up. As I ducked and dove forward, his deadly club glanced off
the stone face behind me with a shower of sparks.

I back-pedaled as he turned, slower this time, stalking me. The shad-
owy brightness of the moon, like the light beneath the water, was still
bright enough for me to see that Dennis was gone, as well as the sleeping bags and the ground cloth. Had he been clubbed, wrapped in the
cloth and dragged away?

The silent Mohawk warrior, though, was not gone. In the space of a
heartbeat, my eyes took him in from head to toe. Scalplock, paint, tattoos, and war club. Deerskin loincloth and moccasins. Everything about
him, including the round wooden shield held in his left hand, marked
him as a man of the mid-1600's, including that cold dead look in his
eyes.

There was no more than the space of a heartbeat before his muscles tensed and he sprang at me again. He spun the shield at me in a motion meant to knock my arm aside, opening me for the killing blow with the war club in his other hand. But I was ready. I swept the shield past me with an open palm, following with a spinning kick that struck him in the back of his head and sent him rolling down the slope.

I shifted into a *t*-stance and waited, trying to make my brain work faster than his feet as he charged back up the hill at me.

The days when Mohawks fought Abenakis had been gone for more than two centuries, ended by the war between King George and his children. Maybe the Mohawks weren't our best friends. There were some issues between us about land claims, seeing as how they tended to believe that everything east of the Mississippi was Iroquois land. But for a long time we'd shared similar histories. Together we'd been deceived, despoiled, despised, and generally dissed by a succession of American governments. Like us, they were native people made to feel like immigrants in their own homelands. When we formed our Wabanaki Confederacy, there were Mohawks included in it. Abenakis and Mohawks walked together on the Trail of Broken Treaties. During the siege at Oka, Abenakis went to support the Mohawk warriors who were trying to keep the Québécois from turning a sacred forest into another golf course. Hell, Alanis Obomsawin even made a movie about it!

I had my own share of Iroquois acquaintances, some from my heavy drinking days in the Indian steelworker bars of Brooklyn. (I can show you the scars.) Others were clients who had come to me with the kind of problems that a non-Native detective couldn't understand, much less solve. (I can show you more scars from that.) I'd done good by my Mohawk brothers and sisters. Now, though, I was in imminent danger of being bludgeoned by a very large—about two hands taller than I— discouragingly determined anachronism who had clearly not been informed that the bounty on Abenaki scalps was no longer being paid.

Or was it?

19

*The sharpest knife
cannot cut itself*

The war club arced down again. I didn't try to stop it, just speeded it past me in another aikido block as I leaned to the side. My antique assailant didn't go sprawling as expected, however. Somehow he managed to keep his balance, turn, and swing his wooden shield at my legs. Good move. I was impressed. I was also doing a cartwheel away from it before it could make contact.

My intention was to open up a little breathing room between us. But the grim-faced Mohawk stuck to me like a burdock to a bearskin. He had tossed away his shield now, but that made him no less deadly.

He shifted the war club from one hand to the other, feinted a strike to my left, then came at my right. But I'd expected that. I caught his wrist in a double-handed block, locked, twisted the club from his grasp and threw him. He landed on his back hard enough to prove to me that he'd never taken a semester of Oriental martial arts. It should, at the least, have knocked the air out of him.

It didn't. He was back on his feet in a heartbeat. That worried me almost as much as the memory of how his wrist felt—like a tree limb— as I locked it and threw him.

His hand whipped down to his belt, to a beaded sheath I hadn't noticed before. A bone-handled knife flashed in his hand. I felt strangely relieved that the knife—Jim Bowie size—was made of steel, not pressure-flaked flint. Whatever time warp my new playmate had emerged from, it was at least post-Columbian.

I looked at the war club in my hand, then hurled it away from me as far as I could with a backhanded throw. Its weight had felt strange. Using another man's weapon gave me no advantage. I held up my hands in what I hoped might be read as the universal gesture of peace.

His response was equally wordless and just as universal—a snake-quick thrust of his knife toward my heart that I barely managed to dodge.

Dodge. Strike. Dodge. Thrust. Spin. Block. The pattern of our movements was as intricate as the weave of a spider's web in the moonlight. I did have a plan. Keep him striking at me, tire him, wear him down. Great plan—except I was the one wearing down. I'd managed to pull off my shirt and wrap it around my right arm to protect me from getting an artery severed, but blood was trickling down my cheek from one slash of that razor-sharp blade. And the pain I'd been feeling in my knee had been steadily getting worse as sometimes happened when I pushed myself to the limit. I wasn't sure how long it would be before it locked up in a spasm.

But before my knee gave out, something else happened. There came a pause then, the kind of moment that occurs in a fight to the death. It was like that moment when the wolf and the deer not brought down by the first attack face each other, when the predator stares into the eyes of the prey and sees that look of weakness and final surrender.

There was no such weakness in the calm, cold gaze of that Mohawk warrior. But, then again, he was not the deer. No matter how many times I had thrown him to the earth, he had bounced up like an Iroquoian Antaeus. Each time I'd tried holds and throws that should have broken bones or disabled him, he'd either found the leverage and the strength to resist them or risen from the ground unharmed.

However, he had fought like a man from the past. Nothing that he had done indicated a knowledge of the martial ways I had spent two decades of my own life learning.

His knife going back and forth as he stood there, weaving a pattern in the air as fascinating and deadly as the motions of a snake. He was crouched low, feet spread wide, one arm held out to the side. I would not be able to sweep his legs out from under him again. His teeth showed in a tight, mirthless smile. He still had said nothing.

But I heard another a voice I had not yet heeded speaking to me. Disarm him, subdue him, take him alive. That had been my intention. But Sifu Huang's voice was insistent now.

Not this time. Kill him, or he will kill you.

Our fight had carried us downhill to the edge of the trees where Dennis had parked the jeep. But, like Dennis, the jeep was gone. Even the logging trail seemed to have vanished.

A small wind moved through the branches of the hemlock behind me. A huge moth, its wings marked with patterns like eyes of the night, fluttered in a beam of moonlight above the head of the one who wanted to take my breath. And I heard the call of the cat owl.

20

The memory of a dream—
is it a dream as well?

I dropped my hands, as if I could hold them up no longer. I turned my eyes away. I'd once seen a caribou in the Arctic Wildlife Refuge do just that. Surrounded by wolves, one leg hamstrung, it had dropped its head to the Alaskan tundra and begun grazing on the last grass of late summer.

I heard the quick intake of the Mohawk warrior's breath. He was about to strike the coup de grace, just as the wolves attacked the throat of the caribou that had finally given itself to them.

But I was not the caribou. I was komodo, the giant lizard. In *pentjak-silat*, komodo strikes only when the time is right. Strikes out of stillness. I drew the breath from the center of my body, feeling the warmth of *tji* move down my arm in my left arm, in my hand, into my index finger.

The one who sought to take my breath leaped forward with a panther's grace. His blade darted toward my heart like the beak of a heron stabbing an unwary fish.

But just before that knife dove into my flesh, just barely before, I dropped low and pivoted. And as I did so, I shouted. In martial arts, that shout, which is more than a shout, is called the *ki-yah*, an explosion of breath and force from the diaphragm. It channels the projection of that invisible, but palpable energy called *ki* or *chi* or *tji* that is centered within all of us, but seldom sensed by most humans. Old people who were known as mteowlin learned a similar scream. So powerful that it could shatter the stones, so charged with an indescribable energy that it could kill.

In the great echoing center of that great shout that froze the air around me and slowed all motion but my own, I struck as the point of his knife slid past me, drawing a line of blood across my abdomen. But my hand had found his throat, my finger was driven into that hollow between the carotid artery and the windpipe.

I felt the collapse of cartilage and the cracking of bone and saw, brief as the sparkle of a mote of dust in moonlight, the surprise in his dark eyes. Then, like the explosion of a puffball mushroom crushed by a foot, he was gone. A cloud of dust billowed about me and out of it came flying the eye-winged moth.

It flapped up as if trying to escape. But as it did so, the cat owl flew up out of the hemlock tree. Dived. Struck. A single brown moth wing fluttered past my face as the owl flew back into the trees, its talons clenched tight about a lifeless piece of the night. And then, just as before at the end of my dream of running from something unseen, I sensed a malevolent presence withdrawing, felt the sticky pull of a spiderweb across my cheeks.

I took a stumbling step back, my knee locking up as I did so, but before falling I was stopped by something solid, cool, and metallic. It was the fender of the jeep. I looked up. The moon was gone and the first light before dawn was trembling through the hemlocks.

"Podjo, what the hell? That yell was loud enough to wake the dead!"

I looked up the slope. Dennis was sitting where I had last seen him asleep. A blanket around his shoulders, his hair sticking out in all directions, he resembled an overgrown version of the Scarecrow in *The Wizard of Oz*.

He stood up, licked the fingertips of both hands and combed his hair back with his fingers, took his glasses from his shirt pocket, cleaned them with the tail of his shirt, and put them on. Then, blanket still over his shoulders, he walked down to me.

"You call that a *kata*, right? Pretending to be fighting with an imaginary opponent like that. Man, you were moving like a wild man. Your eyes were shut the whole time!" Dennis looked closer at me. "You knew what you were doing, right?"

"What?" I said.

Dennis shook his head. "Sleepwalking! No, sleep-fighting! You must of run into some of those low branches. Look, you got a scratch on your cheek. One on your stomach, too. Man, that must have been some dream!"

"Some dream," I agreed, looking down at my knee that was starting to unlock, though the pain in it was not lessening.

And that was when I saw something on the ground next to my foot. I watched as the dawn wind blew it away—the tattered, large-eyed wing of an io moth.

21

We do not see the wind
until the trees are moved by it

I was doing slow stretches, to loosen my knee and let go of the tension I still held in my whole body from the combat that took place somewhere in the uncertain terrain between reality and a bad medicine dream.

My old T-shirt, which I'd finally unwrapped from my arm, had been a bit too much the worse for wear. With all the blood on it, it was no longer easy to read the message emblazoned above the image of a grizzly with an Uzi. SUPPORT THE RIGHT TO ARM BEARS. The clean T-shirt that I now wore, selected from my pack, bore a picture of Geronimo in a Cadillac—REBORN PAGAN arched above his head.

By the time I finished stretching, Dennis had stowed everything in the jeep, rinsed out my T-shirt in a nearby brook, cut half a dozen oranges into sections, and placed out four peeled and bisected bananas next to two bowls of dry trail mix. Dennis had always loved housework and cooking. He and Patty Jean took equal turns at it in their home. Whenever one of the many kids in their house called out for "Mom," they weren't surprised when he responded. Dennis came as close as any man could to being what every woman really needs—a sturdy wife.

"I was just thinking," Dennis said.

"A dangerous pastime."

Dennis ignored my comment.

"I was just thinking," he repeated.

"I thought I smelled smoke."

Dennis looked over his glasses at me. *Enough.*

"I was just thinking"—he paused while I kept my mouth shut—"that it's time to leave the jeep. They got helicopters up. It'd be harder for them to pick us out on foot."

Both Dennis and I had been trained by the best in the ways to go through the woods without being seen from behind, in front, or above. We'd been trained by Uncle John and Tom Nicola. The little stint we did later in Marine Recon was like a little extra edge stropped onto the razor.

We took it slow and quiet, jogging steadily, our feet making very little noise as we went. Big as he was, Dennis moved through the woods like a bear. If you've ever sat in a forest just listening for an hour or two in a place where there are no other humans around, you may hear a lot of noise. But most of it is from the smallest animals: chipmunks, squirrels, the occasional shrew. Sit long enough and you might hear the feet of a deer walking, pausing to listen, then continuing on. But you won't hear a bear, even if one is stirring somewhere and watching you.

We both knew the way, but Dennis had been here more recently, so by mutual unspoken agreement, he led. The sun was two hands' width above the trees when he stopped. I followed his eyes to what he was looking at. It was a pile of large brown marbles, still steaming. More than twice as big as deer droppings, it was moose scat.

"Extra-large, bite-size," I said in a soft voice

Dennis let a smile play over his face. He knew I was referring to the joke Penacook guides sometimes played on flatlanders who came up from the cities to hunt deer. It was not the kind of joke you played on everyone—just those whose attitude made it clear that they were the Head Bwana and you were the indigenous equivalent of pond scum. Before you take them onto the trail you sneak out from the camp and lay down a handful of round chocolate candies.

"Hunh," you'd say to your unwary employer, "deer poop. Me check and see if fresh."

Then you'd scoop up a few of them and eat them . . . which has been known to make some grown white men turn even paler, or lose their cookies.

I bent over the tracks the moose had left behind.

"Just ahead of us?"

Dennis nodded.

"Cow, maybe five years old?"

"Got a little one with her."

"I saw the tracks."

We both sat and waited. The moose and her calf had to be close, moving up the trail just ahead of us. It was best to give them time to move away. The wind was blowing our way and we might come up on her without her knowing we were there. Not a good idea with a cow moose who has a calf to protect. I'd seen big brown bears in Alaska give very wide berths to cow moose with little guys behind them.

"I ever tell you about the moose car?" I said to Dennis.

"Tell me."

"Just outside Fairbanks, on the Alcan highway. This guy had driven all the way up from Seattle in his new Toyota. Came around a bend and there was a big bull moose standing in the middle of the road."

"Moose get big there."

"Really big. So the guy stopped and waited. But the moose didn't move. This guy was in a hurry."

"Wanted to *get there*."

"So he pulled up closer to the moose and revved his engine. Moose didn't move. So, you know what he did."

"He honked his horn?"

"He honked his horn."

"Bad idea."

"Bad idea. Moose do not like horns. So that big bull moose turned its head and looked down at the Toyota, kind of the way the animals in Gary Larson's *Far Side* cartoons look sometimes. Then that moose jumped on top of the car, did a little dance, hopped off, and strolled away. The guy wasn't hurt, but the roof was flattened and he couldn't get the doors open. The car was still running, so he drove it the rest of the way into Fairbanks. When he pulled into the first garage he saw, the mechanic just looked at that flat car and said to the guy . . ."

I paused. Dennis finished it for me.

"Moose, eh?"

The wind had shifted and was behind us now, carrying our scent down the trail. The moose and her calf had been given enough time to amble back into the birch and beech and maples. We slung on our packs and continued at a ground-eating dogtrot.

The land was rising now and we were getting glimpses again of the Mountain. As we started up toward the crest of a rocky hill, Dennis lifted up a hand with his thumb and forefinger held an inch apart. We were almost there.

And someone was waiting for us.

I grabbed Dennis by the shoulder, stopping him. I pointed with my chin to the pile of rock just ahead of us at the top of that hill. It would be enough for anyone to lurk in ambush behind that ancient rubble left by the glacier as it shrank back north.

Dennis nodded. We would wait.

One heartbeat, two, three, four.

Then the one who had been concealed behind those stones stepped out and looked at us.

I took a quick breath between my teeth. His Mohawk face was that of the deadly warrior I had defeated in my dream.

22

The enemy of my enemy
is the enemy of my enemy

As we came closer to the Mohawk man whose face was straight out of my late-night nightmare, I began to feel a little reassured. The face and build were pretty much the same, but not the rest of him. No Mohawk haircut, just what looked to be shoulder-length raven hair pulled back into a ponytail with two feathers from a red-tailed hawk tied onto the braid.

His clothing looked strictly "Nowaday Indian." A black baseball cap with the bill turned backward, emblazoned Go Bulls, a black velvet jacket embroidered with the kind of stitchery favored by those who've served in faraway places with strange-sounding names after joining the American armed forces to see the world, meet interesting people, and kill them.

Below the tightly zipped coat, a silver belt buckle was partially visible. It was cinched under the comfortable bulge of an abdomen obviously formed by a dietary regimen of fry bread and Navajo tacos. Although this Indian guy seemed shaped from the same template as my previous night's attacker, his own plate was much fuller. If any abs were rippling with muscle, that muscle was well-concealed by a good twenty pounds of padding.

No loincloth, just fashionably faded Lees. No moccasins, just Air Jordans. It was enough of a difference from my dream date to make me feel slightly reassured. Why only slightly?

Did I forget to mention the AK-47 that he was holding with the same efficient familiarity of a logger cradling his favorite Husqvarna chainsaw? Plus that the AK-47 was pointing in our direction?

There was a time, in the not-so-recent past, when the Russians claimed to have invented everything first. The airplane? Forget the Wright Brothers. The first manned flight took place outside St. Petersburg, I mean Leningrad, I mean St. Petersburg. The telegraph? Komrad, we do not call it Morse code. The telephone? Reverse the charges. Alexander Graham Bell was a decade late. Electric lights? Vacuum tubes? Television? Buttered toast?

Perhaps some of those claims were true. Maybe others were an understandable result of overcompensating for a Slavic inferiority complex. But there is one thing that the world has no trouble in granting the Ruskies a full semester of credit for—the world's best military rifle.

Because of his invention of the weapon that some prefer to refer to by its maker's name, General Kalashnikov became a hero of the Soviet Union. By all accounts, a quiet modest man with the strong hands and the decent morality of a peasant, he never made a ruble from his creation. He had not done it for money, but to help his homeland. And, oh my, he did.

After World War II, his AK-47 proved as successful in the arms export market as it was in the hands of Soviet soldiers. Dealing death has always been a growth industry, especially when you're offering a reliable portable killing machine, which the AK-47 was in spades. Unlike the American M-1, it didn't jam—even when its barrel grew so hot from repeated firing that it began to glow. Mud, ice, snow, water—it didn't matter. It could also use different ammunition designed for other weapons. (Some joked that it could even be retrofitted to shoot rocks!) From Angola to Iran, from Vietnam to the Philippines, from Central America and Brazil to Northern Ireland and the Balkans, it was as welcome as a gift-bearing wedding guest. For longer than most of us have lived, it's been spitting out death as reliably as an influenza epidemic.

"Pizza Man!" Dennis said.

Huh?

Was it time for us to request our last meal? Did takeout cover this section of the forest primeval where the murmuring of the pines and the hemlocks was about to be drowned out by the rattle of gunfire?

"Yo, Captain Crunch," answered the Mohawk with the gun. His voice was as deep and melodious as that of Floyd Westerman, the famous Lakota activist, musician and—like most surviving members of AIM—Hollywood actor. He smiled and slung his weapon back over his shoulder.

"Captain Crunch?" I said.

"I forgot to mention," Dennis said. "We all got code names. The idea was that when they listen in on the conversations on our walkie-talkies it might confuse them."

There was no time for me to debate the relative merits of having your adversaries take you seriously when you sound like a junkfoodie in a supermarket. The big Indian guy, as tall as his nocturnal counterpart, had stepped forward and held out a paw. We did the Red Power handshake. Like all Indians, we didn't squeeze each other's hands as we did so. To Indians, a handshake is never supposed to be a contest or a sign of superior physical strength. Two hands relaxing into each other's gentle grasp is better proof of the trust and mutual respect a handshake is meant to convey.

"Pizza Man is just my handle on patrol," the big Mohawk said, grinning. "My Indian name is Falling Rocks."

Falling Rocks. It's one of the oldest Nowaday Indian jokes. Usually told at great length before getting to the punch line. The short version is that at the end of whatever Indian war with the white-eyes, there was one warrior who refused to give up. Undaunted, he retreated to the hills. He was so fierce that signs were put up by the sides of mountain highways to warn people that he still might attack. WATCH OUT FOR FALLING ROCKS.

Did he not recognize me as a fellow Skin? Maybe it was my brown hair. At first glance, maybe even first and ten, a lot of people don't see that I am Indian. Or maybe he knew that I'd get it. After all, I knew the secret handshake.

"I'm Jacob Neptune," I said. "But you can call me a cab."

A smile spread down from the corners of his eyes to cross his craggy face.

"My real name's Pete Cook," he rumbled. Then he slapped me on the shoulder with his open palm. "Good to meet you."

He turned to Dennis. "Got some smokes in that backpack, brother?" he asked as they shook hands.

Dennis pulled out a pack of American Spirit cigarettes.

"My brand," Pete Cook said. "If you are going to abuse the sacred, do it with an Indian cigarette."

He unzipped a front pocket on his jacket, stuck the cigarette pack in, and zipped it back shut.

"Glad I happened to run into you guys!"

"Didn't you come out to meet us?" Dennis said.

"No, I'm out looking for someone." Pete Cook's face was not smiling now. "She vanished two nights ago."

A cold feeling went down my back like a load of snow dumped from a hemlock branch.

"Was she wearing a silver bracelet?" I asked.

23

The one who runs
is the one pursued

Pete Cook didn't answer. His dark Mohawk eyes stared into mine as the centuries swirled around us.

Three hundred years ago there were two old Abenaki men. Their names were Beaver and Muskrat. They lived in one of our villages along the big river. Though they were not related by blood, they were as close as brothers. They were both mteowlin.

One night, as they walked by the river, they saw a strange light. It came from the island in the middle of the river.

"Maybe that light is a Mohawk spy," Beaver said.

"That may be so," Muskrat agreed.

So they waded into the river. They took the form of the animals of their names. As a beaver and a muskrat, they could swim easily to the island. They swam upstream against the current. When they were close enough, they saw a party of men camped around a small fire on the river island. They were Mohawks.

"We should swim closer," Muskrat said.

"They may see us," Beaver said.

"We must hear what they plan," Muskrat said.

So the two of them swam closer. Now they could hear voices. The Mohawks were holding a war council. A tall Mohawk whose face was blackened by paint was speaking:

"When the sun rises tomorrow, we will attack the village downstream."

"We must go now, brother," Beaver whispered.

Muskrat did not listen to him. "No," Muskrat hissed. "We must hear more."

One of the Mohawks in the war party was also a man who had power. He stood up and walked to the edge of the river. He looked out into the dark water.

"An enemy is listening," the Mohawk man who had power said. "This will kill him."

Then he threw a war club made from a human thighbone. The war club whistled through the air and struck Muskrat in the head. It wounded him fatally. But before he could cry out or struggle, Beaver pulled him underwater. That way the dying struggles of his friend would not be heard. Then he swam back downstream, taking his friend's body with him. He swam back to their village.

When the Mohawks attacked our village at dawn, an ambush was waiting. The fighting was fierce. Only two Mohawks survived and were taken prisoner. Our people cut the heads off the dead enemies. They stuck poles in the ground on the island and put the heads of the dead enemies on those poles. So, to this day, that island is called Heads Island. Then they cut off the tips of the noses of the two Mohawks who were captured.

"Go home," they told the two Mohawks. "Tell everyone this is what they will get when they put their noses into our village."

That is how the story goes. That is how Tom Nicola told it to me when I was a kid.

As Dennis and I stood there with Pete Cook, that old story of enmity between our nations retold itself to me. But, even as I remembered it, I also remembered that nothing is ever that simple.

When Rogers's Rangers raided St. Francis two and a half centuries ago, many of the Abenakis who survived took shelter among the Mohawks at Akwesasne. They stayed there and married in. Not only had the Mohawks been closer to being friends than enemies since then, many of them were our relatives.

Despite being a Mohawk, this Pete Cook had been trusted enough by Mikwe and his Children of the Mountain to be chosen as a scout. I wondered, though, just where Pete Cook stood on the whole gambling question that lay under the surface of everything we were doing. Our activities were like the punji sticks Tom Nicola told me about—sharp poisoned stakes placed in the bottoms of tiger traps set in the middle of trails and covered by thin layers of branches and leaves that would give way under the weight of one who walked without caution. After all, the Mohawks at Akwesasne had a casino of their own now, despite having fought a miniature civil war between the gambling and anti-gambling factions two decades ago. Yet some of those Mohawk warriors who defended traditional land at Oka against the Québécois Sûreté and the Mounties had been on the side of the gamblers.

You can't tell the players without a program. And even then, you're never completely sure what side they are on. So what else is new in Indian country today?

"Who was the woman who vanished?"

Pete Cook took a deep breath. Maybe he would ask me later how I knew about the silver bracelet and then I'd tell him about seeing it in my dream of pursuit. Or maybe not.

"My sister Ruth," he said.

I looked at Dennis. He nodded his head. Getting to the camp could wait.

"We'll help you look," I said. "Let's go."

24

To see the heart
see through the heart

As we walked, Pete Cook answered the question I'd had in my head since he'd told me that his sister had been missing for two nights. Why had no one noticed she was gone?

He explained: "Things been confused at the camp. After the two deaths."

"Killings have a way of doing that," I said.

"Tell me about it. Felt like back in Afghanistan," Pete replied.

I nodded. Torturing prisoners and leaving their mutilated bodies where their buddies could find them was an old tactic of the Taliban. The objective was to taunt and panic the survivors. Was that what the two killings had been about? Except I didn't recall ever hearing about Afghanis eating hearts and livers.

"So, two days ago, a dozen people said they wanted to leave the camp," Pete Cook continued. "Mikwe told them they were free to go. Things were so crazy after they found Louise's body that when I didn't see Ruth the next day I thought she'd gone with them. It would have been just like her to do something like that. Ruth is . . . sort of different. She has this way of seeing things and then just acting on them without telling anybody what she's going to do."

He held his hands out, palms up, showing his frustration. I thought I got it. It's not easy living with someone who has dreams and visions or hears voices no one else can hear. It requires the kind of patience and understanding shown by my Uncle John and Aunt Mali.

Pete dropped his hands. "But this morning, Mikwe let me use his cell phone—the only one allowed in the camp—so I could ask how Ruth was. They said she wasn't with them."

"What was she looking for?" I said.

Pete Cook stopped walking. He turned and stared straight into my eyes. A blue jay flew across the clearing behind him. A small spinning wind lifted a few leaves from beneath a beech tree and made them dance up in a whirlwind that was growing larger as it interrupted their journey back into the soil.

It is different among our people than among those raised with white ways. "Always make eye contact, children"—that is what whites tell kids in their primary schools. If you don't look a person in the eye, they may think you're sneaky or ashamed of yourself. But among Indians, in general, when you talk you are supposed to not make eye contact. You look down to the earth, the earth that is always listening and knows the truth of your words. To stare into another's eyes when talking can be seen as rude or challenging.

Dennis cleared his throat, but Pete Cook didn't break his gaze. Then a small grim smile appeared at the edge of his mouth.

"Damn," Pete Cook said, looking down and shaking his head. "You're one of *them*, too, ain't you?"

"How much could Ruth see?" I asked. I didn't mean seeing with her eyes, but that other sort of vision that comes from the realm non-Indians refer to as the supernatural.

"Even when she was a kid, I always felt like my little sister was older than me. She'd guess things that were going to happen, remember things before they happened. What about you?"

"I dream," I said, looking past him. "And I find things."

The whirlwind of leaves was blowing stronger now, even though there was no other breeze in the trees around us—and I knew that Dennis and Pete Cook wouldn't see that whirlwind. The dream of two nights before came swirling back to me as I put my hand to my forehead.

The full moon was shining down on the narrow trail between the trees as I ran, my breath rasping in my throat. At the bend in that trail, I saw another smaller trail climbing up the slope to my right and I turned onto it, my fingers grasping at the soil as I scrambled on all fours, past a small hemlock with intricately twisted branches. There! Ahead of me, above me was an old, old birch tree, its trunk marked with the sign of the thunder beings, its roots twisted into the crevices of a rock ledge. The moonlight glittered from the silver and turquoise of my bracelet that fell off my wrist as I reached to that ledge to pull myself up and I saw the hands that were not my hands. They were slender hands with strong graceful fingers and long, painted fingernails. And just as a roar came from close, far too close behind me, I saw the place I'd hoped was here, reached for it . . . and then the blow struck . . . and I was falling toward a dark mouth.

Something grabbed me by the arm. I opened my eyes. Pete Cook had kept me from falling.

Dennis reached for me, but I raised my hand and stepped free of Peter's grasp. I turned toward the direction we'd just come from.

"We need to go back," I said.

I knelt at the place where I saw again—just as in my sudden dream—that a foot had scraped the red-capped lichen from the granite of the trail. Then I looked to the right. The hemlock tree with its tangled branches was up there.

"This is where she turned off the trail."

There were signs left by her flight. Not that much to see, unless you looked with an eye used to seeing things out of place in nature. A stone turned over so that the darker earth beneath it could be seen, a small branch on a lowbush blueberry broken to expose its green layer of cambium below the outer bark. And here and there, where thin soil had been washed across the trail by the rains of the past season, the partial prints of her feet.

"Here," Pete Cook said. His eyes were good. A branch of a small juniper was still bent back and caught beneath another branch where she had been climbing. I leaned over to touch, caught in a tangle of raspberry bushes, a single long strand of black hair.

She had gone off the trail, but her flight was not that of someone made irrational by fear. She was heading up toward the rock face in front of us.

There was no sign yet of anything pursuing her from behind. But that made sense. Whoever—or whatever—it was had probably been flanking her, cutting ahead to wait for her. She'd sensed that. It was why she'd left the trail to head for whatever haven she could find.

"Caves," I said. "Ruth ever mention caves?"

Pete Cook shook his head. "No, but she spent more time in the woods than I did. You know any caves around here, Dennis?"

"We never spent much time around this part of the Mountain," Dennis said. "Our Little People live in cliffs like that." He pointed with his lips.

"Are they rock-throwers?" Pete Cook said. "Us Mohawks got Little People like that, too. Heave stones at us if we get too close."

Bet they speak Abenaki, I thought. Then I saw something out of the corner of my eye, something small and quick on the steep slope above us. Maybe it was a gray fox—or maybe it wasn't.

"Come on," I whispered, looking in the direction that the little gray one had taken. "This way."

25

The open hand
catches the wind

*O*nce, Aunt Mali said, there was a man who was a good hunter. A really good hunter. Whatever he hunted, he was always successful. One day, though, when he went to the stream to drink, he saw strange footprints in the sand by the water's edge. They looked like the footprints of a small child. But he knew there were no children nearby. It was a place where children did not go.

For three days in a row he saw those footprints. Then on the fourth day he saw something else. Near those footprints he saw little circles and curls of clay, as if someone had been making tiny baskets. So it was that he knew whose footprints he had been seeing.

He went to the oldest man in the village.

"Has anyone ever seen them?" the hunter asked.

"Sometimes we see them from the corners of our eyes," the old man answered. "But when we turn our heads to look at them, they are gone."

"Has anyone ever caught one?"

The old man rubbed his hand across his mouth. "No one I ever heard of has done such a thing. They are too quick. No one can get close enough to catch one of them. It is said, too, that anyone who tries to do wrong to them will suffer. But it is also said that they can give great gifts to anyone they favor."

From that day on, the hunter thought of nothing else but the Mikumwesuk, those Little People whose footprints he had seen. He spent many days and nights watching the streambank. He never saw them, even though new *footprints still were there every morning in the moist sand. Finally, one night as he slept, an idea came to him.*

The next day, the hunter went again to the stream as he had done so many times before. This time, though, he did not conceal himself in the ferns or hide among the willows and water reeds. Instead, he walked backward toward the water, leaving deep, clear prints. Then, when he was almost at the water's edge, he dug a deep hole carefully in the sand at the base of a thick tussock of grass. He crawled feetfirst into that hole and then pulled the sand in around him, covering himself up to his neck. He smoothed the sand with his hands so that no trace of his efforts would be seen. His head concealed in that tussock of grass, its blades dancing in the wind before his watching eyes, he waited.

He waited all that night and all through the next day. The Mikumwesuk did not come, but still he waited. His limbs grew cold and his back felt stiff, but he did not move. Insects walked across his face and animals brushed against that tussock of grass as they came to drink from the stream, but he did not move. He stayed there for three days and nights.

Now he could no longer feel his own body. He felt as if he had always been a part of this riverbank. Like the sand and the water, the grasses and the fish, the sunlight and shade, he had always been there. He barely remembered that he was a human being. All that remained was his determination to wait. So he waited.

Very early, on the morning of the fourth day, the ferns parted at the edge of the woods above the stream. A very small man, a tiny hunter with a little bow and a quiver of arrows, came out. He was following the footprints the hunter had left behind. He saw that the footprints led to the water and did not come out again. From the look on the little man's face, it was a mystery that puzzled him. He followed those footprints, one cautious step after another. As he did so, he came closer and closer to the tussock of grass where the hunter waited.

When Mikumwesu was close enough, the hunter lifted up his arms from the sand and grabbed him.

He was not easy to hold. Though small, he was as strong as a lynx. He struck at the hunter with his bow. He bit and scratched. But the hunter would not let go of him.

Finally the little man stopped struggling. He spoke in a voice as high and clear as the call of a robin.

"Who are you and why do you seek to hurt me?" Mikumwesu asked.

"No, little brother," the hunter said in a soft voice. "I do not want to hurt you. I only seek to hold you as one friend holds another."

"If you are my friend, then set me free," Mikumwesu said.

"Ah, little brother," said the hunter, "I would be lonely without you."

So they continued to speak to each other—the little man seeking to gain his freedom, the hunter always denying it, yet taking great care to never threaten Mikumwesu with harm.

Finally Mikumwesu looked the hunter straight in his eyes. "My friend," Mikumwesu said, "you have my word that I will not run away. You have caught me. Now, because I ask you as a friend, set me free."

Immediately the hunter let go of the little man.

Mikumwesu was so pleased that he began to leap and dance. He sang a little song as he did so. Then he came back to the hunter's side.

"Since you have trusted my word, I see that you truly are my friend," Mikumwesu said. "Now my people and I wish to give you something."

Then Mikumwesu whistled like the sweet song of the hermit thrush. A little woman, even smaller than the tiny hunter, came out of the ferns.

"This is my sister," said Mikumwesu. "She has been watching you each day as you come to the stream and she likes what she has seen. No one has been worthy to be her husband. Now, if you are willing, she will marry you."

"I agree and I thank you both," said the hunter. As soon as he spoke those words, the little woman began to grow in size. She grew until she was a large as a human being. She was a fine, handsome woman with strong limbs and a clear, certain look in her eyes. She reached out and took the hunter by his hands.

"Now," said Mikumwesu, "you will have good fortune all of your life and you will always remember your little brother."

And so it was just that way. And when I last saw that hunter and his wife, they were still living together happily.

It was easy to follow her trail. In part, it was because the tips of branches had been broken and stones dislodged along the way. In part, it was because I had been this way before—though not in my body.

"Down there," I said.

My knee was bothering me again, which made what should have been an easy descent across the face of the hill hard for me—though I was careful not to show it. I stayed ahead as the three of us scrambled down the slope of loose stones that rattled as they rolled around us, clicking like the sound of a turtle-shell rattle being shaken.

When we reached the base of the cliff that rose a hundred feet straight above us, I stopped. I knelt, ignoring the spear point of pain that was piercing my knee, and pushed aside the bushes that obscured the mouth to the cave that I knew had to be there. I leaned close to listen and heard a faint sound, no louder than a whisper.

Of the three of us, I was the only one small enough to squeeze through that narrow opening into a darkness that slanted down and back at a 45-degree angle. As Dennis held my feet, I crawled in, my arms stretched out ahead of me, my hands open as I slid on my chest and stomach, feeling nothing at first, but guided by that sound of shallow breath. Then I touched a limp hand, grasped a wrist.

"Pull me out," I called back. "I've got her."

26

*Five fingers together
make a single fist*

Peeople of the dawn. That is what *Wabanaki* means. The name our Algonquin-speaking cousins such as the Anishinabe called us. Alnonbak, we called ourselves. That just means human beings.

Thirteen or more different nations made up the Wabanaki peoples. Penobscots, Passamaquoddies, Micmacs, Malecites, and all of our other nations in northern and western New England that were driven off their lands. Nations that took refuge in such places as the mission villages of Wolinak and Odanak in southern Quebec, nations whose names were almost lost to history as our league dissolved and our hands no longer held each other tight. It seemed for a time as if our dawnland nations would disappear with the setting sun.

But we did not. By the end of that arbitrary division of sun cycles referred to by the white-minded as the twentieth century, we were growing visible again and still looking toward the sunrise. No one else on this continent saw the sun before we did. Our old people watched it rise, gave it thanks every morning for all its gifts of life and light, for both seeing and being. That is why the doors of our wigwams always faced east—toward the warmth of new life.

The T-shirt I'd put on to face this new day bore the logo SPIRIT OF THE WILD over the image of another returning New Englander—a timber wolf peering out from among the trees.

Mikwe probably would have preferred my wearing a leather loincloth to match the traditional attire he was favoring these days. I'd been forced to listen to a long lecture from him last night on tribal sovereignty, the evils of neocolonialism, solidarity forever, and the importance of not wearing sneakers if you are a real Indian. His way of saying how glad he was I had helped find Ruth.

As I knelt to tighten the laces of my New Balance 585s, I looked up at the faint glow in the eastern sky. Still an hour until sunrise, even the first birds were not stirring yet. I'd done my warm-up exercises. My heart rate was at a good level, my limbs loose. I started to run the long run, run to run up the sun.

Running has always been woven into the lives of our people. Perhaps it is less common now than in the old days, but it remains in our cultural fabric like the thin strands of sweetgrass threaded into an ash splint basket. Running, we run into the heart of our land. Our feet make sweet music as they pound the drum of the earth.

My Uncle John and Tom Nicola taught me to run. Each of them had been great runners in their day. But nothing like our old people, they said. They could *run*. Those two modest men, both of them with legs still as strong as the roots of the ash trees, taught me what they knew. They saw how easily running came to me, how I was called to it the way the sky calls the wings of a young hawk.

Uncle John taught me that to run with my hands raised high above my head would build my lungs. He had me fill my mouth with water before I started to run, water that I would hold in my mouth and not swallow till I had gone at least a mile. That was how I learned to breathe through my nose, even and strong.

Tom Nicola taught me about carrying stones to the mountaintop. It was really just a big hill, the closest thing to a mountain we had near the reservation. Pick up a small stone, run with it to the summit. Place the stone there and run back down again. Keep doing that stone after stone until you have built a pile knee high. Then, stone by stone, carry them back down the mountain again, running all the way.

In the old days, our runners were the ones who carried news and warnings from one village to the next. In our oldest stories, heroes have such names as Swift Runner.

Each morning of my life, I've run unless I have been kept from it by travel or danger, or a stiffness in that one knee that sometimes even stretching can't remedy. The land under my feet has changed, living soil to dead asphalt, grass to sand, cushioned pine needles to the concrete of a city walkway, but the heart of the run has remained the same, as familiar as my own heart beating and the throbbing rhythm of my soles. I run as the sun starts to redden the sky, as small birds begin to fly up, twittering with their songs of praise.

My run was not taking me along the trails through the forest. Caution and the need to stay close to the campsite just in case anything else happened kept me off those mountain trails. Instead, I followed the grassy edges of the miles of driveways and parking lots that had once been used by motorized campers in Winnebagos. No tourists now, though, since the state had closed down the campsite prior to the now-postponed public auction. Just us Indians here since the Mountain had been declared Indian Land Forever by Mikwe and Co.

But even along the paved roadways, this was still far from the feel of New York City. My morning runs there always took me through Central Park, where the stones that lift up through the soil are as ancient as anything solid on the surface of our planet. But even though the trees there may fill with the songs of migrating warblers and red-tailed hawks circling overhead, there's always something in the air that is not quite right. It might just be the haze of pollution drifting in from the million cars passing on Park Avenue and drifting down from Con-Ed's smokestacks. Or perhaps it's that wrongness of heart and spirit emanating from dealers dispensing stupefying poison under the statue of a Latino Liberator, or the homeless wrapped in rags and newspapers, or the drunken father beating his child to death in a tenement twenty blocks away . . .

This place was not the city. But I had to admit to myself that death was still walking close here. Where there's life, there's death in balance. And wherever I went, I'd always be near that border where the two come close—or cross.

My legs were carrying me up a slope where I would have a clear view of the rising sun. I guessed that I was doing seven-minute miles, three in a row so far. Not that bad, though before my knee was crushed I used to be able to do a dozen miles in five minutes or less each. I wasn't clocking myself with a stopwatch, but I knew my own pace better than the high school and college track coaches whose angry or despairing faces matched their voices when they would ask yet again why a boy with God-given natural talents like mine didn't care enough to want to *win*.

The answer was easy—it was because I loved to run, just run, not beat anyone else at it. When you run for yourself, it doesn't matter how fast another runner goes. I wasn't built the way a classical long-distance runner is supposed to be built. I had too much upper body muscle and bulk, yet no one could ever leave me in the dust. Whether it was a mile or a marathon, I was always within reach of the winner. I just never felt justified in sprinting ahead and taking the leader's heart. For a trophy, or some green pieces of paper? Big deal. There should be more at stake than that.

Like your life?

Did I just think that? Or had those words drifted in from some other place? For just a moment both my nose and my mind scented something as strong and sudden as the decaying body of an animal left by the road and it made me stumble as if I'd stepped into a hole.

I stopped, rubbing my knee that had started aching again as suddenly as if someone had fired a dart into it. The smell of death had vanished, but I'd been left with a lingering feeling of imbalance and . . . anger. I rubbed my eyes with my palms, trying to wipe away what felt like thin strands of a spider's web across my face

I began to run again, faster now, ignoring the pain, willing it to burn away. My arms were pumping oxygen into my lungs, my head was lifted up to the sky and the new day. I was awake and alive and angry and a song was coming to me, a war song Tom taught me. It filled my mind as I ran and I felt those spiderweb wisps blow away like mist touched by the sun's warm rays.

I reached the top of the ridge, my arms held over my head. My heart was pounding like a powwow drum. I was drenched with sweat and gasping for breath and fully alive.

27

*One ear hears more
than ten mouths*

Without Dennis taking up as much room as a beached whale, our two-man tent seemed as spacious as a stadium. While I was taking my run, he was making his own slower circuit around the camp. Just looking things over. Dennis had a way of sniffing around like a lazy dog. Not seeming to be aware of much of anything, but taking in every strange and significant scent. We'd talk at noon about what he'd discovered. Then he'd be heading back south later this afternoon. He had too many responsibilities with his paying job, his volunteer work for the tribal office, and his family.

Me? My responsibility was to stay, provide an extra layer of security, and try to figure out why—and how—the Children of the Mountain, already surrounded by state and local cops, now seemed to be under attack from another direction that was not logically explained.

I stripped off the sweaty T-shirt and selected yet another from my pack. This one bore upon its breast a reproduction of my second favorite Gary Larson cartoon. It showed an arrow the size of an ICBM stuck in the side of an army fort. The caption was the sentry reporting: "There's only one Indian out there, sir. But he's a big one."

I ran a comb through my hair and stepped outside in time to almost knock over the man who had been sent to rouse me for my morning chores. He looked disappointed and, I suppose, so did I. His disappointment was because he'd been robbed of the opportunity to prod me out of bed while making sarcastic comments about urban Indians being used to sleeping all day. My disappointment was that I knew him. It was Mook Glossian.

I hadn't noticed Mook in the circle of people who had gathered around the night before when Dennis and I had walked into the camp behind Pete Cook, who carried his sister Ruth cradled in his arms.

As soon as we had pulled her from her hiding place, her brother had taken over. He'd wrapped his shirt around her to warm her, washed her face with water from Dennis's canteen. The huge Mohawk's gentleness showed such protectiveness and love for his little sister that Dennis and I had just stepped back.

It brought back to my mind the unforgettable image of that gorilla and the kid. You know, the one that picked up a little child who had fallen over the wall into an enclosure and been knocked unconscious. The gorilla had picked the child up and cradled him, protecting the little one until keepers came. Then, a look of concern on its dark face, the gorilla handed the child—who turned out not to be badly hurt—over to them. That was sort of how it looked with Pete Cook and his sister Ruth, except for two major differences. First, the gorilla was female. Second, the ape was better looking. But then it wasn't Mohawk.

As Pete held Ruth, Dennis and I doing what we could to be helpful, I'd noticed that size and gender were not the only differences between the siblings. There was nothing tough or rough-edged about Ruth's face. Whereas her brother's face looked to have been hacked out of a block of flint, hers was even-featured and smooth as a piece of wood washed into a graceful shape by wind and waves.

Maybe it is that women and children in distress make the Galahad syndrome kick in with some men. All I know is that the way Ruth looked made me feel incredibly protective, too, at that moment. And Dennis, too. If some hapless man-eating monster had chanced to fall upon us at that moment, the two of us would have ripped it apart with our teeth to protect her.

Atavistic, yes. But we thugs do have our uses from time to time. Think of us next time you are in trouble.

As Ruth lay there unconscious, I felt protective until she coughed and opened her eyes to meet my gaze. For just a second, I found it hard to breathe.

What was it that hit me? Was it the lack of fear in her eyes, the quick intelligence I saw there that told me she was seeing the humor of her situation as she was being hovered over by three huge men? I'd gone

from feeling protective about a woman I'd never met to being aston-
ished, practically knocked over by the personality that radiated from
her face. Such radiance nearly gave me a sunburn.

Somehow, though, as she regarded me with the kind of feminine
poise that proves men are a million years behind the opposite sex, I
controlled myself. I didn't squirm onto my belly or babble "I am not
worthy."

"Hi," I managed.

"Hi," she said back. Her voice was weak, but she still said it so much
better than I did.

She turned her eyes to Dennis and her brother.

"Thank you," she whispered

That was all she said then. She was too weak to say anything else and
kept her eyes closed all the way back to the camp.

As Phil carried her into the infirmary tent, he'd paused for a moment
in the doorway. "Tomorrow?" he'd said. "Talk to her then?"

Even though all I wanted to do at that moment was to curl up at the
foot of Ruth's bed and listen to her voice say just about anything, I
nodded.

"Tomorrow," I'd agreed.

❧

That tomorrow had come. But instead of Ruth Cook, who did I get to
see first thing in the morning? Mook Glossian.

Mook was my age, even though he looked a decade older. Other than
that and the Chingachook outfit he was wearing, he hadn't changed.
His stringy black hair still was unwashed, his eyes were still close together and shifty. His fingernails were still black and broken, hands
stained from years of work in a local garage. A couple of years ago, I'd
heard, his wife had finally left him. Good for her! After years of enduring verbal abuse daily, black eyes and bruises every other weekend when
Mook had too much to drink, she'd found refuge in a women's shelter
in Boston.

Long-armed and heavy-shouldered, Mook was six feet tall, but looked
much shorter because of the sideways, hunched-over way he walked. It
made me think of the old story about the Glossian family. Before they
were human beings, they were toads. Toad or not, you didn't want Mook
Glossian mad at you. He'd say nothing for weeks, then sidle up to you
one day in a bar and break a bottle over your head.

In my drinking days, when I was just back from Iraq, he did that to me once. That had been inadvisable. Back when I, too, drank too much, I was not a nice man, far from the confirmed pacifist I am now, as I'm certain you have noted.

I'd taken offense at the shards of glass stuck in my scalp and the blood trickling down my face, but had said nothing. Before Mook could swing a second time, my training had kicked in.

Lock the wrist, shake loose the neck of the beer bottle from his hand as he tries to slash me with it, sweep his feet out from under him, press him face-down on the floor, and bend his arm behind his back.

All that in less than three seconds. Then I slowed down and started counting out loud in Japanese.

"*Ichi*." Snap!

"*Ni*." Snap!

"*Sahng*." Snap!

By the time Dennis pulled me off him, I had broken three of Mook Glossian's fingers.

Mook Glossian. What surprised me most about seeing him was seeing him here. Even as a kid, Mook had been ashamed of being Indian. He'd even been known to claim his family was really Italian. Mook Glossian in buckskins was a rare sight to see.

He stepped back, maybe a little nervous at the way I was eyeing his left hand, whose first three digits looked just as good as new. He looked up at me sideways.

"Don't call me Mook," he said.

I hadn't, so I didn't.

"My name is Malsum."

Malsum the wolf. How slanderous of the lupine species. If I heard wolves howling later that night, I would know what they were saying.

Nooooooooooooo! Noooooooooooo!

But I kept quiet, which I could see was making Mook Malsum nervous and was thus a good reason to keep on saying nothing.

"Mikwe needs to see you," he snarled.

Mentally, I thought *Oh No!* Was I going to be subjected to another lecture like the one he delivered to me last night about the righteousness of our cause, about how we were not going to back down, and so on and on, sprinkled with semi accurate quotes from such figures as Red Jacket, Geronimo, and Oren Lyons, the Iroquois activist?

But all I said was "Okay."

I made my way to the one small permanent building that had housed the administrative center for the former state campsite and was the only place with electricity. The power lines into the Mountain had been cut off by the blockading forces of law and order, but the chugging gas-powered generator on the side of the building provided sufficient current for the building.

It looked strangely out of place, surrounded as it was now by a variety of wigwams and longhouses that had been built to resemble those in our pre-Contact villages. When I walked into the building, another incongruous sight awaited me. There, in the far corner of the room, still dressed in pre-colonial garb, Mikwe was sitting in front of a laptop computer typing. His asolkwan, the traditional headdress our elders wore, sat on the desktop next to him, the heron feathers bobbing in the breeze from the electric fan he'd placed facing himself. It was a hot morning, so I understood the practicality of it, but it was still hard to keep from chuckling, especially when I noted that, long as Mikwe's hair was on the sides and in back, he was suffering on top from the male pattern baldness brought on by the white genes present in every Penacook of our generation.

Mikwe looked up at me and then quickly back down at his typing.

"*Kwai kwai bidoba. Wliwini,*" he said. "Hello, my friend. Thank you."

"*Nda kagwi,*" I answered. "Don't mention it."

I was, to be frank, a little surprised. Part of it was the subdued atmosphere in the room. Rather than the soapbox he'd been the night before, Mikwe looked more like a tired and uncertain parent today than anything else. I was also surprised that Mikwe actually knew how to greet me in Indian, though I suspected that he had pretty much exhausted all the Penacook language he knew. Maybe there was more depth to him than I'd given him credit for.

He sighed, pushed himself back from the desk and turned his chair toward the window.

"I've only t-told a few people w-why you're h-here," he said. "People I trust like D-dennis and M-m-malsum." He paused, clearly trying to control the stammer that had been the only weakness he ever showed to the world when we were kids and he was killing himself to be the valedictorian of our high school class. It never showed up when he was in front of an audience, but in private it returned when he was feeling stressed.

He took a few breaths, looked back over his shoulder at me, then turned again to the window. "I know you had some history with Malsum, but he's ch-ch-changed. He really b-believes in our cause."

"Okay," I said. There was no point in arguing about the past, even if I had no intention of forgetting about it. The past, like the roots of a tree, holds up the present. Trace those roots and you may find the source of whatever it is that is going on now, especially when some of those roots turn out to be rotten.

"I thought you might b-be able to learn m-m-more if people just think you're another volunteer and not some k-k-kind of investigator."

"Good idea."

Mikwe nodded and pressed his lips together. "So I've assigned you to a w-work detail." He paused again. "Okay?"

"Sure."

That day, I reported to work. A cabin was being built of logs and I was assigned to the fitting and lifting crew. I quickly noticed that very few of the other Indians who were part of the Children were wearing anachronistic traditional outfits. Jeans, shirts, and sneakers abounded. It was only Mikwe and his closest associates who dressed like bit players from central casting. Making a visual statement, Mikwe called it. Always ready for the TV cameras. Neither Pete Cook nor his sister Ruth was anywhere in sight, nor was the one person that I was certainly not eager to see.

Malsum, the toad wolf was there, but not dirtying his paws. He seemed to be staying at the edge of things, peering around corners, listening in. He'd been like that as a kid, too, always looking for something someone else did wrong so that he could tell on them.

"Malsum's keeping busy," I said to one of my fellow-workers as we manhandled a beam.

"Right," the man said with a grim smile that verified my first impression of the toad wolf's role as Mikwe's main informer.

I knew Mook was watching me closest of all. But even when he thought he was out of sight from me, I could sense where he was. I remembered that as a kid, he'd been big for his age. He'd used that size advantage to bully the girls and the littlest boys, but he would never pick on anyone his size.

One day I tried to intervene when he chose Katlin as his target. Back then I was skinny and a head shorter than all the other boys, smaller than most of the girls.

"Stop it," I said, stepping up to him and looking up into his face. "Leave her alone."

Mook Glossian stared at me that day like I was a worm. But then he turned away as if he would leave us alone. For a brief happy moment, I thought I'd won. I didn't see him swing the stick at my head. The next thing I knew he had me down on the ground and was sitting on my chest with his knees on my elbows. My head was ringing.

"Want some, sissy?" he said. Then he started sticking his long filthy fingers up my nose, one after another.

Past turned into present as I stopped work and turned quickly to look over my left shoulder. Mook froze for a moment from where he was peeking out from behind the far corner of the half-built cabin. I nodded and wiggled my fingers at him in a happy greeting. He ducked back out of sight.

Fingers, I thought. How symbolic our subconscious minds can be.

28

Look for the tiger,
the tiger looks for you

"You lift?"

I looked over at the speaker, a man who had just spent the last half hour helping me move logs that weighed about as much as your average piano. He was no more than thirty years old, perhaps 5′9″, and built like an Olympic power lifter. His features were classically Abenaki—Indian with just a hint of French ancestry. He had deep-set eyes, round ears, a broad forehead and a strong chin. His complexion was brown, his hair thick and night-black.

The longhouse we were building was just that—long. Each course of the wall was a single tree trunk. The pines that the Children of the Mountain were taking had originally been slated for a clear-cut by a commercial firm. The Children had not been going through the forest like a harvester through a wheat field as the loggers would have done, but in their selective cutting they'd been taking the tallest and straightest trees. Neither the government nor the commercial logging firm were going to be pleased about that, but as long as the roadblocks were up and the impasse still going on, there was not much they could do.

"You lift?" the man said again.

"Hunh?" I said, wiping the sweat from beneath my nose with the back of my hand.

"Weights, I mean."

"Oh."

I wasn't sure what else to say. My working companion's simple question had thrown me at first—since I was already lifting my part of the log. Then, when I realized he was talking about pumping iron, I became even more uncertain of how to reply to a question clearly meant to establish common ground between us. I've never seriously lifted weights in my life. No bench press, squats, reps, or rows of whatevers. I'd come by my physique through a combination of genetic good fortune, tree climbing like an ape when I was a kid, and an adult life immersed in the martial arts.

"Thought so," he said, taking my silence as confirmation rather than confusion. "I pump some iron, too."

He held up a palm for me to slap, which I did. Then, as our right hands took hold of each other, despite the accompanying ripple of deltoids, pectorals, biceps, and triceps that went with that motion, his grasp was Indian-gentle.

"Nick Sabattis."

He'd waited all morning for that. The two of us had been sweating together in the sun for three hours without pause, working together with an ease and rhythm as he'd sized me up before giving me his name.

"*Pakwenogwisian*," I said. It means "You appear new to me."

"P`kwenag`wsian," he said back. A little different accent in the way he said it.

It's that way with our language. Scholars call it Western Abenaki, but it is made up of more than a dozen different dialects. Sokoki, Missisquoi, Cowasuck, Penacook, Norridgewock, Wawenock, Pigwacket among them—names of peoples and the places they were sometimes forced to leave behind in the bitter fighting that took place in the seventeenth and eighteenth centuries. Back when bounties were paid on Indian scalps.

Two and a half centuries ago, posters had been put up around New England. They offered bounties of a hundred pounds for a dead Indian, male or female, young or old. Then it had gone up to two hundred pounds. Finally, in 1772, it reached four hundred pounds. Four hundred pounds for the head—or the scalp—of an Indian, if taken by a private individual and not a member of the armed forces. Four hundred pounds was roughly the equivalent of $40,000 today, about what might be paid for a professional hit.

I shook my head. Next thing I'd be doing would be reciting "Lovewell's Fight" from memory again, the narrative poem written in the eighteenth century to glorify one of those scalp hunters who started a war. I'd been assigned to write a paper about the poem in my colonial literature class at Dartmouth and what I came up with both horrified my instructor and earned me a grudging *A*.

"Of worthy Captain Lovewell, I purpose now to sing," I murmured.

"Something wrong?" Nick Sabattis said.

"Just something stuck in my ear," I smiled. "Jake Neptune."

"Good to meet you, Jake. I come from upstate New York, around Long Lake," Nick Sabattis said.

I smiled a little broader. "Direct descendant of . . ."

"Mitchell Sabattis." Nick Sabattis was really grinning now.

"The greatest of all the nineteenth-century Adirondack guides."

"Don't get me started," Nick Sabattis said.

I nodded. I hoped he would get started on tales of Mitchell Sabattis, who was one of my heroes. Maybe later tonight if there was time. I directed that thought at him. He nodded back. Maybe later.

"You a guide, too?" I said.

"In a manner of speaking." Nick Sabattis pushed back his shoulder-length hair. He pulled a red kerchief from his back pocket, shook it out, folded it with care over his knee and then tied it around his sweat-beaded forehead. "Before I took a leave without pay to come here to the Mountain, I was a systems engineer with Big Blue."

Our brief break over, we went back to work. Nick might have been expecting me to tell him why I was here. Rather than speak a lie, something I hate worse than going to the dentist, I'd just said nothing, which was probably enough.

As far as my new buddy Nick and about everyone else was concerned, I was just another aboriginal recruit. Probably one on the wanna-be side, seeing as how I looked more white than red.

I was fully in agreement with Mikwe that such unspoken deceit was necessary. No one knew who or what was behind the murders. People in the camp might be part of it and probably were. In the short time I'd been present it had become clear to me what an incredibly mixed group of people this was. There was plenty of room for an infiltrator from the pro-casino crowd that opposed Mikwe on the one hand, or on the other hand from such agencies as the FBI, the BIA, the Division of Alcohol and Firearms, and the state police. Then there were other regional enemies of tribal recognition and Native sovereignty such as non-Native casino owners like Donald Trump (whose recent declaration that he was more Indian than the Mashuntucket Pequots rings like a proud anthem in Native ears), the lumber companies, and the League of Northeast

Regional Real Estate Developers. There were also others too numerous to name, including the nameless dark tingling presence that had
now cast its web at me several times, enough possibilities to make my
head spin. The only good thing was that being paranoid means that you
are never lonely.

Of the hundred or so Children of the Mountain who had remained
after the killings, no more than two dozen of them were people from
our own little tribe. There were Micmacs, Nipmucs, Penobscots, Pas-
samaquoddys and Wampanoags, and Mohawks. Mikwe had not been
picky about accepting whoever answered his call as long as they were
Indians from the northeast. So far, they all seemed like decent people—
with one notable exception. Strangers for the most part, they seemed
to be getting along well.

Then again, maybe it was because they were mostly strangers. When
you have families that have been living in the same town for a hundred
generations, you begin to understand what it is to hold a grudge.
"There's no feud like an old feud" could be the national anthem for your
average Indian reservation.

As Nick and I continued to work, there was no more talking between us other than the occasional "Ready?" and "I got it!" But the
internal dialogue inside my skull was deafening. Had the murders
been a way to force the Indians to invite in the outside authorities? Once
they were in, there'd be no way to ease them out again. For all intents
and purposes, the Indian takeover would be over. The state and the
feds would love to be asked to come in to a place that Indians had declared Indian land because this problem was too big for the Indians to
solve.

As cold and heavy-handed a tactic as it was, the murders were a clever
way to end the occupation, especially because of their sensational nature. When the national press got hold of the story, there would be a
public outcry and plenty of pundits offering their anal-retentive opin-
ions on everything they know nothing about.

Unless there was a solution, fast, to the killings, the Children of the
Mountain would be history. But what worried me just as much was
the distinct possibility that before any government intervention, there
would be more killings. I felt that in my gut. Already a third of the
people who had been here a week ago had been frightened off. All it
would take now would be more blood. The mind behind the murders
saw human life the way a market hunter sees a herd of deer. Killing
Indians for profit.

I felt a cold wind blow through my soul. It was all so familiar. It had happened before.

"Jake, hey?"

"Hunh?" I wrenched my mind back from the sadly familiar past to look over at Nick Sabattis.

"Sun's in the middle of the sky, Bro. Break time."

29

Even when you cannot see them
the stars remain in the sky

I walked with the others in the work crew toward the army surplus tent that still served as the main meeting place for the Children of the Mountain. When finished, the big longhouse we were building would take its place. People talked and joked as we walked along. But that talking and joking seemed half-hearted, subdued by the knowledge of all that had been happening.

I understood their uncertainty. Those who had left jobs, homes, and families to come here had done so because they believed in something, or at least wanted to believe. For hundreds of years our Penacook people had watched their land being taken, their good leaders being killed, their weak leaders selling out. They'd seen our forests clear-cut, our rivers polluted, the birds and plants and animals that sustained us just about wiped out. They'd been wounded by racism and neglect, seduced by materialism, and confused by television. They'd watched their families being torn apart by unemployment and alcoholism. And then, to top it all off, they'd been told that they were half-breeds at best and pretenders at worst. Everybody knows all them real Penacooks died off two centuries ago.

Yet somehow, in the midst of all that, they'd still wanted to believe in the old dream. Our people and the land are one. A broken circle can be mended.

And so, when someone stood up and begun speaking those clichéd words, there were still people willing to try. Tears in their eyes, their feet moving awkwardly to the old rhythm of the drum, they were risking it all for that beautiful dream, even though when the one speaking those words had only recently been reborn as a "noble red man."

I wasn't looking forward to hearing a public lecture from Mikwe. No doubt our midday repast would provide the occasion for another of his inspirational talks. Perhaps he was perusing *Touch the Earth* even now to pull out the requisite unoriginal aboriginal aphorisms with which he liked to pepper his pronouncements.

In the first half of the meeting I'd had with Mikwe the night before, he'd shown a different face from the uncertain one I'd seen this morning. Last night—with Dennis, Mook, and me as his audience—he had immediately switched the focus from our rescue of Ruth's unconscious body from that cave and the unsolved deaths to a defiant speech indicting Columbus and Caucasian original sin. Maybe he'd been reading *The Conquest of Eden.*

I had nodded and silently gritted my teeth. However, if I'd had to listen to Mikwe's Red Power platitudes much longer, I would have needed a good dentist.

To be honest, though, I was probably mentally raining on Mikwe's parade because I had known him way back when. In fact, only three years ago he was still Paulie Attean, the same Paulie Attean who made fun of people like Uncle John and Tom Nicola because they were living in the past. During high school, being Indian, despite being from an unrecognized tribe, had meant being able to check a box on his college application form that got him preferential treatment for admission and a scholarship. And after graduating from BU, his main interests had been getting out of the Island and getting ahead in a Boston law firm. How he had made the transition from writing legal briefs to becoming a Native activist was as great a mystery to me as why UFOs existed or why the French worshiped the movies of Jerry Lewis.

As I walked, my mind went to the dream that had overtaken me last night.

It came last night as soon as I closed my eyes. It had been waiting for me. I was in the forest again. Again I was running and again something was following. This time, though, it was different. I was in my own body, not experiencing what Ruth had, but going through it myself. It was also different because I knew two things as I ran. The first was that it was a dream, but the second thing I knew, with terrible certainty, was that the mteowlin *who was*

sending me this dream was not sending it as a warning or a prophecy, but as a weapon. If I died in this dream, that death would be for real.

I ran hard, but without the panic that had slowed the limbs of the others who tried to escape the long-armed horror that wanted to embrace me. I ran with fear, but not from it. My long years of running were part of the reason for the calm I was able to maintain in my stride. It did not matter if it was a mile or ten miles, my pace would be the same.

And because it was a dream, because I knew it was a dream, I could shape it—fighting the direction my enemy wanted it to go. So it was that, within that dream, both my knees were as strong as they had been when I was as yet unwounded, as hard as ash wood, as untiring as those of the running men who had hunted for our people in the old days. Alni Alnobak, *Right Men, they were called, men whose bodies and thoughts were clean and focused. They would run the deer with no weapon, running in pursuit, running day and night until the animal collapsed. Then they would end it by thanking the deer for agreeing to share its flesh with the people and then use their hands to cut off its breath.*

As I ran in that dream, I drew strength from the spirit of all those men who hunted for the people. Those strong runners never tasted the meat of the animals whose lives they took, but gave it to the old and weak, and those who could not hunt for themselves.

Fast as I ran, the thing following me was getting closer. I saw that the path led down through a thick stand of hemlocks and I sensed that death was ahead of me, waiting in the evergreens.

Then the air seemed to burst around me, the ground seemed ready to shatter beneath my feet as a scream filled my ears. It was a scream so terrible that it seemed as if my heart would burst, a cry meant to freeze me in place.

No, I said in my dream. No. I will wake now.

And that was when I had opened my eyes inside the tent. Dennis had still been asleep. I had lain there without moving or speaking, but without going back to sleep again. I lay there knowing the next time I dreamed I would see whatever it was that had hunted me.

"J-jacob."

It was Mikwe, heading toward me. I'd hung back from the others heading for the meeting tent when I'd noticed him half-hidden behind the makeshift wigwam of poles and elm bark. Whoever had built it had not known what they were doing. The bark had curled like a bad perm and it looked more like a fishnet than the skin of a house.

"Mikwe," I said.

He stopped in front of me and took me by the hand.

"Sh-shit, Jacob," he said. "You don't know how g-g-glad I am that y-you're here. W-we need to t-t-t-talk."

Stuttering is a funny thing. When you are speaking someone else's words, a stammer can completely disappear. Left alone with your own uncertain thoughts, though, trying to express what you truly feel, your tongue can tie itself into knots. For the first time, I felt true sympathy toward him. After all the years of disliking him for his self-centeredness, it was a strange feeling.

I let him walk me back away from the tent where the community had gathered. As we walked, I studied him out of the corner of my eye. He was wearing the same traditional clothing as when I'd first seen him. A smoke-tanned deerskin vest on his upper body, a deerskin loincloth worn over a pair of khaki shorts, leggings and low moccasins. He'd left his asolkwan with the heron feathers behind. Aside from the shorts, he was attired in close to pre-Contact style.

He was as skinny as he had ever been. Long arms, knobby knees. His face was still narrow, his eyes still bulged out, his teeth prominent, his chin a little weak—just like all the Atteans. His black hair still had a couple of cowlicks that no amount of bear grease would ever slick down, and he stuttered like a squirrel when he was excited or nervous. He'd chosen the right name for himself. Mikwe is the red squirrel.

Finally, close to the edge of the woods, we stopped.

Mikwe shook his head. "I j-just wanted to d-d-d-do the right thing," he said. "And n-now it's all t-t-turning t-to crap."

It was at that moment that I remembered Mikwe's family had been a family of chiefs for more generations than I could count. I unclouded my vision, looked within him and there I saw his sincerity, his pain, and the depth of his feeling. I felt ashamed of myself for my judgmental thoughts. Mikwe had grown from being a seemingly selfish—but maybe just overcompensating and self-conscious kid—into a man. Perhaps he wasn't ready to be a chief, but then again most people who turn into good chiefs aren't at the start.

I put my hand on his shoulder.

"I'm here," I said. "I'll do what I can."

30

*The old ones ask
is history your story?*

Our talk took no more than a few minutes. Somehow, don't ask me how, but whatever words I spoke cheered up Mikwe. It was one of those rare times when I found myself being absolutely sincere, speaking straight from the heart—like being at an AA meeting. No wonder I can't remember my part of the conversation.

Unfortunately, Mikwe's summary of everything that was wrong with the grand statement of Penacook sovereignty, with the meaning of the takeover of the Mountain, stuck with me. With a smile on his face, ready to inspire his people, Mikwe sailed off to the noon gathering, while I stood there leaning against a birch tree and thinking, "It *is* all falling apart."

Perhaps you know something about the string of occupations that marked one path taken toward the assertion of American Indian rights since 1969. The year 1969—that was the year of Alcatraz. The Indian takeover of an abandoned prison island in San Francisco Bay with no water, no power, inadequate shelter and sanitary facilities, no arable soil, indefensible borders, no potential for employment. The perfect definition of a reservation. It was a foolhardy, valiant, inspiring, heroic, poetic, and often poorly thought-out effort that ended up not with a bang but a universal whimper as the Indians left, and rather than becoming Indian land forever, perhaps even the site of an Indian university, Alcatraz became a federally administered tourist attraction. The occupation is only a historical footnote to most of the millions who want to see Al Capone's cell or the block where Clint Eastwood stayed.

1972. The Trail of Broken Treaties, an American Indian Movement protest walk across America ended with the temporary takeover of the Bureau of Indian Affairs building in Washington, D.C. Meanwhile, for decades thereafter, money supposedly being held in trust for the tribes kept disappearing—to the tune of billions of dollars.

Then it was 1973. The big one at Wounded Knee. Gunships circled overhead and heavy ordinance was fired at the outgunned Indians, who had circled their wagons in the little church near that graveyard where Big Foot and the other disarmed Lakotas had been slaughtered by the Seventh Cavalry in the last decade of the nineteenth century. There was enough fire power to make some of the Vietnam vets inside the perimeter feel as if they were back at Hue during the Tet offensive.

At least that is how Tom Nicola told me he felt when he was at Wounded Knee. But he crouched behind the barricades like the others. Drawn in by the dreams of the American Indian Movement and protected by the good medicine of Leonard Crow Dog, the Indians did the ghost dance against the government's helicopters. And, through it all, with all that gunfire, only one Indian was hit by a stray bullet and killed. But in the end, the two-month-long occupation was ended and the Indians walked away—just as at Alcatraz, to be followed by a reign of terror led by right-wing tribal chairman Dick Wilson's goon squads at the nearby Pine Ridge Reservation. Many of those who had been at Wounded Knee, trying to organize the community and bring social justice, wound up dead. In the course of the years that followed, dozens of AIM supporters were murdered. Like Anna Mae Acquash—a Wabanaki woman who left our dawnland to disappear into that western sunset.

I remember the look in Tom's eyes when he spoke about Anna Mae. No one was ever convicted or even arrested for Anna Mae's death or for any of the dozens of other unsolved homicides of Indians during that dark time. Only the Lakota activist Leonard Peltier still sits in a jail cell, unjustly convicted with manufactured evidence of the murder of two FBI agents, the only white men killed during that period of darkness. By the end of the '70s, most of the leaders of AIM had shared the same fate as the Black Panthers, as a result of the government's Counter Intelligence Program (COINTELPRO).

At times, it has felt to me as if our people have been nothing more to the government than bugs hitting the windshield of progress. An unpleasant smear, occasionally blurring their vision, but easily washed away. Except that image, central to W. D. Snodgrass's white-liberal-guilt poem "Powwow," is not exactly accurate. For one thing, our people have not been fragile butterflies, but hornets with stings.

Beaten? Is that an accurate description of our Native American nations at the start of the twenty-first century? Or does that describe the fledgling United States government in 1775? Or the Denver Broncos in the fourth quarter when they are two touchdowns down and John Elway has the ball?

Because, bit by bit, some things have changed for the better. Land has been returned, Native rights upheld. Even though there are those who would still like to wipe us out, such as those politicians who want to put women back into the kitchen, white men back in the driver's seat, and multiculturalism into the fire under the melting pot, we remain. In the words of the Menominee poet Chrystos, we are "not vanishing."

Enough contextualizing, aside from a mention of the First Nations occupation at Oka in Canada. There, ordinary Mohawk people protesting a golf course planned for their traditional forestland inadvertently found themselves under siege in 1990. They were surrounded in the Reserve's Treatment Center by one thousand police and four thousand Canadian soldiers, and engaged in long negotiations with the governments of Quebec and Canada. Fax messages were used to keep in touch with the international press and other tribes across Canada who closed roads and set up blockades of their own in sympathy. As a result of those negotiations, three agreements favorable to the Natives were signed by the Canadian government.

And now the Mountain. But, as Mikwe had outlined it to me and as I'd already seen, it was different here. Dumb as bureaucracies may seem to those who suffer under the weight of their irrationalities, government agencies are good at keeping records. Especially when it comes to being able to *prevent* people from doing something, or using those records to learn from the past how best to confound the will of the masses.

As a result, one of the first tactics employed by the assembled hordes outside our gates had been to cut off all access to the media. To put a near total blackout on the area. No phone lines meant no faxes and no immediate e-mail. Aside from one cell phone that Mikwe controlled, there was no direct contact with the outside. All negotiations between the Indians and the besiegers were being done face-to-face in a fifty-yard strip of land that had been declared neutral ground.

For another, Mikwe hoped, the lessons of Waco and Ruby Ridge were also being applied by the forces of law and order here. No loud music being blared in over loudspeakers. Perhaps they knew that repeatedly hearing Frank Sinatra's "My Way" might whip us Indians up into an uncontrollable bloodthirsty frenzy. There were no snipers trying to draw a lethal bead on the leaders of the takeover. There had been orders given to avoid casualties. Dead people make bad PR. After all, we held no hostages and there were no endangered minors among the Children of the Mountain.

However, the blockade was firmly in place and, although it had been possible for a few people to slip in and out by the route Dennis and I had used, the Children of the Mountain were short of food and medicine.

Also, the actual assembled weaponry of the camp was much more limited than I had first presumed—or the government forces knew. The perimeters were being guarded by a pretty well-organized contingent of Indian veterans of Vietnam, the Gulf War, Afghanistan, and Iraq. But those twenty men, including my new buddy Nick Sabattis, had only twelve guns between them. Why so few? Mikwe's original idea had been to stage an unarmed takeover, a protest that would rely on moral force (and much publicity) to make its point. He had talked it over with Chief Polis first (and that was news to me!) and they had agreed it was worth the risk.

The news blackout had changed everything. If no one saw it or read about it, what would be the point of the state police holding back? But, when the state police had made their first attempt to move in and take back the Mountain, the appearance of the few guns overlooked even by Mikwe had forced the agents of law and disorder to beat a retreat.

"After that," Mikwe had said to me, "we'd d-decided the g-g-guns were a n-necessary evil."

So the Children of the Mountain began to bluff the police into thinking they were better prepared than they really were. Makeshift spotlights were rigged by taking the headlights out of several of the park trucks that had been left behind and hooking them up to batteries. It was possible for us to illuminate our perimeters off and on at night—though not for long because the batteries would have been drained—in case they tried an assault after dark.

Vehicle parts and items from the former campground's toolshed had been used to create what looked like weapons—phony rocket launchers made out of truck mufflers, machine guns that were really just metal pipes with makeshift wooden stocks. The sight of it all had helped deter any assault.

And Mikwe's one cell phone had been put to good use in contacting the media. As a result, the government's hoped-for news blackout evaporated and stories were regularly appearing in print and on television.

Now, though, with the deaths in recent days, things had changed. It wasn't that we were an embarrassment to the state and an impediment to progress. Now it looked like we Indians were *in danger*. They might have to rescue us from ourselves. That had been the historic logic applied by the American government when they'd established the boarding schools in the nineteenth century with the objective of "killing the Indian and saving the man," of "holding the Indian underwater until he is immersed in civilization," as Captain Pratt, the founder of the Carlisle Indian School, put it.

Regarding Penacooks, that brought us to our other little sticky problem. Officially, in the eyes of the federal and state governments, despite our petitions for recognition, we weren't real Native Americans. Despite the presence of Natives from other tribes, ours was not a Mohawk or Lakota or even "Indians of All Tribes" takeover. It was nominally Penacook. It opened up the possibility that the powers-that-be might decide to write us off as a band of kooks with guns, discontents playing Indian, no better than a bunch of gate-crashers.

It also meant that the stakes were higher. If Mikwe's takeover move had brought publicity of the right kind, then the wheels that were grinding toward recognition might have been greased by public awareness and sympathy. It had even been Mikwe's thought that martyrdom wouldn't have been a bad thing at all. But things were far from going as planned.

"And n-n-ow, the s-s-senselessness, the p-p-pointlessness, the b-b-brutality of those killings . . . ," Mikwe said.

Plus the cannibalism, I thought. But again I didn't voice it.

Or repeat my agreement to help enough to bolster Mikwe's spirits. As I said before, he had sailed off to the meager midday meal with the assurance of a man who once again knows, like Lincoln on his way to a comedic play, that this is going to be a fine day after all.

I stood there leaning against a tree and wondering how I always got myself into things like this, and about the other small problem Mikwe had laid upon my shoulders before he sauntered away, leaving me a sadder but a wiser man.

"I haven't told anyone else," he said, "b-b-but the w-well went dry this morning. By tomorrow we'll b-b-be out of d-d-drinking w-water."

31

*The bird that flies
leaves the tree*

I hadn't expected it. But when I walked into the meeting and found everyone not eating but sitting instead around a portable television, I shouldn't have been surprised. I gathered that the TV was also under the control of Mikwe and the Leadership Council, and that with limited battery power it was used sparingly to give the community an occasional window on the world—as offered by the national and local news and the series *Third Rock From the Sun*. The reception was pitiful—only two local channels came in clearly enough to be seen and heard at the same time. No cable.

But everyone was glued to the screen. Native American stepchildren of the global village suffering from a case of media deprivation. The local commentator, feeding off CNN (which still had a truck parked on the other side of the primary roadblock near the state highway), was reporting on our situation.

"In the fifty-seventh day of the siege at Mount Wadzo campgrounds, confidential sources have informed CNN that violence has broken out inside the camp. The so-called Native Americans, who have been described by local law enforcement as 'nothing more than a kooky cult,' may be fighting among themselves. If this is true, what began as a minor annoyance may be developing into another Waco or a Jonestown."

The local commentator paused for effect as the camera pulled in closer. A little too close. Even with the weak reception on this communal book tube, I could see he was a member of the Good Hair Club for men.

"However, a statement just received by e-mail at our station, purport-edly from 'Mikwe,' the leader of the dissident group, insists that the situation remains under control and that their aim of drawing atten-tion to legitimate Penacook grievances and the struggle for Indian sov-ereignty in this state has only just begun. Well, Liz, does that mean we're going to be paying rent on our condos to the Indians? Ho, ho."

With the exception of the warriors guarding our defensive perime-ter, everyone was glued to the TV. As I stepped back from the group of intent viewers, gathered like acolytes around a shrine, I noted that all of the Leadership Council members were there. Mikwe had told me their names last night and showed me the photos of each of them, kept neatly in a folder. Some were people I knew, especially Katlin, who was the speaker for the Women's Council. All that I could see of her now was part of her profile, her dark hair swept down across her face like the wing of a hawk, but that was enough to make my ventricles start working overtime. Once upon a time and far away, we had promised to be together forever. Her face started slowly to turn in my direction. Per-haps she felt my gaze . . . or heard my distressed heart trying to pound its way out through my rib cage.

Katlin had always known what I was thinking or feeling. We had al-most spoken last night, but she was the official nurse for the Children of the Mountain, as well as one of the most visible members of the Lead-ership Council. As I entered the infirmary tent she'd greeted me in Penacook. Her voice always sounded like a bird singing when she spoke our language. I'd answered back and for a moment it seemed as if the old bond was there. Then the moment passed as she focused her atten-tion on ministering to Rose Cook.

Our lives were like two canoes going in different directions on the Big Otter River. Hers floating downstream. Mine, of course, being pad-dled upriver against the current. Not that Katlin's passage thus far along the stream of life had been easy. After I left for my Ivy League edu-ma-cation, we kept in touch through letters and a few phone calls. But even though Dartmouth was not that far from the Island, she turned down all my invitations for her to visit during the first year I was there.

I didn't go home for vacations. After all, my parents were gone, my aunt and uncle and even Tom had passed on. My best buddy Dennis was a fellow Dartmouth Indian. So what was there to draw me back? Katlin, of course. So I kept inviting her to visit me. And, in the middle of my sophomore year, she finally did, once. It was a long bus trip. Her face looked gray with exhaustion. I checked her into the motel room.

"I just need to sleep," she said. It wasn't like her. Katlin, who could run up a mountain and back and then still be ready to canoe ten miles, worn out by a simple bus ride? But I didn't push it. Katlin was never one to be pushed.

The next day things seemed better. I picked her up at dawn. She wanted to see everything. Every building where I had a class, the football field, the places to eat in town. She listened to me play my new guitar. She met my first martial arts instructor, Sensei Yamamoto, who was also a tenured Japanese philosophy professor. A deeply gentle man who burned like a tiger in the dojo, he was the one who began my long journey into the discipline of martial arts. I had just earned my yellow belt and I was trying not to show how proud I was of that. I remember how he looked at her and then at me as he took her hand.

"Sword and wild rose," he said. He looked sad.

I didn't understand why at the time.

She kept repeating my own words back to me each place we went. Not words I spoke while we were together that day, though. It was as if she had memorized every sentence I'd spoken to her over the phone and every page I'd written so faithfully every other day during my first semester at college. She'd been living those experiences with me all that time. But only during my first semester. And it was April now. After Christmas, our letters had been far fewer, much shorter. Our phone calls—aside from the last one inviting her to come—had become nonexistent.

I realized that as we were trying to converse. I was trying so hard that I wasn't making any jokes. She just kept saying how proud she was of me. How proud she was of me. That night we didn't go to the Indigo Girls concert, even though I'd gotten the tickets weeks before. We went to her motel room together. Neither one of us got undressed. We lay down together on the bed with our arms around each other. She kissed me once, on the cheek.

"I'm just a little Indian girl," she said. "I need to go home."

I didn't say anything.

Katlin nodded as if I'd said it all and hugged me harder. We fell asleep together like that, like the two children we had once been.

I woke up before she did, but didn't move. I kept my eyes closed as she woke, slipped out of bed, and went into the bathroom. I still kept them closed as I listened to her packing her suitcase. Then I felt her breath on my cheek.

"I'm ready to go," she whispered.

When she got on the bus, she looked down at me from the steps. The sunlight reflecting off the window of the bus framed her head like a halo.

"*Wlipamkaani*," she said in her clear, lilting voice. "Travel well."

"*Wlipamkaani*," I said back. "I'll be seeing you."

Until the night before at the infirmary tent, that was the last time I saw Katlin. She had gotten married a year after that, had her first child a little less than a year later, and then a second one. Her two daughters were staying with her mother and father for now. Their names were Katherine and Margaret. No little baby Jacob.

I'd heard about it all from Dennis. How her marriage had taken her to Boston until her husband's drinking problem got so bad that his abuse escalated from verbal to physical. He began to push her around and threaten the babies. Then, one night, he hit her. But he only did that once. The second time he tried to hit her, Katlin picked up his softball bat and slammed a home run off the side of his head. When he woke up in Boston General with a concussion, he was served the divorce papers. He didn't contest it. Just as when we were kids, it took a lot to make Katlin angry, but when she finally did it was wise to get out of her way.

Driving her unconscious and soon to be ex-husband to the hospital had given her an idea. She began taking a nursing course. Public assistance and child support were barely enough, but she got by. And when she got her degree—just a year ago—she had moved back to the Island with her girls. She had been working in the clinic when the occupation began, and she had decided to take part.

Knowing that our chief had been a quiet backer of Mikwe's plan made me understand why a responsible mother with two daughters in elementary school might leave a good job. Katlin hadn't left it. I was willing to bet that she was still pulling down a paycheck from the clinic while carrying on her nursing work here among the Children of the Mountain. This occupation was not like a wildcat strike at all, but something thought out by Chief Polis and Mikwe together. That put a whole different light on things.

Mentally, I breathed a sigh of relief. Instead of continuing to beat myself up about losing the love of my life, I was starting to piece a few things together again and acting like a real detective. Except, where was my giant economy-size Watson?

Dennis was nowhere to be seen. That bothered me. I looked again fruitlessly among the assembled multitude. For a moment I thought I recognized someone who should not be here, someone who went out the backdoor before I could get a better look. If it was who I thought it was . . .

That familiar feeling went down my spine, like a cold bone knife touched lightly to each vertebrae in turn. An image of a face filled with hatred flashed before my eyes and then was gone. As we stand on this hilltop we call the present moment, most of us look only at the ground just before our feet. Some of us, blessed or cursed with longer sight, lift our eyes to discern what lies ahead . . . or turn our heads to look farther back. Then we must be prepared for what we see.

I blinked my eyes and I was back in the present moment. The TV was being turned off. Mikwe was standing up and getting ready to give a before-lunch talk.

I turned and went outside. I wasn't that hungry.

32

*Big or small,
all fish swim in the water*

Pete Cook was standing fifty yards away listening to a walkie-talkie. All the men on guard duty had them. They checked in at regular intervals, using the code that included their deceptive culinary handles and the device of referring to the four points of the compass in Penacook terms. East was yellow, for the dawn. West was red, for the sunset. North was white for snow, and south green for the plants of summer. Maybe it confused those who listened in. The walkie-talkies were easy enough for anyone to access, owing their origins to Wal-Mart. Every deer hunter in the state owned a set.

"How's Ruth?" I asked.

Pete pointed with his chin toward the small tent that was his sister's. I had the feeling he was pleased I had asked about her.

"Doing okay. Wants to talk to you later."

I nodded. We stood together without saying anything, Mikwe's high-pitched and impassioned oratory drifting out to us. He was saying something about there being nothing to fear but fear itself.

As one, the urge took the two of us to stroll a bit farther away. When the sound of Mikwe's voice could no longer be heard over the songs of the chickadees and the rustle of the wind in the small pines, we stopped.

"Seen Captain Crunch?" I asked.

"He's not back in there?"

I shook my head.

"Let me check."

He lifted the hand-held transceiver to his mouth, pressed the talk switch.

"Pizza Man here. 4D all clear?"

"White's all right."

"Yellow's still mellow."

"Green is keen."

"Red's not dead."

I raised an eyebrow. Pete shrugged back at me, as if to ask what more I could expect. At least the codes rhymed. And, as we both knew, the Indian sense of humor has been known to drive the authorities to the point of self-immolation.

On the other hand, I liked poetry. I held out my hand for the walkie-talkie.

"May I?"

"New guy has a question. Give him the skinny."

Pete handed me the walkie-talkie.

My question was a simple one. It was not "what's the frequency, Kenneth?"

"Anybody seen Dennis?"

The answer from all four directions was even more terse. *Nyet. Nein. Non. Nada.*

It's hard to lose a whale inside a goldfish bowl. It likely meant that Dennis was outside the defensive perimeter of the camp, an area which had shrunk down from most of the state campground to a piece of land less than a mile square, a contraction like a brief recapitulation of recent Native American history.

Did that mean that someone had Dennis? Or something? I pushed that thought aside. It was broad daylight and the other attacks had come with the evening and the dark.

Big though he was, Dennis was woods-wise and not an easy man to find once he got into a forest like the one on three sides of the campground. The only really clear area of any size was between the main roadblock and the state road. Since that was the easiest area to guard, that was where most of the fuzz had been inserted like a bad hair transplant. Roving patrols of less-than-woods-wise state and federal gendarmes circled the camp regularly. But nervously. Slipping past those roving patrols and the six static checkpoints set up around the camp was as easy as running water through a fishnet. On our side, the warriors were more focused on anyone trying to get in, not anyone sneaking out.

I decided to defer any serious worries about my amigo. After all, Dennis and I had agreed to meet around noon. "Around" tends to be a bigger circle for an Indian when we're talking about time.

The meeting, I knew, was not going to be a short one. After Mikwe's initial remarks there would be reports from the Men's Council and the Women's Council and the representative of the Warrior's Circle. Some of the talking would be in Penacook. That would be painful. From what I'd heard in the room, the only fluent speaker of our language would be Katlin. Our language isn't taught in the schools in this state, even as an elective, and the use of it in our homes has grown less common. With the old ones like my aunt and uncle and Tom gone, who was left to teach the children?

On the other hand, here at the Mountain they wanted to change that. Katlin was also acting as a language tutor. Penacook greetings were now more common than "Hi, how-ah-ya," among the Children of the Mountain, though when the conversation went beyond the hellos, the yes's and no's, there were plenty of pregnant pauses and long gestation periods before any further phrases could be born.

I needed to do something useful. Finding things was my specialty. What did they need to find now? Aside from such obvious stuff as a solution to two murders and a way out of an impasse with a police force armed to the teeth and eager to start chewing?

Water. *Donde esta agua? Toni nebizonbik?*

I looked around the campgrounds with more than just my eyes, trying to sense as well as see. The water pipes had been turned off by the authorities and, as a result, the storage tanks were almost empty. There had been no rain, so no chance to collect water that way. A solar still could collect the dew, but not enough for a hundred people.

Running water? The nearest stream was a mile into the woods outside the defensive perimeter. And, Mikwe had told me, there were no springs here.

But there should have been a spring. Everything about the lay of the land whispered that to me. I took my buck knife from its sheath and cut a green forked branch from one of the beeches. A willow would have been better, but I'd seen Tom do it with a bent coat hanger. I'd even seen him do it over a map, telling people who lived a hundred miles away where to dig.

I peeled the stick, grasped it by the forks, and held it out in front of me. I could still feel Tom's hands around mine.

"You'll recognize the pull," he'd said.

The stick trembled back then and it trembled now. I walked with it until it pointed down at a pile of rocks in the slope of the hill at the very back of the camp.

"Want a shovel?"

I'd forgotten that Pete Cook was behind me.

I shook my head. I started to roll the rocks away. Even without the dowsing, I should have seen it. Pete clipped the walkie-talkie onto his belt and began to help. It took us only a few minutes, especially with Pete's huge paws shifting stones like a human backhoe. By the time we were done, the flow of the disused spring was strong and kept from pooling only by the hidden drainpipe that led into the storm drain and took the water out of the campground.

I bent and tasted the water. It was sweet. Block the drainpipe, build up a berm around the base, and there'd be a little pool in no time. There was more than enough for the hundred people in the camp.

I stood up and wiped my hands on my knees.

Pete Cook was looking at me.

"I find things," I said.

"No shit, Sherlock," he replied.

33

The open hand remains empty
when the eye is shut

"Old times," my aunt said, "old times it was easy to get fish, get berries, get meat. Easy as it is now to walk out in winter and gather a handful of snow. Old times."

And here I was in the here and now.

Pete had gone off to tell the others about the spring I'd dowsed. I decided to walk on alone, toward the perimeter. Maybe I'd see some sign of Dennis.

Further sign, that is. While picking out a forked stick I'd seen something—a pile of fresh little shavings of wood flicked from Dennis's knife as he whittled while walking. I relocated that pile of shavings and strolled on a bit farther. Just as I'd hoped, I soon found another pale curlicue of pine, not yet darkened by moisture, its color proof of how recent it was.

I kept walking, not making it obvious that I was following a trail. In addition to the telltale shavings, I was able to pick out the track of Dennis's right foot every now and then. A few others in the camp had shoes as big as his—Pete Cook for one. But the tread patterns, the wear on the bottom left toe box, and the slash across the back three studs on the left heel of Dennis's shoes were unique.

Tracking is part of our old Indian way. Not that many of us still knew how to do it. Ever hear the one about the three urban Indians who went out hunting? They didn't really know much about finding game, but they found a clear set of tracks.

"These here are bear tracks," said the first urban Indian.

"No way, Cochise, those are deer tracks."

134

The third Indian, he never got a chance to say anything because just then the train came along and damn near hit them!

The farther I went, the more I realized there was more than one set of tracks going this way. The other set was not a running shoe. It was smooth-soled, but with a visible shank. Probably one of those pairs of modern moccasins that have a heel glued onto the moose-skin uppers. Someone else was walking with Dennis, just a little ahead of him, every now and then turning back to talk to him. I could see that as clearly as I could see that the little pine shavings were not just falling by accident. Dennis had been dropping them deliberately, probably just in case whoever was leading him wherever couldn't be trusted. It was typical of Dennis to act oblivious while his mind was racing four steps ahead.

The trail led toward the back perimeter of the camp, in the direction of the Mountain and the trail we'd followed coming in the night before. But the second set of tracks turned back before crossing the perimeter. I looked around. I was not yet within the line of sight of the warrior on patrol. A good place to turn back if you didn't want to be seen.

I had a mental image of the person—for some reason I pictured Mook Glossian, although there was now at least one other suspicious character here among the Children of the Mountain. Whoever this Judas goat was, he'd been telling Dennis about something, pointing the direction for him to go before turning back himself.

Why had Dennis gone out alone and not come back to get me? The answer was obvious. The big guy always liked to have something he could tease me about. If he could find something out before me, out-detective the professional P.I., that would be a one-up for sure.

I could almost hear him thinking. "I'll check this out quick and then hustle back for old slow Podjo."

Why had he not been suspicious? Obviously, he had. That was why he'd left that trail of shavings that were like a set of road signs for me, like the crumbs dropped by Hansel and Gretel.

Was a witch waiting at the end of this trail?

34

*What one wants
is not always what is wanted*

Before long I came to the place in the perimeter where a sentry had been posted. I saw him long before he saw me, and it was easy to slip past him. If it had been Pete Cook or one of the former NativeRangers, it might have been another story. But the person on duty here, a Penobscot guy from Bangor, was a different story. It was like the difference between pemmican and a Big Mac.

When Dennis and I ran down the roster of his scouts with Pete the night before, he'd shaken his head about this one. His name was Sammy Loron and he was a veteran, so to speak, of Bosnia. But he was Army National Guard, a weekend warrior back before the Guard began pulling extended tours of duty as a result of our being in not one but two regional conflicts. Sammy had been in and out without firing a shot.

Mikwe had already come close to kicking him out of the camp. Someone had accused him of smoking on duty. From the smell on the wind, that someone had deduced it was something with less tar, but more kick than *nicotiana rustica*. Sammy Loron had denied it. He'd claimed he was burning a little sacred sweetgrass to keep away evil. With no other witness, they'd let it ride, after a careful search of his person and his belongings to make sure he didn't have any joints stashed. He'd protested, but hadn't left the camp. He was here to serve his people, man!

It was as easy for me to slip by him, cross the small field, and make it into the woods, as I assumed it had probably been for Dennis a few hours before. And there, where the trailhead began, I found a few more strategically dropped wood shavings.

Now that I was in the woods, it was so much easier for me to take things in. It was like removing a set of headphones and a pair of dark glasses. Around groups of people, it isn't always easy to hear or see clearly. Admittedly, it was better in the camp than in a big city. If you're an Indian in the big city, you may feel buried alive by all that that weight of steel and glass and concrete, people moving like herds of the walking dead everywhere around you. It makes you think of taking your own last exit to Brooklyn by flying with the Thunderbird, answering the call of Wild Turkey, losing yourself in the sick-sweet scent of Wild Irish Rose. Cheap wine is fine, makes winter feel like summertime.

Dampening my senses with alcohol was not anything I wanted to accept anymore—even though I found it necessary to live in the metropolis. Keep your wants simple and they may equal your needs. Sifu Huang shared those words of wisdom with me years ago. I was grown up enough now to understand, if not always follow, that advice. I still had a problem with knowing exactly what it was that I wanted.

Be careful what you want, Aunt Mali said. Then she told me about Gluskonba and the four wishes.

It is said that, long ago, after Gluskonba sailed away in his canoe made of white stone, people would sometimes find their way to the distant island where he built his lodge. He sat in that great white wigwam making arrowheads for the day when he would come back and kill the monsters that were threatening the people. As soon as his lodge was full from top to bottom with powerful arrowheads, pressure-flecked from flint, he would return.

In the meantime, though, it was known that Gluskonba would grant your greatest desire if you could succeed in making that hard journey to his door.

Once there were four men who made that journey. It took them four years as they crossed the great distance, over land and water. Finally, they came to the door of Gluskonba's lodge. A great pillar of smoke billowed up from the smokehole. It showed them that the giant was within, smoking his pipe. Then a deep voice rumbled from within the wigwam.

"Enter my lodge one at a time. Tell me your desire."

The first man went in. Gluskonba sat there beside a roaring fire. A huge stack of arrowheads was piled behind him to the height of four men. But it only reached a short distance toward the top of that huge wigwam. A white wolf sat on Gluskonba's right side and a black wolf on his left side. To the first man, it seemed that Gluskonba was bigger than the hugest whale. His pipe was so large that, if it had been a pot, a whole village's meals could have been cooked in it. It was an awesome sight, but that first man was not without courage and his desire was great.

"My wish is to live forever and never grow old."

Gluskonba looked at him. "This is truly what you want?"

"Yes," the man said. Then Gluskonba turned that man into a large granite rock.

"Now," said Gluskonba, "you will live forever and never grow old."

Now the second man came into Gluskonba's lodge. Gluskonba looked down at him.

"What is your desire?" Gluskonba said.

"I want to be taller than all men."

Gluskonba bent closer. "That is truly what you want?"

"Yes," said the man. Then Gluskonba turned him into a big white pine tree.

"Now," said Gluskonba, "you are truly taller than all men."

Next into the lodge came the third man.

"Gluskonba," he said, "this is my desire. I want to always be surrounded by women who wish to make love with me."

"That is truly your wish?" said Gluskonba.

"It is," said the man. Then Gluskonba pulled a bag out of the great pouch that hung at his side.

"In this bag," Gluskonba said, "are all the women in the world you would ever want to make love to. Whenever you want one, you have only to open this bag. But you must take care and not open it until you have reached your village."

"I shall do as you say," said the man, who then left Gluskonba's lodge. The fourth man saw him come out.

"Where are our two companions?" asked the fourth man.

"Do not worry about them," said the third man, clutching his bag close to his chest. "I am sure Gluskonba gave them all they wished for and even more. Hurry up and go inside. I want to get back to my village."

Slowly, the fourth man entered the lodge. Just within the door, a big stone with a familiar shape stood on one side. A tall pine tree stood on the other, swaying back and forth, even though there was no wind. Gluskonba sat before him, a big man but not that much bigger than most others. A white dog and a black dog sat by Gluskonba's side and as the fourth man approached they wagged their tails and came up to him.

"It is good to see that you are well, Great One," said the fourth man as he petted Gluskonba's dogs.

"I thank you," Gluskonba said. "But don't you want to tell me what you desire?"

"Great One," the fourth hunter said, "just to see that you are alive and well is enough for me."

"Come," said Gluskonba, "surely there is something that you wish for."

"Great One," said the man, "I am ashamed to bother you with my small troubles. But for years I have tried to be a good hunter. I have tried to bring home food for my people. But I have failed. I have been no good to anyone. So, at last, I have come to you. I would like to be useful to my people as long as I live."

"Is this all that you wish?" Gluskonba said. "Do you wish nothing for yourself?"

"Forgive me, Great One, for I am small and foolish. But I do not understand what more anyone could want than to be of use to his people."

Gluskonba smiled. "Listen," he said.

Then he told that man all the secrets a good hunter must know. He told him the ways to find game and what to do to make the spirits of the animals willing to sacrifice their bodies for the people. The man listened and his heart was filled with happiness. When Gluskonba was finished, the man laughed out loud.

"Thank you, Great One," he said. "I will remember all that you have taught me." Then he left Gluskonba's lodge.

At first he saw no sign of his companion. But, looking far ahead, he saw the man climbing up a distant ridge. He hurried to catch up to his companion, who was carrying a small pouch very close to his heart as if it was very precious and also very heavy.

"I could not wait for you," said the third man. "I am in a great hurry to get back to my village with this gift."

"Yes," said the fourth man. "I understand. I, too, am in a hurry to get back to my village."

They traveled hard. By the time the day ended, they had gone back as far as it had taken them a whole year to come. Darkness fell and they made camp near a big white pine tree. Just before they slept, the fourth man thought he heard the voice of one of their companions, the one who had been the second to enter Gluskonba's lodge.

"Do you hear that?" he asked. But the other man was not interested. He was curled up in a ball around his pouch.

"It is only the wind blowing through the pine branches," the third man said.

The next day they traveled hard again. By nightfall they had reached the place it had taken them two years to reach on their journey to Gluskonba's lodge. They camped that night in the shadow of a big granite boulder. Once again, the fourth hunter thought he heard a voice, this time the voice of the first man who had entered Gluskonba's lodge.

"Did you hear that voice?" he asked. But the other man was not interested. He was crouched over and pressing his face hard against his pouch.

"It is only the wind in the rocks," the third man said.

On the third day they traveled hard once more. Just as before, they went as far as it had taken them a whole year to go on their way to Gluskonba's lodge. This time, darkness came upon them as they entered a forest. The hunter, or fourth man, was so tired that he fell asleep at once.

As soon as he saw that his traveling companion slept, the third man could wait no longer. He sneaked off among the trees until he was sure no one could see or hear him. Then, his fingers trembling, he opened the pouch.

Out of the mouth of the pouch came clouds of smoke that formed at once into women. Some were slender and pale as the birch tree. Some were as full-bodied and lush as the blossoms of the wild rose. Their naked forms were all around him. The man's knees grew weak with desire as he looked with hungry eyes at their outstretched arms and their thighs. Then they were all on top of him, grasping at him, pressing him to the ground, all of them trying to grasp him at once as they ripped away his clothes.

There were too many of them. He tried to speak, to tell them to wait, but his mouth was filled with their long black hair. He tried to scream, but he could not breathe. For a brief time, he struggled. Then darkness filled his eyes and a wind came through the trees to blow away the few sinuous wisps of smoke that still clung in the air near his dead face.

The next morning, the hunter woke and found that his companion was gone. He did not search long, for he was certain that the man had risen before dawn and gone on to his village, eager to share whatever gift Gluskonba had given him. So the hunter took the trail. He traveled hard and reached his village before the end of the day.

All of the people greeted him with joy. His parents embraced him as the people sang greeting songs. From that time on, that man hunted for his people. He remembered all the lessons Gluskonba taught him. He shared whatever he caught with everyone. He never took more than was needed. He respected the animal spirits and gave them thanks. He became known as the greatest of all hunters and lived a long, happy life among his people, leaving behind him children and grandchildren who passed his secrets on after him.

And the greatest of those secrets was the knowledge that the only things one should truly desire are those gifts to be shared with all those who share life with you. That is how the story goes.

35

Tree becomes forest,
forest becomes tree

I hadn't gone more than half a mile into the woods before a tingling feeling at the base of my neck told me I was being watched. Most people have had that feeling at one time or another, but have been civilized enough to ignore it. Being civilized, though, is a luxury that people in my line of work can't afford. Our lives could be on the line, like the lives of our ancient ancestors who paid attention to that feeling on the chance that the eyes fixed on their backs belonged to large carnivores that saw them as the catch of the day.

You don't believe people can sense they are being watched? Then try this. Next time you are in a crowd, say a subway, pretend you are a hungry predator. Fix your gaze on the back of someone's head and see how long it takes for him or her to start fidgeting. It's wise to do two things if you chose a male subject, however. The first is to pick someone considerably smaller than yourself. The second is to shift your attention quickly away when he finally wheels around to see who's been watching him. If you don't, you may find your pretend hunger sated by a real knuckle sandwich.

It's actually harder in the woods to figure out who or what is watching you than it is in a subway car or even on a crowded city street. Most people who don't spend much time in the forest think of it as something like a park, only with more trees. But one of our northern forests may have as many ripples and waves in its surface as a frozen ocean. The land dips and rises where trees have fallen and are slowly sinking back beneath the surface while bushes and small saplings have climbed up to perch atop their burial mounds. That is one of the reasons why the best vantage points in the woods are not from ground level, but from above.

Look up, dummy.

I looked up. Like an overfed hoot owl, Dennis was perched in the high fork of a big pine tree. He smiled and wiggled his fingers at me. His one raised eyebrow was clearly asking me why I had taken so long to figure out he was there.

Before releasing the branch that he had pulled back to make himself visible, he made our ancient Indian sign-language gesture for silence by pretending to close a zipper over his lips and then crooked his finger backward toward himself. I got the point. I left the trail quickly, but carefully, and quietly made my way over to the tree, whose thick stubs left by broken low branches were like a ladder. Dennis took up much of the available space, but there was just enough room for me to wedge myself in next to him.

He leaned close. There is a way of talking in the woods that cannot be heard from far off, a low tone of voice, almost like a song.

"But don't feel sad," Dennis crooned softly, "cuz two in a tree ain't bad."

"Can it, Meat Loaf," I hummed back. "What's up? Aside from you and me?"

He patted the pocket of his blue jean jacket. I could see there was something inside it, folded like a piece of paper. I was curious about what it was and held out my hand. But Dennis held up a finger. Wait. He pointed with his chin, directing my eyes to a place a hundred yards away, just around the corner and following the trail I'd just left.

"C-o-m-p-a-n y-o-u-s-e," he thrummed.

"Mickey Mouse, for sure," I hummed to Dennis. "That old gang of mine."

"You know those guys?" he rumbled back.

I smiled. I was so pleased by the prospect of a reunion with my four old buddies that I was at a loss for words.

Alphonse, Gaston, Rene, and Pierre. There they were, easily recognizable, though no longer in their biker disguises. Instead, they were wearing standard issue SWAT Squad gear.

It was so good to see them. It reassured me that my original deduction about their attitude toward me was correct. It wasn't about a parking space, after all. Keeping me away from the Mountain had been their intent, plus the added innocent fun of breaking a few strategic bones, such as those located between occiput and metatarsals.

However, their appearance in FBI standard issue told me a few more things. The first was that if they were, indeed, in federal employ, much money was changing hands somewhere down the line. The second was that the federal government was using its tax dollars wisely. Contract labor thugs from the former Soviet Union were a much better bargain than full-time employees. Third, my departure through the porous picket lines emplaced about the camp had not gone unnoticed after all. Shame on me. Fourth, there was indeed an enemy in our camp with the ability to communicate with the outside world. Probably one with a hidden cell phone, who used it to tell the hit squad below, outfitted now with automatic pistols and a sawed-off shotgun, where to find their clay pigeon. I was beginning to feel a bit more certain about who that enemy just might be. It was someone whose treachery would break at least one heart and I didn't feel good about it.

I focused in again on the party of four approaching without reservations. It had taken them a while to get this far. Especially since they tended to stop every now and then to mill about and apparently make sure they stepped on every stick in the path. The four refugees from a bad James Bond flick (any not starring Sean Connery) were not only packing deadly force, they were almost as loud as a brigade of bagpipers.

There they were, heavily armed, obviously trained in lethal combat, vicious, men totally without scruples, ready to kill or be killed. And then there was Dennis and me, both of us unarmed. It was an unfair matchup, so we took pity on them and let them walk by.

The sound of their heavy feet grew fainter as they continued on along the trail. Dennis looked at me. I shook my head because I'd heard a faint sound that told me it was not yet time for a recapitulation to the forest floor, which was not yet the optimal home for us disoriented descendants of anthropoids.

"We must be in Missouri," I said to Dennis in a low voice.

"Why?" he asked. Since childhood he'd never minded playing the straight man for any knock-knock joke.

"Because Missouri loves company." I directed his gaze toward the path yet again.

Déjà vu all over again again. Ever had that feeling? Déjà vu all over again again. Ever had that feeling?

Never mind. Our lofty gazes, like the gazes of stout Balboas with eagle eyes, took in two more familiar figures toiling up the trail. Looking even more out of place in the woods than the Ukrainian Mod Squad had, they were sweating, cursing audibly, their feet slipping in the leaf litter.

It was Gray Suit A and Gray Suit B—Greg, the moonlighting policeman, and his equally flatfooted buddy.

Dennis and I smiled at each other as they passed by beneath us.

After you? I asked.

Might be, he mouthed back, trying to look modest. *Nice to be wanted.*

36

One is hard to discern,
many easy to see

Pete Cook was manning the perimeter where Sammy Loron had been snoozing with his eyes wide open. Pete's gaze, though, fell upon us while we were still a hundred yards away among the trees. As we approached, he lifted his walkie-talkie to his mouth.

"Pizza Man here," he was saying as we got within earshot. "I have delivery, one double-cheese, one jalapeno."

Double-cheese? Dennis mouthed at me.

I shrugged.

Pete hung the radio back on his belt and cradled his AK-47 in the crook of his left arm.

"Wait here?" he asked.

It was one of the politest commands I'd ever been given. The three of us stood there without speaking for a while, Dennis patting that lump in his jeans jacket every now and then and smiling like a canary-filled Siamese.

I turned toward the sound of soft footfalls. The other man who co-captained the warriors appeared from behind a tree. He'd been using it as cover while he walked toward us. A rail-thin Canadian Abenaki from Odanak in his late fifties, named Ely Joulette. He hadn't let a little detail like Canadian citizenship get in the way of his volunteering for the U.S. Marines and serving three tours in Vietnam. We'd never met in person, but I already knew him by name. He and Tom Nicola had been together for a brief time during the Tet offensive, pinned down behind a ruined wall for three days in Hue. Sharing C-rations, playing poker with a deck that had only fifty cards and seven aces, and drinking out of a rain puddle. Since I'd heard he was here last night I'd been looking forward to finding time to sit down with him, to mention Tom's name and then listen.

But now was not the time. He and Pete nodded to each other as he took over Pete's post. Then, as one, Dennis, Pete, and I turned and started back toward the camp.

"Natives getting restless out there?" Pete said as we started down the hill.

"A veritable convention of traveling salesmen," I ventured, using my best W. C. Fields accent.

"We saw them," Dennis said.

"But they didn't see us," I added.

"They never do until it's too late," Pete deadpanned. Then we all did laugh.

By the time we reached his tent, we had briefed Pete and he had filled us in on what had taken place while we were gone. The meeting had broken up inconclusively. Everyone was staying put, at least for tonight. The spring I'd found was flowing steadily and Mikwe had taken credit for it. There was more activity than usual among the assembled hosts massed at our front door, but no overflights yet with copters. Maybe they actually believed our silver-painted drain pipes really were Stinger missiles.

The big news Pete had was of some substance. During the meeting a messenger had been sent up on foot to the second barricade at the front gate. It was a state policeman with a white flag that he carried over his shoulder like a pitchfork, who looked as if he'd rather be eating donuts and ticketing speeders on the interstate. A negotiating meeting was requested and agreed to. It would take place between the authorities and the Children of the Mountain at 1600 hours near the second barricade in neutral territory.

I looked at my watch. It was one P.M., 1300 hours for those who prefer military consistency.

"Mikwe wants you there," Pete said. He held out a black ski mask to me. "We'll all be wearing these."

I nodded. It was not just to protect my secret identity. In my line of work, it always helps when certain people can't prove you've been somewhere. There is an old tradition among law enforcement agencies of collecting candid snapshots of certain gatherings. At some later date, they can pull out those photographs to wax nostalgic about the good old days, and then pick out your face and throw your ass in the slammer.

Of course, in other countries being identified that way has even worse consequences—such as in Chiapas, where they just shoot you for having been among the Zapatistas—which is not much of a departure from what has been happening for the last few hundred years to the Mayan people there and in Honduras and Guatemala.

I wondered if I should change my clothes for that upcoming masked ball. Perhaps put on my T-shirt that reads I JOINED THE WITNESS PROTECTION PROGRAM AND ALL THEY GAVE ME WAS THIS LOUSY T-SHIRT. Luckily, I had four hours to decide on my wardrobe. I lifted up the ski mask to try it on.

Pete held up his index finger. "Don't put that on yet," he said. "Ruth said she's feeling well enough to talk with you now."

37

Look into the past,
remember the future

When we reached the door flap to Ruth's tent, Pete Cook called out a quick word in Mohawk. Ruth's voice answered from within, also in Mohawk, and then the three of us entered.

The tent that Ruth had set up for herself was a blue North Slope, longer than it was wide and almost tall enough at the peak for us to stand upright. I took in—in my own way—the space Ruth Cook had clearly made her own. There's this thing I do that I call taking a mental snapshot. It involves closing my eyes, imagining the shutter of the camera closing, and in that brief darkness saving in my mind the image of what I'd seen.

I have to admit that what I mostly saw was Pete's sister, Ruth.

She was sitting in one of those ground-level folding canvas camp chairs. Her eyes were bright, her chin tilted up, the glow of health from her face so vivid that she no longer looked—as she did the night before—like a wounded saint. Her back was very straight, her long black hair combed to hang loosely over her shoulders. She was wearing a turquoise blue tank top that left her shoulders bare. Her shoulders and arms were relaxed as she sat holding her knees with her palms. Her white shorts were immaculate and plain, except for a bundle of white pine needles clinging to the right hem, her brown legs long and shaped like a runner's, her thighs and calves like her arms—smooth, supple, muscular. The image of the gracilis muscle of her inner thigh rippling as she straightened her leg slightly vibrated in my medulla oblongata like a tuning fork. *Down, boy!*

Her neatly folded down sleeping bag lay to her right, an L. L. Bean sticker still attached, a small foam pillow in the exact center of it. Behind her, just below the closed window flap was a backpack and another tightly zipped bag that held the clothing and possessions she had chosen to bring with her. There was nothing visible that might disclose her inner life except for one thing. It was there on her left, on the floor—a small portable CD player with three CDs next to it. I might have expected Joanne Shenandoah (always a good choice, American Indian Recording Artist of the Year in 1996). Instead, the three recordings were among my own favorites: Putamayo's *The Best of World Music: African*, *The Dalom Kids and Splash Collection*, and *Talking Timbuktu*, on which Ali Farka Touré and Ry Cooder recorded what I still considered one of the most delicate and lovely songs in the history of world music. "Soukora."

I closed my eyes as I heard the kora begin to play in my mind and I was back in Africa, once again in the mudbrick houses of people so poor that all they could offer you was the hospitality of their hearts, their meager food. They gave up their own beds for you, they shared their healing songs, gifts better than I had ever been able to give anyone.

Soukora. The gentle repetitious rhythms, like the night wind over the edge of the desert, the thum of the drum, the trembling strings of the kora and Ali Farka Touré's tremulous, plaintive voice weaving, the warp and weft of a cloth made of moonlight and longing.

I kept my eyes closed a little longer than I intended. The African music had been the kicker.

I opened my eyes. It took every ounce of self-control I possessed to keep from throwing myself down on my belly and babbling, "I am not worthy."

Instead, though, I looked at her hands. Her right hand was folded over her left one so that her fingers on that hand were covered. Ruth looked up at me with a little smile as if she knew exactly what I'd been thinking. She slowly slid back her right hand to show me what I hoped was there—namely nothing. No wedding ring on her third finger.

Yes! I thought.

But as soon as I thought that, another inner voice said *Not now!*

If not now, then when? asked another of my multiple inner voices.

Later, my logical self replied.

Oh yeah, sure, sneered the most sarcastic of my inner monologists, the one I'd like to locate and strangle.

Ruth patted the ground just in front of her. I quieted my mental tur-
moil, more or less, by looking down and keeping my eyes there as the
three of us sat—Hollywood Indian style—on the tent floor.

"How are things now?" she said to her brother.

In a few words, he filled her in on the meeting and the upcoming
negotiations.

"Can we trust them?" she asked. Then she smiled. "I can't believe I
just said that!"

"Hey," Dennis said, "It's only been five hundred years. They're slow
learners. We just need to give the white folks a little more time."

I wished I'd said that. It made Ruth laugh.

"Oh," Pete said. "Almost forgot. Jake here located a spring for us. So
the camp has plenty of water."

Ruth reached out and grasped my hand, which immediately felt so
hot I thought it would start glowing.

"That's really good," she said. "Are you a water witch?"

"No, more of a ham sandwich," I said.

Wasn't that brilliant? No one said anything. But at least I didn't laugh
at my own joke and I covered my awkwardness with the more direct
reply that question had deserved.

"Some of the old people in my family could do it," I said. "I just took
a stab at it and got lucky."

"People don't just *get* lucky," Ruth said. "They earn their luck."

No way to answer that one. Ruth squeezed my hand and then, alas,
let go of me.

"Can we talk about what happened last night?" I said. Reasserting
my role as an investigator was my last hope before I went down for the
third time and was forever lost.

"Okay," Ruth said, her voice suddenly subdued. She bit her lip and
then took a breath. "Usually I can remember everything. But last
night . . ." She stopped talking and began rubbing her hands together.

I looked over at Pete. Were we pushing her too soon? He nodded. It
was okay. He knew his sister. So we waited.

Ruth took another breath. "I'll start at the beginning," she said, holding up her right hand.

"Okay," I said in an encouraging voice. It seemed clear she needed
reassurance just then.

The small smile she directed at me confirmed that, and made my
heart thud like a bass drum.

"I had this feeling that I knew where it had happened to Louise, where she'd been killed. I felt that I just had to go there. Louise and I had been getting close. We'd talked and gathered medicine." She paused again and made the forward motion with her hand that stands for traveling. "So I went there. It took longer than I thought it would. Sometimes when I see things the distances seem shorter."

"I understand," I said in a soft voice.

Ruth looked up at me. "I know," she said. "By the time I got there it was almost evening. The place where the largest birch trees grow. I found footprints. You know it hasn't rained since it happened. There were her footprints and also the same footprints we'd seen where we found her body."

"Bigfoot," Dennis said.

She nodded.

"There were a few other tracks, too, like those of a large animal of some kind—but perhaps those came later. I've been told there are bears around here, though we haven't seen any. I followed Louise's tracks until I came to the place where it must have happened. There was blood, little pieces of her clothing. And when I touched one of those torn pieces of her blouse, I could feel what it had been like. There was also something else—a piece of birchbark that had been folded together and looked almost like a little envelope, and when I picked it up I could feel that Louise had dropped it there. I had just started to unfold it when I heard something. Rocks were being knocked loose by someone or something coming down the hill toward me and there was an awful growling sound. I didn't wait to see what it was. I just shoved that piece of birchbark under my bracelet and started to run."

Ruth stopped again. As she wiped her mouth with her fingers her hand trembled.

"It's okay," Pete said. "That's enough."

"No," Ruth said, looking down into her hands. "There's more. I need to tell it now. I ran for a long time and as I ran I knew that it was following me. One moment it was on one side, then it was on the other. It was as if it could be in more than one place at the same time. But as I ran I began to sense something, something helping me and showing me which way to go. That was how I knew that somehow, one way or another, I had to get to the cliff."

"Did you ever see what was chasing you?" I asked.

"Not really, though I . . . felt it. It felt like it wasn't a human. But not an animal, either. At one point I thought maybe I'd lost it. But that was when, when . . ."

"When it screamed."

Ruth looked up at me. "Yes. It was a scream like something from a nightmare or an old, old story. You understand, don't you? I felt as if my legs would collapse when it screamed, as if my heart would burst. But I kept going. I'd almost reached the cliff. My bracelet caught on a branch and was pulled off my wrist. Then there was something in front of me, so large that it blocked out the moonlight. I couldn't make out its shape, but I could smell its breath and it smelled like death as it struck at me, but I managed to duck down and it missed me. That was when I caught my foot and fell and started rolling. All I could think to do was keep rolling, knowing that if I stopped I'd be killed. I rolled and rolled and then . . . it was as if the ground opened up to take me in."

"Maybe it did," I said.

Ruth smiled. "Maybe. I guess the opening to that cave where you found me was too narrow for it to get in and reach me. As I rolled inside I seemed to hear little voices singing and something like water drum playing just before my head struck something and everything just went dark."

She nodded her head twice. "That's it," she said.

The four of us sat there for a while, none of us speaking, all of us—Ruth included—thinking about the story she'd just shared of her narrow escape. It was a story that, in certain respects, meant a lot more to us than it would have to the average white person.

"*Niaweh*," I said, using one of the few Mohawk words I knew to break the long silence. "*Niaweh*. Thank you."

"Thank you for finding me," Ruth said, emphasizing each word in a husky voice that made my body thrum like a plucked bass string.

"It's . . . what I do," I managed to reply.

"No shit, Sherlock," Pete Cook said. He was going to have to find some new lines.

Dennis, however, was smiling that little Buddha smile he sometimes indulges in. He put his hand up to his jeans pocket and took something out that remained hidden in his catcher's-mitt-sized paw until he folded back his fingers to disclose his treasure.

"Recognize this?" he said.

It was a delicate silver and turquoise bracelet.

Ruth reached out and took it. "Where did you find it?" she said.

"Just above where we found you in that cave," Dennis said. "When we found you, I thought I saw something glinting near where you went down off the trail. So I went back. I found this hanging from a bush right at the edge of the trail." Dennis shook his head. "Funny, though."

"What's that?" I asked.

"The way it was right in plain sight like that. I don't think that was where I first saw it. The other thing is that, hard as I looked, I just couldn't find that cave again. It was like it wasn't there anymore."

Ruth and I shared a quick look. When the Little People shut their door, no one can tell it has ever been there. Ruth turned the bracelet over to look inside. She gave her head a little shake of disappointment. But Dennis was reaching into his pocket again. He pulled out a small piece of folded birch bark.

"This was still wedged inside the bracelet when I found it," he said. He handed it to Ruth. She carefully unfolded it and then handed it to me. Three letters were scratched—with a twig or a fingernail—into the brown undersurface of the bark: C H E

38

The bird does not
see lines on a map

It was 3:45. Or 1545 hours, military time. Fifteen minutes till zero
hour, when we would meet with the representatives of white law and
order. I stood a bit behind Mikwe and the unarmed primary negotiators, who included Katlin as the head of the Women's Council and
an older Penacook man in his sixties whom Mikwe called by his Indian
name of Mdawela, which means loon. But almost everyone else just
called him Frank. Frank Bowen, aka Mdawela, was the best barber in
the county. Frank Bowen's Barbery Post was the name of his shop, complete with candy cane–striped pole out front. I'll never forget the first
time my aunt and uncle took me to Mr. Bowen to get my hair cut. I
was eight. Halfway through his snipping, he pinched my ear with one
finger and then dropped a crimson-splattered rubber ear in my lap.

"Ooops," he said. "Just hate it when that happens. Least you got one
left."

He also had a store of scalping jokes ready and waiting for his occasional non-Native customers, which made some of them get a little nervous when Frank started stropping his razor.

As befitted the best Indian barber in the Northeast, he had the
worst haircut of anyone at the camp. Tufts of hair stuck out from the
back of his head almost like quills. Despite his appearance and his
macabre sense of humor, people were genuinely fond of Frank, who had
a well-deserved reputation for charity, honesty, and level-headedness.
His heading the Men's Council and Katlin's place at the front of the

women gave me more respect for Mikwe and the Children of the Mountain.

I still hadn't found a chance to talk with Katlin. After our visit to Ruth, Dennis (who had chosen to stay for one more day) and I had used the remaining time before the tête-à-tête with the white law and order boys to take a quick trip into the forest to locate a place that might be right for the foolhardy plan we'd hatched for later that night.

I looked over at Katlin. This was the closest I'd gotten to her since my arrival. I no longer wondered if she was trying to avoid me.

My job at the meeting, like thousands who at His bidding speed to post o'er land and ocean without rest, was to stand and wait—hang back a bit and see what was happening. My ski mask was in place, ensuring that none of the assembled John Laws—federal, state, county and bounty—might recognize me and create an embarrassing scene by begging for my autograph.

Dennis was not with us. Even concealed in a ski mask—or a pup tent—his bulk would have given him away. He'd chosen to remain near the rear perimeter with Ely Joulette, who was a professional chef and a connoisseur of fine cuisine. Food was one of Dennis four *F*'s, the things he loved best: the other three being family, firearms, and fishing. The two were back at the cook tent comparing recipes.

Mikwe was using binoculars to scan those waiting below. All of them wore wide-brimmed hats and the kind of silver sunglasses that make your face look like that of a giant bug.

"I don't like it," Mikwe said. "That one might be Chief Baxter. That little one might be Osini, the head federal. The clothes are right. But something about them looks wrong."

And feels wrong, I thought. I had a tingling feeling in my spine that suggested something was afoot. But what it was I could not tell. It was like those three letters hastily etched onto that piece of birch bark by Louise Brooks as she tried to escape whoever or whatever killed her.

CHE. What did that message mean?

I felt certain that it was a name or part of a name. But no one in the camp was called Che. Was it a reference to the ghost of a South American Marxist? I felt like an idiot because I couldn't figure it out, knowing the answer was there, was hiding at the back of my mind.

It was now time to go down the hill, to cross over the border between Penacook dreams and bureaucratic reality, but Mikwe was still hesitating.

Wise idea, I thought.

Nick Sabattis slipped past me, heading for Mikwe's side. He'd made a quick recon down the hill, out of sight of the feds, but close enough to get a better look. He whispered into Mikwe's ear.

"That's not Baxter. It's somebody else in his uniform."

Mikwe looked over at me.

I nodded back. What was waiting down there was a setup.

Like most dumb ideas, it was a simple one. When it comes to situations involving a bunch of armed people whom you have surrounded, there are always different factions to consider. There are ATF people, FBI, local and state law enforcement personnel. There are hostage negotiators and special weapons and tactics teams. Everyone wants to operate in his own way and everyone knows that he is really the one in charge. Plus, after long enough with nothing happening, after you just sit around outside day after day, cleaning your weapons and drinking bad coffee and eating stale donuts, you get pissed and bored. Boredom is the greatest enemy of rationality.

Damn it, you think, *I have to do something.*

Anything, even if it is something dumb.

I looked over the terrain. What would be the proper dumb thing to do here? I considered history for an example. In 1712, when the Tuscarora leaders of North Carolina went out under a flag of truce, they were taken prisoner and then sent to the West Indies as slaves. It was a tactic that was repeated again and again across the continent over the next century and a half, as with Captain Jack and the Modocs. Lure the Indians in to negotiate and then grab their leaders.

That had to be their plan. Dress up a few people as their negotiators, send them out as decoys. Deploy one or more teams into place, maybe in those little ravines, to set up the ambush. And even as I thought that, I saw, in the ravine off to our right, a bush move when there was no wind.

I looked back up the slope toward the camp. Ely Joulette and four other armed warriors who had been left behind were coming toward us. When Ely was close enough, I raised a questioning eyebrow at him.

"Lot of shit going on out there," he said in a terse voice.

"What now?" I said.

Ely smiled. "Wanta come along?"

I turned back to Mikwe, pointed at my chest with my thumb and then flicked it off to the side.

"Go ahead," Mikwe said.

Then he sat down on the hillside. The seven others with him, including Katlin and Frank Mdawela Bowen, lowered themselves to sit next to him. The four warriors with automatic weapons placed themselves in a circle around them, facing the four directions.

In the valley below, the decoy negotiators stayed where they were. They probably could tell something was up, but like stupid persons trying to be deceitful didn't think that they'd been found out.

Ely and I started up the hill, walking along the road that wound its way into the camp. We hadn't gone far before we met another small group of people from the camp, plus one who certainly was not.

Was it my superior sleuthing skill that enabled me to quickly grasp the purpose and profession of the previously unknown individual who now confronted me? Well, yes. Certain subtle clues enabled me to pierce the veil of mystery about this recent arrival among our ranks. Said clues included the battery packs on his belt, the earphones around his neck, the mike in his left hand, the remote TV camera on his shoulder, and the plastic badge clipped to his shirt pocket that identified him as "Jim" from Channel 14.

"Jim Garble, Action News," he said in a hearty voice, extending his hand to take mine in a bone-crushing grip.

Time to scoop the national media.

I went with the men who escorted Jim while Ely went to check the perimeters. Our news buddy had been smuggled in on one of the side roads that led through the porous net woven around the camp by the gendarmerie, which was even more porous now. The camp's entire eastern perimeter had been emptied of black, blue, and camouflaged uniforms.

"Is it coming through?" Jim said to the microphone he had lifted up in front of his mouth.

"Loud and clear," a tinny voice buzzed back loud enough for us to hear through his earphones.

"Great." He winked at us and mouthed two words: *Live feed*. Then he panned the camera over us, lingering on Ely's rifle and my ski mask.

When we reached Mikwe and the others, still sitting in the grass, a brief interview took place. Mikwe rose to his feet and then, without a single stammer, explained in sound-bite clarity why we were here and what the Children of the Mountain hoped to accomplish.

He mentioned the Federal Non-intercourse Act, which had forbade the states or private individuals to buy or take Indian land. He explained how, in 1877, the state had granted the Penacooks ten thousand acres to be chosen from any state-held land anywhere in the areas to the north—ten thousand acres we never got because they said we no longer existed. But here we were, like Mark Twain, disputing the rumor of our collective demise and laying claim to a little of our own land that included our most sacred mountain.

"But what about the white people who come here to vacation at the park every year?" Jim asked.

Mikwe nodded. "Remember, the state closed this campground down, so no tourists could come here as it stood when we arrived. As soon as the state recognizes our legal title we will reopen the park to tourists just as before. But with one difference. We'll cut the entrance and camping fees in half."

Jim loved it. He kept nodding his head while Mikwe was talking. Meanwhile, down in the valley, the federal, state, and local forces were hanging their heads. They'd seen the camera, the first one to make its way into the camp, and it looked as if they were watching a TV monitor next to one of their trucks.

"There's a rumor that someone died up here. What about that?" Jim said.

Mikwe didn't miss a beat.

"I can confirm the tragic death of one of our group. But the authorities have been keeping it a secret—and holding her body, which has prevented us from giving her a traditional burial as her family wishes."

Jim swallowed audibly. This was an even bigger story than he'd expected. But he managed to keep his voice level as he asked the next logical question.

"How did she die?"

"She was murdered outside our territory by a person or persons unknown. The brutal method leads us to conclude it was done to frighten us. Further, instead of cooperating with us in finding the killer or killers, the authorities have harassed us. Instead of negotiating honestly with us, they now appear to be planning an assault on our camp."

"What!" Jim said. He was so excited that his voice trembled. But he somehow kept the camera steady. He was probably already mentally packing his bags and imagining what it was going to be like based in Atlanta and not the New Hampshire sticks.

Mikwe looked down the slope, lifting his head up to show his profile beneath the two tall heron feathers attached to his headband. Dramatic—a good shot.

"We have attempted to negotiate in good faith. Now it is up to them to show that same good faith. Let them call off their cowardly attack. *Ni ya yo*. So it is."

I looked back up the slope. Ely was coming toward us, grinning broadly. I looked down the slope. A man wearing a flak jacket and carrying what had to be a portable phone was making his way toward us with a white flag held high. Meanwhile, in the ravine to our right, the bushes and small trees seemed to be dancing the conga as concealed SWAT team members were making covert departures.

"They're all pulling back," Ely said.

39

If we are aware,
we wear what we are

The man with the portable phone was red-faced and puffing by the time he reached us. The flak jacket looked a little too tight for him and he was not in a talkative mood. He put the phone down on the ground in front of Mikwe, who stood with his arms folded. Then he turned and walked back down the hill. He'd gone no more than a hundred yards before the phone rang.

"Telemarketing?" I asked.

Mikwe picked up the phone.

"I am here," he said.

That was, of course, self-evident. But it didn't sound bad. Nor, for that matter, did Mikwe look bad. The traditional clothing he wore fit him well. He looked like a larger, stronger, more dignified man than he had ever looked in a three-piece suit as Paul Attean, affirmative action hire and potential future law partner. I finally had to admit that I liked him better as Mikwe.

I also recognized the clothing he was wearing. There was no mistaking it. It had been Tom Nicola's. Every piece of it made with loving care and infinite patience by the man who had been a second uncle to me. It was not Tom's favorite regalia. He had given that to me. It had arrived by UPS, carefully packed in a large cardboard box, not long after Tom's funeral. I've never worn it. For one, it would be a little small for me and would need some serious alternations. More than that, though, I've never felt worthy enough to wear it. Nothing I've ever done has ever made me feel that I deserve to walk in his beaded moccasins.

Recognizing Tom's clothing, a gift with such deep meaning, made me remember something I'd forgotten, namely that Paul Attean had once been my close friend. Paul and Katlin and I had been inseparable when all three of us were eleven and twelve winters old. We'd spent as much of our time as possible around Tom, listening to his stories, copying his every move.

But the next summer had been different. Hormones kicking in and other kids starting to pair up made our little threesome really awkward. It became clear—even though Katlin seemed unaware of it—that we both had a crush on our former tomboy playmate and that created tension. It finally erupted one day when Mikwe said something about my being too white to be right. So I showed him red—spurting out of his nose after I popped him.

It had never been the same for us after that. Our friendship was over. I was too young then to be truly forgiving of Mikwe for what he had said. Tom tried to get us back together, but finally gave up when he saw that both of us had dug our heels in about being enemies. It looked as if it was just a matter of time before we came to blows again and I would really hurt Mikwe—me being so much bigger and stronger even back then.

The situation led to Tom giving me a talk about fighting.

"A warrior never attacks those who are weaker," Tom said. "A real warrior always prefers peace. A real warrior always tries to protect others. When you must fight, be compassionate until you have no other choice. Then, and only then, do what must be done."

I was too young to understand most of it. It would take me another fifteen years to begin to really understand. And I am still in that beginning stage. But I understood just enough of what Tom told me to know that I'd been wrong to hit my friend. That was when I did try to apologize, but Mikwe would have none of it. He just walked away from my outstretched hand and kept on walking. So I gave up on it.

And although I never hit Mikwe again with my fist, I started on beating him up in my mind, mentally putting him down, mocking his pretensions when he became an academic star and seemed to turn his back on being Indian.

Tom Nicola, I thought, *you old fox*. Leaving your two best sets of traditional regalia to Mikwe and to me, knowing that both of us would eventually get the message. As I looked at Mikwe, relaxed and natural in that regalia which was now his, looking as if he had been born to dress that way, I got it.

Mikwe's moccasins were made of moose hide. Designs in the shape of flowers had been sewed onto them in moose hair. A moose that Tom Nicola hunted and killed, not with a gun but with a bow and arrows in northern Quebec while visiting the Mistasini Crees. The moose stands for the eastern wind, which comes up out of the ocean dripping water just as a moose lifts its head to let the water stream off its wide horns after dipping below the pond surface to browse on underwater plants. Each of Mikwe's leggings was made from the entire skin of a big otter, the hair tanned on the skin, the otters' tails used as garters to tie the leggings to his belt made of woven basswood. Tom had trapped those otters in the big river that bore their name. Otter, another creature at home in two worlds. The way we Indians had to be to survive.

Mikwe's vest was made of soft, smoke-tanned deerskin, smoked over the fire that was kept always burning in Tom's backyard. Winter or summer, it burned. The smoke kept open that path between earth and sky, that road the spirits could travel upon. On that deerskin vest was painted the double-curve design that stands for the unity of the people. It had been Tom's favorite design.

Above it all was his headdress. Not one of those many-feathered Plains Indian war bonnets that tourists expect all Indians to wear. Feathered, but not with the plumage of the eagle. Instead, it was a coronet of long feathers taken from the gull and the heron, the two tallest heron feathers in front. Heron, as Tom told the three of us, is a very powerful bird, a sacred one. Heron stands without moving, its beak in the sky, reminding us to pray, telling us to look up to the Giver of Life.

Mikwe finished talking. He clicked a button on the phone, opened his hand and let it drop onto the ground. Mook Glossian scooted in like a crab to pick it up. Mikwe shook his head.

"Leave it there," he said.

He looked at the small group of people gathered and waiting. He let his eyes take in each person in turn. Maybe it was from his training to be a lawyer, learning how to look over a jury, win people to his point of view. Or maybe it was just real sincerity. I noticed how his gaze lingered a little longer when it hit Katlin's. I also noticed how their eyes met and held each other.

Seek no further for an explanation of why Katlin has been avoiding you, Dumbo, I thought.

Then, to my surprise, instead of a jealous scowl, a little smile twitched the edge of my mouth. *Those two,* I thought, *Katlin and Paul. Of course.*

Those two had always been fated to be together. My little smile got bigger as a warm protective feeling began to take over. If a grizzly bear had tried to attack the two of them at that moment, I would have ripped it apart with my teeth.

At that exact moment, Mikwe and Katlin both turned to look in my direction. They saw my smile. I shrugged my shoulders and nodded, giving them my blessings. It was as if a sigh of relief had been breathed and shared between us. And for a few heartbeats the three of us were all twelve again.

40

*With strategy one
defeats one thousand*

Jim Garble was edging in for a close-up of Mikwe.

"Could you please turn that off for a moment?" Mikwe said.

To his credit, Jim did just that.

Mikwe smiled at him. "Thank you. You can spend the night here among the Children of the Mountain if you'd like."

Jim looked like a puppy about to be given a whole box of milk bones. "I'd like," he said.

Mikwe nodded and gestured toward his right. "Mdawela will show you around," he said.

Frank Bowen nodded. "Unh-hunh, nidoba," he said in Abenaki, placing his hand on the cameraman's shoulder and steering him away. "And might I inquire," I heard him say in English just before they were out of earshot, "when the last time was that you had a good haircut?"

With the exception of Katlin and Mikwe, the rest of the group followed, leaving the three of us alone.

Katlin came up to me first. She reached out with her left hand to touch my arm. The same left hand that bore an engagement ring on the third finger.

"*Paakwenogwisian,*" I said. "You appear new to me. Both of you."

"*Paakwenagwisian,*" Katlin replied. Her eyes were sparkling. She reached up to my shoulder and pulled me down so that she could kiss my cheek. "Thank you for understanding, Jake. My kids love him."

"Unh-hunh," I said. "Congratulations to both of you."

"I have to meet with the Women's Council now," Katlin said.

"There's one thing you can do for me," I said. "It's about one of the women on the council."

I explained it to her in a few words. I could see how Katlin's quick mind took it in. She understood my suspicions.

"I'll see what I can find out," she said. She patted the back of my hand, just as she used to do at age eleven. "And we'll talk later."

"Later," I said.

Then, like a bright leaf blown away by the wind, a leaf that will never come back to the branch again, she broke away from us and was gone.

Mikwe was studying an extremely interesting tuft of grass by his feet. I stood and studied it with him, neither of us saying anything. Finally, he broke the silence.

"I d-d-d-don't deserve her."

No need for any reply to that. We were on the same page.

"Eh-eh-anyhow," he said, biting his lip, "Will you k-k-k-kill me if I ever h-h-hurt her?"

"I'll kill you if you ever hurt her."

"Thank you," he said.

Then, while both of us still looked down at that tuft of grass, which had begun to appear a bit blurry and misty to me for some unexplained reason, he held out his hand. And I took it.

As we walked back to the camp he filled me in on the conversation he'd just had on the portable phone with Agent Baxter, in charge of negotiations. The unexpected arrival of the local TV guy—and the fact that Mikwe was being guarded by armed Indians—had blown the snatch-and-grab maneuver. Baxter insisted the plan had not been his but Homeland Security's. The idea had been to take the leadership and then the rest of the camp in order to protect the Children of the Mountain from whatever or whoever had killed one of the Indians. With things not going so well now in Iraq, where the mission had clearly not been accomplished, there was a lot of pressure from the vice president's office to clear this thing up and put the focus back on foreign affairs.

But now things were being rethought. No, the Indians would not be allowed to bring in food and medicine. No, they would not have their power and phone lines turned back on. But they would be given forty-eight hours. And that was a firm promise. But when those forty-eight hours were up, if the murders were not solved, they would have no choice but to vacate the premises. One way or another, the feds were coming in.

When Mikwe finished his summary, I looked back down the hill.

"Wh-wh-what do you th-th-think?" he said.

"They might not even give you the full forty-eight."

"I thought so," Mikwe said. The stammer was gone and his voice was firm. His right hand was also resting on my shoulder, the way we used to stand back when we were kids together. "How long?"

"Maybe a day. But they're not the first thing we have to worry about. We still have to get through another night."

Mikwe nodded. Neither one of us had to say it. Whoever or whatever had killed twice and almost added Ruth to its hit list would try to kill again.

"What should we do?" Mikwe said.

"You're sure you want my advice?"

"I'm sure."

"All right, then. Let's assume that the boys in blue are just as spooked about what's out there going bump in the night as we are. That means they won't be prowling our perimeters again until well after dawn. So, as soon as it's dark, we shrink our own circle. There's too much space to cover. Bring everyone into the big meeting tent. Everyone sleeps there tonight. Post the warriors around the tent, no one goes more than fifty feet away. How close are the pit latrines?"

"A lot farther than that."

"Remember what Tom told us about Nam? More people got ambushed going to the latrine than walking down the trails. Anyone needing to go to the toilet after dark has to have an armed escort. Pants down, rifles locked and loaded."

"We can dig new latrines on either side of the meeting tent."

"Good. That way people should be relatively safe tonight."

"Safety in numbers," Mikwe said. He nodded.

It was at that exact moment that a certain Anglo-Saxon epic elbowed its way out of the dark crannies of my overactive cerebrum. Safety in numbers, indeed. All the king's men asleep together in the great hall of the Danes while Grendel slipped in with a toothy grin, like a kid let loose in a candy store.

And then, the image of that ancient Anglo-Saxon boogeyman was replaced by another, one out of our own native nightmares.

Che, I thought. *Louise had time to write only the first three letters.*

Mikwe must have felt the way that I stiffened when that thought came to me. He took his hand off my shoulder.

"Jake," he said, "what are *you* going to do tonight?"

41

Eye open and blind
Eyes closed and listening

I sat down to make a list. It was a slightly more descriptive one this time, a summary of the problems facing me.

1. Monstrous person or thing (or both) lurking in the forest.
2. One or more traitors among the Children of the Mountain.
3. Attack by unidentified monstrous person or thing to take place tonight.
4. Forces of law and order waiting to swoop in. (48 hours?)

As I sat in our tent looking at that list, Dennis was engaged in one of his favorite pastimes. He'd put aside the piece of wood he'd been carving—which had begun to disclose a shape that I found chillingly familiar. He was now taking apart and cleaning a gun, an AK-47 that some foolhardy warrior had loaned him. He lifted up the barrel and squinted through it.

"Time me," he said. His big hands blurred as the constituent parts of the weapon were slapped back into place.

"Thirty seconds," I said, lying back on my sleeping bag.

Dennis shook his head. "I could do better."

"So could I." I wasn't talking about putting guns together.

Dennis nodded.

"What do you think it's about?" I asked him. "The casino? The land? Or the succession to the chieftaincy?"

"Well, Podjo," Dennis said as he tossed the rifle from one hand to the other. "How about a little bit of everything?"

I sighed. "That's what I'm thinking—which means we have more than one problem to deal with."

"Unless we deal with them all at once."

"Put all our eggs in one basket."

"And then make an omelet?"

"*Kwe-kwe*," a soft voice called from outside the thin wall of the tent next to me. It was Katlin.

"You were right," she whispered through the tent wall. "There's a cell phone hidden under her sleeping bag."

Then she was gone. I looked over at Dennis, who had raised one eyebrow.

"The plot sickens," I said.

42

The story told,
not the storyteller

If you think you're funny, other people won't. It was plainly time for me to get serious.

But first we had to get through dinner. Despite the roadblocks, food had managed to keep trickling into the camp and there was still enough for everyone. The fare was pow-wow standard. Corn soup, Navajo tacos on big greasy slabs of fry bread (the Pan-Indian flag), and coffee. There were plans, should the takeover last long enough, to be more self-sufficient. But the gardens they'd planted had been a disaster, stunted by the rocky soil and then drying up from the lack of rain.

The symbolism of their return to the old ways, as Mikwe explained it, was more important than the reality of their reliance on such twenty-first-century hunter-gatherer subsistence techniques as stalking the best bargain in ground beef at the supermarket (never take it all, always leave some of the meat for another generation).

But the meal did begin with a traditional prayer of thanks in our language. It was a good one, delivered by Frank Mdawela Bowen in a voice that was so quiet that everyone grew silent to hear his words, so strong that it seemed as if the trees outside were leaning in to listen with us.

The spirit of sharing among the Children of the Mountain was real. People here cared about each other and about the dream this place represented to them, to their families, to their people. Their eyes were, to use the old words that still choke me up from the Civil Rights Days that my father told me about, "on the prize"—but not so much for the three individuals I'd marked out, whose eyes looked shifty. Aside from me, though, no one else seemed to notice. But, then again, why should they? Until I'd figured it out, the answer hadn't been that obvious to me, either. And what was even more ironic was that those three—I was convinced—were not acting in concert. Each thought that he or she was singing solo.

Thinking of singing, I had earlier taken note of the guitar case off to one side in the dinner tent. The owner of the guitar had turned out to be Ely. After a little conversation about the relative merits of Gibsons Guilds, Epiphones, and Yamahas, I modestly mentioned that I *had* written a song or two. He asked me if I wanted to borrow his ax to share a tune or two around the fire tonight.

I looked across the circle of people that was gathering now around the fire and my eyes met those of Ruth Cook. Funny how I wasn't at all resentful now about Katlin and Mikwe being a couple.

Anyhow, as my heart punched holes in my rib cage, I knew what was going on. Maybe this time it was real. And I found myself in the all-too-familiar position of the man who fell off the fifty-story building and was heard to shout as he plummeted past the twentieth floor, "So faaar, so gooood!"

But, before I was to sing my serenade to the lovers with their arms 'round the grief of the ages, storytelling would come first. And Katlin was the one who stood to tell a story. It was one that Tom Nicola had given us when we were kids together. I remembered that, and so did Mikwe. With a smile, I acknowledged his nod of pride when she began those familiar words.

There was a young woman who went out alone to swim. "Be careful," her mother told her. But she went alone into the woods, to a pond deep in the woods. She took off her dress and waded into the water up to her waist. As she stood there in the cool water, bubbles began to rise to the surface far out from her. They rose and rose until they formed a shape in froth on top of the water. It was the shape of a baby. The wind began to blow. That shape made of froth moved across the water toward her. The girl was frightened. She turned to run, but the water was too deep. The froth washed against her legs and was gone.

The girl went home. From that day on she did not go back to the water. She became very quiet. Her mother grew worried. Then, after the passage of two moons, that girl's belly began to grow. She had no husband and was going to have a child. Her parents became ashamed. They moved away and left her alone.

The girl sat on the ground and began to cry. "What will happen to me?"
she said. Then Kingfisher flew up and landed on a branch near her.

"Do not cry," Kingfisher said. "It is not possible for you to die of starva-
tion. I will feed you. Our grandmother will be here soon. She will help you."

That made the girl glad. That evening an old woman came to her. The old
woman wore clothing made of forest moss. It was fastened around her with a
belt made of strips peeled from the basswood tree.

"Granddaughter," the old woman said, "I am Grandmother Woodchuck.
I shall take care of you."

As Katlin continued the story, I no longer heard her voice. Nor did I
hear the voice of Tom Nicola. Instead, there was an older voice. It was
the voice of the story itself, a voice that surrounded me and carried me
again into that world I had loved more than almost any other when I
was a child.

The boy who was born to her was known as Froth. He grew up to be a great
hunter and a hero. He fought the Great White Bear, a monster that threat-
ened to wipe out all of his people. The White Bear was so tall that it reached
halfway up to the treetops. It seemed as if nothing could defeat the terrible
creature until Chickadee flew down and told Froth the secret place to aim his
arrow, the place where the white monster was weak. There is always a place
where every monster is weak. If it had no weakness, it would not be a
monster.

There are more lessons than one to be heard in our stories. When Katlin finished, I was not the only one who was quiet and thinking.

But Ely broke the silence.

"Hey," he said, "you know we got a musician here with us? I talked
him into singing a song or two. Right?"

Ely's guitar was placed into my hands a lot sooner than I'd expected.
I strummed it, shaped a chord or two, and began to fingerpick. A simple progression. *D, A, E, A.*

Ruth was sitting next to me. I cleared my throat and started to sing,
trying to put my heart into it.

> The Creator first shaped people out of the stone
> But their hearts were as cold as the clay,
> So he made men and women step forth from the ash,
> They are growing and green to this day.

Then Gluskonba was shaped from the dust of the land
With his hands he made rivers and lakes
And he learned all the lessons his Grandmother taught
How to live for this Earth's sacred sake.
It all happened that way,
So my ancestors say.

When the new people came from out of the east.
They were starving and we gave them food.
We taught them the ways our people thought best
That to share with each other was good.

But their leaders were greedy and wanted our land,
They said all the Indians must go.
Their drums were all tuned to the rhythm of war
And their hearts seemed as cold as the snow.

It all happened that way
so my ancestors say.

I don't have a great voice, but I can usually pull off a song, talking it
as much as singing it. More like reading a poem. When I was done, a
few people applauded while others nodded.

"Unh-hunh," Mikwe said. There was a smile on his face.

I bowed my humble head.

Then Ruth put one hand lightly on my shoulder and placed her lips
close to my right ear.

Be still my heart, I thought.

"Your B string is flat," she whispered.

In the movie of my mind, Elvis *has* left the building.

43

Seasons change
and remain the same

Three hours had passed since the campfire. The full moon had not yet risen. The night was quiet. Everyone except for Dennis and me was inside the big tent, bedded down for the night. But Dennis and I were sitting on either side of the big cedar tree at the edge of the camp. We had other things to do. Like Dennis cleaning his glasses for the twelfth time in the past two hours.

And as I sat there, a story came to me.

Here is where my story camps. Many years ago a woman and a man lived alone in the forest. They had only their little son to keep them company. As he grew up, they could see that he was strong and clever. They were proud of him. One day, when he was almost a man, he went to his parents.

"I wish to see other people," he told them.

His parents were sad, but because they loved him they told him he could go and look for other human beings.

The boy set out on his journey that same day. He walked far. He slept all night in the forest and when he woke he saw a rabbit standing up on its hind legs and looking at him.

"Ehe!" said the rabbit. "How are you?"

"I am well, my friend," the boy said. "I am going to look for other human beings."

"That is good," the rabbit said. "I will go with you."

Together they traveled a great way, far toward the direction of the summer land. Finally they came to a big village. They looked down at that village from the hilltop. They could see that the people were in great distress.

"I will creep close to the village and see what is wrong," the rabbit said. Then he went down the hill and came back to the boy.

"Kiwakwe has come here," said the rabbit. "Soon it will return and then the chief must give his daughter to the monster. No one knows how to save her from being eaten by the Kiwakwe."

"I will try," said the boy.

"That is good," said the rabbit. "No one has tried to take the girl away. They know the Kiwakwe can follow any track with the speed of the wind. Go now and speak to the people. Then come back here with the daughter of the chief and I will help you."

The boy went down into the village. At first, no one would listen to him. What could this strange boy do that even the strongest men in the village could not do? But when the chief heard that someone wanted to save his daughter, he had the boy brought to him.

"If you can save my daughter's life," said the chief, "you may take her as a wife, if she agrees." He looked at his daughter. She looked at the boy and something passed between their eyes.

"I agree," said the girl.

Then the two of them left the village. They went straight to the place where the rabbit was waiting. In his paw, he held a tiny toboggan. He put it down on the ground.

"Blow on this," he said to the chief's daughter.

She did so. Immediately that tiny sled became large enough to carry them. The rabbit held out his other paw. In it were two tiny squirrels.

"Pet these," he said to the boy. The boy did so. They quickly grew as large as wolves. The rabbit hitched them to the toboggan. The three of them climbed on and the squirrels began to pull. The toboggan sped across the snow.

But a terrible cry came from behind them. It was the Kiwakwe. It had found that the girl was gone and now it was on their trail.

The squirrels ran as fast as the wind, but the cries of the monster grew louder. The Kiwakwe was catching up to them. The rabbit stopped the toboggan.

"Keep running," he said to the boy and girl. "Help is waiting for you by the river. I will make a track that will confuse the Kiwakwe."

Then, as the toboggan sped on with the boy and girl, the rabbit began making tracks going in all directions. When the Kiwakwe reached those tracks, it became confused. It went first one direction and then the other. Meanwhile, the toboggan had reached the river. There by the water an old woman waited.

"Grandchildren," the old woman said, "your death is close behind you. Do as I say and I will help you."

Then the old woman stepped into the river and lay down on top of the water.

"Get on my back," she said.

The boy was uncertain, but the chief's daughter urged him on. Together, they got onto the old woman's back. Just like that, she turned into a canoe and carried them across the wide river.

When they climbed out of the canoe and looked back, the old woman was gone. Only an old duck was floating there in the water.

"Go up the bank," the old duck said. "Your friend is waiting for you."

The boy and girl did as she said. At the top of the bank they found the rabbit and the squirrel toboggan waiting for them. Once again, they hopped on and sped away.

In the meantime, the Kiwakwe had found their trail and reached the river. It saw the old duck floating in the water.

"Take me across," the Kiwakwe roared.

But the old duck just flapped her wings and flew away. So the Kiwakwe had to search upstream and downstream for a shallow place to cross.

Now the squirrel toboggan was going like the wind. They traveled far this way until they saw the shape of a mountain before them.

"The old gray mountain will help us," said the rabbit.

Even as he spoke, the terrible howl of the Kiwakwe came from the forest behind them.

Faster and faster the squirrels pulled the toboggan until they came to the base of a great steep cliff. The rabbit jumped off the toboggan and picked up a long pole.

"Climb this," he said.

The chief's daughter and the young man began to climb. As they climbed, the pole grew taller and taller. It grew taller than the tallest pines. It lifted them up to the top of the cliff before the Kiwakwe could reach them.

Reaching the bottom of the pole, the Kiwakwe looked up. It saw the young man and the chief's daughter step off the pole at the top of the cliff. It began to climb the pole.

The pole, however, continued to grow, carrying the Kiwakwe right up over the top of the cliff. Higher and higher it grew, until it was above the clouds. All that the Kiwakwe could do was cling to the pole.

The rabbit came to the base of the pole. He pushed and the pole began to tip and then fall. The Kiwakwe fell with it, striking the ground so hard that the monster was killed.

So it was that the rabbit helped the young man and the chief's daughter escape from the Kiwakwe. And when I last saw the three of them, they were still living together happily. That is how the story is told.

❧

As I finished the story in my mind, despite what it made me consider, I did feel a little better. I had to admit that what Tom Nicola had told me years ago was true.

"When you are feeling confused or alone, just tell yourself a story."

Though Tom Nicola had added that his own particular method of finding peace in a stressful situation, such as being pinned down by Viet Cong fire in southeast Asia, had been a little different. He recited the traditional names of the Penacook cycle of moons.

Hard Moon. Moon When Food Runs Out. Moon When Wind Scatters Leaves over the Crusted Snow. Egg Laying Moon. Moon of Spring Fishing. Moon of Planting. Moon of Hoeing. Moon of Ripe Berries. Corn Moon. Moon When Deer Mate. Moon When Leaves Fall. Ice Moon. Moon of Long Nights.

I pictured Tom as he was that night—a lot worse off than I was now—a K-Bar knife grasped in his bandaged and badly infected right hand, his left arm hanging useless by his side, no ammunition left for his rifle. Yet he had the presence of mind to whisper those words in Penacook. One part of his mind picturing those living seasons while another part listened for the scrape against gravel and stone of the belts of small black-clad men creeping up on their bellies to try to kill him.

I thought about Tom's old story. It was apropos, as well as being anthropomorphic and anthropophagous.

The Kiwakwe is the cannibal giant who walks the northern forests of night, a human being before it was inhabited by an insatiable spirit of hunger. Perpetually in pain, howling like the storm wind, it is so hungry that it devours the flesh from its own lips and its arms and shoulders. The northern Crees call that one Windigo. Our Pasamaquoddy cousins—like Louise Brooks—call him Chenoo. CHE.

Was it a Chenoo that she saw, or someone using that monster of our Wabanaki bad dreams as a guise for the kind of murders that not only can end a movement, but kill the spirit as well? I couldn't answer that yet. Only by risking my understandably uninsured neck might I find the answer.

44

*Who sees the border
between waking and dream?*

When people live in cities, they learn to lock all their doors and windows. Including those of their senses. Next time you walk through the human-crafted canyons of Manhattan, try to be aware of how much of your surroundings you usually ignore. True, you do look to see if the lights have changed, if the flow of traffic will allow you to cross the street. And you may also take note of those who approach a bit too closely. But after you have closed yourself in for the night, bolted, dead-bolted, locked, chain-locked, and padlocked your reinforced steel door, how much can you remember of what you saw, smelled, and saw? The civilized person learns to block out most of the city world in order to survive it.

It is different in the forest. To live there—not just make a brief visit—to survive as we all did not that long ago, you must open the doors of perception. Allow in all the notes in the great symphony being played around you, especially in the darkness. Hear the bat's wings fluttering overhead, the slow rustling steps of the deer's hooves fifty feet away in dry leaves. To recognize and identify those sounds is like being able to pick out the individual drumbeats in a familiar recording.

There is a way of listening that Uncle John shared with me that he called "opening the wind." He learned it from a Cherokee friend named Norman Russell, who was both a botanist and a published poet.

We would sit on the back porch in the dark with our eyes closed. First we'd listen to the close sounds within a small circle, no more than the distance of our outspread arms. Then, once we'd listened long enough to hear everything that close, we'd double the circle. It took a long time, many nights, for me to begin to do that well. Bit by bit, we'd widen the circle of our listening that way. Finally, by the end of the first summer Uncle John had introduced me to that way of listening, I could identify things I heard from more than half a mile away.

So now, as I sat beneath the cedar tree with Dennis, I listened and heard, beyond the sound of our own breathing, beyond the rustle of a shrew in the leaves, beyond an owl calling in a distant clearing, the sound of human voices—two voices talking to each other. One had the Indian's distinct way of speaking of an Indian, the other was a white man. I caught only stray words and the tone of their conversation, but that was enough for me to grasp that what they were planning would bring nothing good our way.

Then the night wind shifted and those faint voices were gone. But I could hear something else. It was a heartbeat sound, deep, threatening, growing stronger. Though the night sky was clear, I experienced the skin-prickling sensation you may get when you sense an approaching storm.

Ethnologists have pointed out that our old stories about monsters are used for the purpose of making children behave. Obey me, or the forest monster will come for you.

But our aboriginal hearts know that there is more to these stories than the fright factor. They are elemental. There is still something held in the earth and stone of this continent that is older than humans, stronger than wind, colder than ice, hotter than fire. It is power, analogous perhaps to that energy locked into the ore that can be refined into Uranium 235.

It is dangerous. If your heart is right, then you might use such power well. But few know how to control such power after finding it. It may shape or destroy the one who tries to use it. If your heart is wrong, if something within you is not straight, that power will push against the weak place. It will bend you further. It will use you.

Scientific explanations start at the surface and usually end there. But what if they go deeper, beyond elements and molecules, beyond atoms and subatomic particles? What if they dive into those waves of energy that no human being is supposed to be able to see? At that point, physicists tell us, logic fails. Quantum mechanics. At that point we can only rely upon faith. So the physicists say. And so, too, say the shamans. Those we called mteowlin.

"One who is mteowlin," Uncle John said to me one spring morning when I was thirteen, "knows how to see that power, sense it. Call helpers. Find things."

He looked at me. I nodded as if I understood. But I didn't want to understand. I didn't want to be different from anyone. I didn't even want to be myself. I wanted to have black hair like the other kids and not look so white. I was the worst kind of student, one with as much resistance as talent.

Uncle John knew that. "You've seen television? Everybody has seen television, right? But how does it work? And if a TV is broke, can just anyone fix it? White people make TVs and transistors and microchips, but if one of them things is broken, can most of those white folks fix it? An ordinary white person can only change a burnt-out light bulb."

"No," I said. I figured it was a safe enough answer. Then maybe we could get back to getting ready to go fishing.

"No," Uncle John said. He smiled. "They have to know how and they have to have the tools. And when it comes to medicine power, the one who is mteowlin is the one who knows how. That one has the tools. That one knows how to touch the light that is at the heart of all life."

"I see," I said, thinking that I didn't. But Uncle John's smile got broader. It made me nervous. Then he nodded.

"Now let's go fishing," Uncle John said.

It was later that I learned not all mteowlins use their power for good things. And when a mteowlin's heart goes really bad, that mteowlin may turn into a Chenoo. All the power he controlled begins to shape him. He grows larger than any human being should grow. His hair grows long and unruly like that of a bear. His teeth get bigger and his fingers curl into claws. His heart turns into ice and he rides on the wind, filled with an emptiness, a never-ending hunger.

My eyes closed, I heard that heartbeat grow stronger, that dark presence move closer. I stood and began to run. I ran through the forest, the bright moonlight showing me the way through the night. I leaped over branches and fallen trees. My bad knee didn't bother me. Only the wind could go faster than I ran. My hands brushed the flanks of deer as they stood amazed. And as I ran, I kept listening. I could hear something ahead of me. It was waiting.

I don't know how long I ran. It seemed as if the moon should have risen, but there was no sign of its light in the sky that was aswirl with stars. Then I came to a clearing. I stopped running and looked around. It was not here yet. But it would be.

There was something on the ground in the middle of that clearing. I walked forward slowly and picked it up. It was a long spear made of bone, or the single horn of some animal I could not name. Its balance felt right in my hand and its point was sharp.

I should have been ready for it, but I wasn't. When the lunatic laugh came from behind me it almost buckled my knees. Somehow, I remained standing and I turned to look at what stood there at the clearing's edge, less than a spear cast away. It was at least seven feet tall, massive shoulders slumped forward under the weight of arms muscled like those of a gorilla.

Its body, though, did not look like that of an animal. It was like that of a hairy, gnarled old man, muscles knotted, skin wrinkled. The face was the worst part. It was both human and less than human. The intelligence that gleamed from its red eyes was the cunning of a demon mad for slaughter. Its long gray hair was filthy and matted dark with blood. Its mouth was open, lips bloody and torn.

It looked at me, waiting for me to run. Instead, I looked back at it. With all the strength I had, I willed my feet to hold themselves to the earth as if they were rooted like ash trees. Then, amazingly, the Chenoo looked aside. But I had not won much in that staring contest. Less than a heartbeat passed before it lifted its head like a wolf and howled.

Howled!

I'd heard the great breathless moan of a monsoon wind tearing apart a building as if it were made of tissue paper. I'd heard the screams of men after an explosion has ripped through them so that their guts hang out like shreds of tattered flags. But nothing I had ever heard before compared with the full-throated howl of the Chenoo. For the briefest of moments, my mind was washed away from me the way a wet cloth wipes chalk from a blackboard, my body an empty, vulnerable shell. I came back to myself, though I do not know how, to see that the Chenoo seemed larger. But he had not grown in size. In that split-second of blankness that had overwhelmed me, the monster had leaped close, his arms reaching out to take me in a final embrace.

Though my mind had forgotten what I held in my hands, my body had not. I ducked beneath those arms and thrust the sharp point of the bone spear toward the Chenoo's belly. It struck home, but the monster twisted away with a growl of pain.

It circled me, more cautious now as I held the spear. Black blood was oozing from the wound in its stomach. The tip of the bone spear was smoking as if it was on fire. I wondered fleetingly what the chemical composition of a Chenoo's blood might be. Substitute sulfuric acid for amino acid?

Each time it lunged at me, I stabbed back. Its arms were long and one of its clawed fingers raked across my cheek. It burned like fire and I could feel my own blood flowing down over the line of my jaw. But I did not reach up to feel my wound. Every ounce of my concentration had to stay focused.

Lunge, stab. Circle, stab, lunge. It went on and on. And I could feel myself tiring. Even though I had wounded the creature that sought my blood, I knew that I was weakening more than it was. Soon it would come in at me with the force of the storm wind and I would not be able to stop it. It would eat my flesh and swallow my soul.

There was only one thing I could do. I filled my lungs with the clean night air in one deep breath. Sen go no koe. *The before and after voice, as old Musashi called it. Then, from the center of my being, from the depth of the* chi, *I screamed. I drew on the strength of the four winds, on the voices of eagle and hawk, wolf and loon, panther and bear. I took the sound of avalanche and ice breaking on a frozen lake. I touched the ancient power that is known by those who are* mteowlin, *who have paid with dreams and pain, with seeking and the longing to be in balance and to earn a voice that can shatter stone.*

The air shook with the power of that scream. The Chenoo froze, confused by it. And I leaped from the heart of that scream, twisting like an eel, to drive the bone spear deep into the Chenoo's chest. I dove and rolled away, unable to wrench the spear free. The Chenoo stood, looking at it in disbelief. Then it fell to its knees, forward onto that spear, driving it deeper. Gouts of black blood came from the Chenoo's mouth and it toppled onto its back. But it was not fully defeated yet. There was only one place to strike the killing blow—if it is possible to kill that which has already been long dead.

I stepped forward and grasped the spear. It came free as easily as a stick thrust into sand. I aimed and thrust the spear point into the Chenoo's left ear.

Water was rippling and flowing about me, light growing and then ebbing. Beneath me, the Chenoo grew smaller. Like a snowbank touched by the sun, like ice fallen into warm waters, he shrank. I pulled the bone spear free and dropped it. A naked old man lay there. His eyes found mine. His eyes were clear, emptied of anger or evil.

"Grandson," he whispered in a hoarse voice, "it has been so long. I have been so tired."

He spoke those words in our language, but the accent was different. It was, perhaps, the way those words would have been spoken a hundred generations ago.

"Grandson," he rasped.

His face was so familiar. He was no one I had ever seen before, yet he looked like those elders I knew and had loved. Like Uncle John or Tom. Like their great-grandfather many times removed. He coughed and something came out of his mouth. It was a piece of ice in the shape of a human being. I picked it up. It was cold and hot, like dry ice. I squeezed it and smoke rose.

"Thank you, Grandson," the old man whispered. Then he closed his eyes. I opened my hand. The shape in ice was gone.

I picked up the bone spear and placed it on the old man's chest. Then I stepped back. And as I did so, weariness overcame me. My eyes closed and I fell into darkness.

❧

Someone caught me. I opened my eyes. Dennis was holding me under my arms.

"Podjo," he said, "You all right? You stood up and then you just keeled over."

I looked around. I was still next to the cedar tree. The full moon was showing herself above the trees. The weariness that I had felt—or dreamed—was gone. Instead, I felt stronger than I'd ever felt before.

Dennis touched his hand to my cheek.

"You're bleeding like you been in a fight."

"You could say that," I replied.

"Man," Dennis said, "this is the second time in three days. Some-day, brother, you have got to tell me what goes on whenever you have one of these episodes."

"Some day, maybe."

Dennis shook his head. "Ready to go now?" he asked.

"More than before."

45

*When the enemy thinks of the mountain
attack like the sea*

Study the ways of all professions. So Miyamoto Musashi wrote in his book called *Go Rin No Sho. Book of Five Rings.* It was the spring of 1645 and he was sixty-two years old. Never defeated in individual combat, often disdaining even the use of a sword when faced by deadly opponents, he fought and killed more than sixty opponents before the age of twenty-nine. In one case, when fighting Sasaki Kojiro, he used a wooden oar he had just carved into the shape of a blade. So claimed his pupils a generation after his death in their compilation of his early exploits, *Niten Ki (Two Heavens Chronicle).*

I've often wondered, if I spoke Japanese better and could go back 350 years and take on the appearance not of a tall round-eyed *gaijin* but of a young earnest warrior—like Teruo Nobuyuki, Musashi's last pupil, to whom his great book of strategy was dedicated—if I would have recognized something familiar in the master's eagle eyes.

His final years were dedicated not to killing but to teaching, poetry, and painting. In 1643, he retired to a cave in the mountains of the island of Kyushu. There, in lone seclusion, he spent his time in deep contemplation until that spring day in April when he picked up his brush and began to write, in flowing characters as delicate and strong as sword strokes, the book that gave birth to the martial art of kendo.

If you go to Kyushu, as I did, you'll find that cave is still there. It is not far from Kumamoto Castle, where Musashi had been the honored guest of Lord Churi. The cave has a name. It is called Reigendo.

The angular stone floor and rough walls of Reigendo leave little room for anything but contemplation. Try sitting in that cave and see where your thoughts take you, or just stand as I did in front of the carved stone marker, not at all tall, but four-tiered like a pagoda, and read the simple inscription on the wooden post in front of it that says "Grave of teacher Miyamoto Musashi."

On the day I was there, the air shimmered with heat. The breathless cry of a cicada pierced the rocks. It told me not to stay.

My thoughts, as Dennis and I set out, were on Musashi for more reasons than one. First, in that dream which had taken such abrupt hold of me, I realized how much the old warrior's technique had shaped the strategy that I needed to defeat the Chenoo. I also had a very strong feeling that had I not defeated the monster in that all-too-real dream, I would not now be walking around and telling this story.

What we were about to do derived from yet another strategy that Musashi had outlined in the second ring of his teachings, "Fire Book." Mountain-Sea Spirit. Enemy thinks of mountain, attack like sea. Enemy thinks of sea, attack like mountain.

While it might appear to the uninitiated that Dennis and I were about to enter a dark and dangerous forest where we would eventually go in two different directions, thus making each of us vulnerable to attack while we were on our own, what was really happening was that Dennis and I were about to go deep into a dark and dangerous forest and then split up in two different directions, thus making each of us *appear* more vulnerable to attack than if we were still together. We wanted to be attacked. We were ready for it.

For the past two years there'd been a strong rumor that the state lands of the northern forest might be privatized. With a conservative Republican in the governor's mansion and a pro-development majority in the legislature, that seemed even more possible now. That was one of the reasons Mikwe had picked the park for the Children of the Mountain to make their stand. If the state is going to give it up, they should give it back to the Indians.

Certain powerful interests knew exactly where they wanted that land to go. Did I mention the Snowflake Development Corporation with headquarters in nearby Rangerville? Figure out how much profit there is to be had from building a thousand uppity-scale condominiums, three ski slopes, a luxury lodge, and four shopping complexes. There was enough potential profit to make some state or federal officials look the other way or look a little harder in our direction.

There was more than enough money to invest in outside talent who could make us Native American squatters go bye-bye. Bounty hunters, men who enjoyed what they are did, whether it was in Africa or Iraq or the mountains of New England.

Though the ghost of the Chenoo might still walk these mountains, survive in the damaged spirits of people who allowed anger and jealousy to twist their minds, I believed that none of our people had any hand in the killings of Jock Sockabasin and Louise Brooks.

The struggle for recognition, control of our tribe, and the wealth that might come from a casino—those were different, more familiar and familial matters. But not ones that would lead to the kind of homicides that had happened, and could happen again here. Dennis and I were betting on that, betting that the ones responsible for those deaths were hired assassins, outsiders. It meant that, good as they might be, they didn't know our land as well as Dennis and I did and our land did not love them.

46

Ask the mountain
and it might answer

Our plan depended on a couple of things, the first of which involved being seen. Dennis had made sure of that when we left
the dining tent where everyone was congregated for the night.
The second part of our strategy had taken some help from others—
namely Ely and Peter Cook, whose job it was to post guards around the
dining tent. At our request, they had made sure that one person in particular had been placed where he could observe us as we left and then
be able to sneak off unseen to the place where his cell phone could pick
up a signal.

A cellular phone, as you likely know, is actually a two-way radio, its
transmissions ranging between 824 and 894 megahertz FM. That signal has to be received by a cell site, usually an eighty-foot-high antenna
cleverly concealed by being placed in the midst of the most scenic vista
available. Since the effective radius of the radio signal from a cell phone
is twelve square miles at most, that signal then has to be bounced to a
Mobile Telephone Switching Office, travel by landline to the local phone
company's switching office, and finally be routed to the intended party.

Being able to send your voice through electronically excited airwaves
is an amazingly efficient way to engage in long-distance communica-
tion. But there are downsides to cell phones (aside from being in the
car that is about to be hit head-on by the idiot who is having an argu-
ment with his girlfriend on his Jitterbug and has forgotten that he is
going down the freeway at ninety-miles an hour). Too many calls can

jam the cell lines. And then there are such obstacles as being parallel to hillsides, being inside tunnels, or being surrounded by mountains with a high concentration of iron that can block out the cell signal or blanket the transmission static.

It meant in our case that the person reporting our departure had a five-minute walk to the nearest place his call could go out, giving us enough of a head start to go beyond the range of cell phones. It meant that whoever came after us would not be able to call in more troops.

❧

My Uncle John used to say that calling someone on the telephone was not just a poor second to being there yourself, it was also not as good for talking with distant friends as some of the methods our old people used.

I wasn't quite sure what he meant till I heard this story—not from him but from one of his cronies named Gus Panadis.

It seems that about thirty years ago Uncle John and Gus were on an extended hunting trip up north, over two hundred miles away from home. They had left their truck by the road and hiked inland about twenty miles. They'd just set up their tent and were settling down for the night when Uncle John stood up and started patting his pockets.

"Darn it," he said, "I forgot my favorite pipe."

"You sure did," Gus said.

He was amused because he had left Uncle John's house right behind Uncle John and had noticed that pipe hanging there on the wall next to Uncle John's favorite chair.

"Well," Uncle John said, "guess I just better get it."

He stepped out of the tent. Gus looked out after him, but Uncle John was nowhere in sight.

Half an hour passed and Uncle John ducked back into the tent. That pipe was in his hand. He sat down, filled it, lit it, and started smoking. Gus didn't say a word. Uncle John finished the pipe, tapped out the dottle, and stuck it in his pocket.

"Didn't mean to take so long," he said. "But once I got there I found out I was out of tobacco, too. Guess I'm really getting forgetful. Had to go to the store. Saw your wife there and she said to tell you to be sure to be home by Thursday."

Gus figured Uncle John was just teasing him, so he thought nothing of it until he got back home and found his wife hopping mad.

"Where you been?" she asked.

"You know where I been. I been hunting with John."

"Were you with him all the time?"

That made Gus smile since he figured his answer would get him out of trouble.

"I sure was," he said.

Instead of calming the waters, though, that made Gus's wife so angry she didn't talk to him for three days. When she finally cooled down, she told Gus that she had seen Uncle John at the store a full two days after she thought he'd gone off hunting way up north with him. So if John wasn't with Gus, then who was Gus with?

We moved fast as soon as we hit the trail. But just in case we were heading into an ambush set up ahead of time, we had planned ahead. The day before, at strategic points where trails crossed, we had set up tracking boxes.

A tracking box is nothing more than a patch of soft earth that has been raked smooth so that any foot touching it will leave a clear imprint. Made right, big enough and wide enough, it is hard for anyone coming down a trail to avoid or even notice a tracking box. In the woods, everything that doesn't burrow under the surface or fly through the air travels much of the time by the same well-used trails. Most of the main arteries in New York City were deer paths first, then wider trails followed by the Lenape Indians before the earth was displaced by paving and assaulted by wheels instead of caressed by feet.

At the first tracking box, my penlight—concealed by our bodies— showed us deer tracks and the prints of white-footed mice. We flicked the light off as soon as we'd looked. It is easier to travel without a light in your hand when you know the trails. And even if these paths had been less than familiar, the moon was making it seem almost like day to us. Even a man wearing a night-vision rig would not have an advantage over us tonight. Black light is darker than moonlight.

We quartered the trails as we loped along. Not going straight in one direction too long. Turning, then turning again to encircle the area we had chosen. It was not until we returned to our first tracking box again, perhaps an hour later, that we found what we had expected. And more.

Dennis whistled softly under his breath. He took off his glasses and began to clean them.

"Lovely," I said.

There, in the middle of the soft patch of soil, was the deep print of a huge bare humanoid foot—about a size eighteen. From the depth of the track, the one who'd left it had to weigh well over about three hundred pounds. Next to it was an added bonus—two equally outsized prints of what might be either a Great Dane on growth hormones or an overgrown relative of a dire wolf.

47

*One and one
may be more than three*

"How nice for us," Dennis said.

I understood what he meant. The presence of Rin-Tin-Tin from Jurassic Park meant that he and his Gigantopithecus partner would be able to track us by my scent. No need to make any noise or do anything overt to draw them in our direction. Which was a good thing, since being too overt about being the bait, too much like decoys, might warn our potential attackers away.

There's an old Irish story about that. My friend Kiernan Keene told it to me as we picked our way down the steep trail to Lake Bosumtwi in the heart of the African nation of Ghana. His voice was low and quiet as he told the tale. We didn't know how far behind us was the group of well-armed Rumanians who had interesting and unpleasant plans for us. But that's a story for another time.

An old hawk was teaching a young hawk how to hunt.

"Fly down to that farm, grab a baby chick, and then bring it back here," the old hawk says.

So the young one leaps off the branch and flies into the valley. Soon it comes flying back with a baby chick held in its talons.

"What did the mother hen do when you grabbed her chick?" the old hawk asks.

"Not a thing," says the young hawk.

"Ah," says the old hawk. "Then take it back as quick as you can, for as sure as the night follows the day there is something wrong with it."

"And who was the smarter one?" Kiernan said, resting his hand on the buttressed trunk of an odum tree. "The mother hen or the old hawk?"

That was an Irish Zen koan that I never had the opportunity to answer since Kiernan and I found ourselves otherwise occupied at that very point.

When we were finally discharged from Korle Bu Teaching Hospital in Accra, there was not time for us to conclude our interrupted contemplation since Kiernan and I were given quick, quiet, courteous escorts out of the country after Jerry Rawlings, president of Ghana, had finished thanking us for our work. But, as I said, that is another story.

Right now Dennis and I were peering down the moonlit trail.

"Looking for sign?" Dennis said in a soft voice.

"Aside from the one that reads ABANDON HOPE ALL YE WHO ENTER HERE?"

Before he could answer, another sound gave us both pause. But it was not the sound of paws. This game was afoot.

We slipped off the trail to either side and waited—a bit longer than we had expected. It wasn't just that sounds carry at night in the forest. It was also because the beings we'd heard approaching were having a hard time navigating the trails—evidenced by the sounds of them slipping, tripping, and falling.

It seemed that more than one cell phone had been employed because the party of four that came thumping down the bunny trail were quite likely not at all connected to the barefoot giant whose print we'd found. They wore hiking boots—an improvement over the slippery brogans they'd had on before—dark khaki coveralls and black baseball caps with the bills turned backward, making it that much easier for the two in back to peer through the sniperscopes on their rifles and for the two in front to use the night vision goggles.

Those two leaders were our old friends, Gray Suit A and B, meaning Greg and his friend. The two new, heavily muscled men behind them were likely moonlighting from government jobs as weapons and tactical team snipers. As I implied before, a little money goes a long way when renting civil servants on fixed incomes. They were GS-14s at the most, I guessed.

Dennis and I "cast a cold eye" as the "four horsemen" went by. The moonlight sonata of their incessant cracking of twigs (perhaps they carried their own supply so that they could strew them in front of themselves as they advanced), the stumbling thump of their heavy heels, the occasional Anglo-Saxon expletive followed by the requisite

"SHHH!"—everything could be heard for a long time before it gradually faded with distance.

Dennis and I re-emerged from cover, feeling as if we'd been wasting our time doing such a good job of hiding from that crew. We would probably have gone unnoticed if we'd been playing ping-pong in the middle of the path. Put those guys in a city or around a barricaded farmhouse and they'd be something to worry about. But at night, in the north woods? Forget about it.

"Casino moneybags or land developers?" I said to Dennis.

He shrugged. Six of one, half a dozen of the other? There were only two things we knew for sure about that crew. The first was that they were hunting us, the second that they were heading in the direction that our large economy-size barefooted buddy and his puppy had gone.

How nice for them.

One of the unwritten rules of guerilla combat is that if it takes two to tango, it takes three to get caught in a crossfire. That was one reason why just Dennis and I had set out together that night. There were other competent and trustworthy men—and women—in the camp. But adding even one other person made it that much easier for something confusing to happen.

It was also the reason why the only one armed with a rifle in our fishing party of two had been Dennis. He would be, when the occasion called for it, the shooter. As for me, I had planned to be the goat staked out to lure in the tiger.

Our plans might have to change. Instead of decoying in a single adversary, it appeared we now had two. Dennis and I looked at each other and nodded. It was time to follow our quartet of clumsy nimrods, who might soon themselves become prey.

48

The night sees
Do we see the night?

We followed, but not too closely. The trail was a winding one, going up and down so much that it reminded me of the path we took to the well one summer when my parents and I stayed with friends at an old cabin near Long Lake in the Adirondacks. It was uphill all the way to the well and uphill all the way back to the house.

Ahead of us, the trail began to drop into a narrow divide between a steep rocky slope and a cut made by a nearly dry stream. Dennis and I stopped, looked at each other, and nodded. The place a quarter-mile farther, where that narrow path bent around the hillside, was where it would likely happen. That was the place we would have chosen for an ambush. It was time for us to wait.

Have you ever seen a double curve design? If you look at Wabanaki birch bark baskets, you'll see etched into them the delicate, often intricate scrollwork of the double curve. The simple design is a shape of a fern, lifting up and starting to uncurl, like a *J* turned upside down. It reminds us of the way new growth comes forth again after winter, of the way the circle opens into life. But it is more than that for a hunter. Tom Nicola explained to me how a hunter sees the double curve.

"That's the path an animal takes when it's being pursued. A deer will do that. Instead of just going straight, it'll curve off the trail and go up to a hill where it can look back and see what's on its tail."

193

I was thinking about this kind of cunning when we stopped on a small rise, a sand hill formed by the ancient retreat of a melting glacier, the terminal moraine of gravel scraped from antediluvian mountaintops released here at last from the icy flow. I moved a few yards off the trail, leaned back against a white pine and listened.

Dennis was crouched beside me, his hands cupped behind his ears. The notch between the mountain and the dry stream could still be seen from where we were. I looked at him and raised an eyebrow. He nodded. Those four hired guns should about be there soon, even moving as haltingly as they had been. They thought that with their technology they could see better than the night. But they were dead wrong.

Then there were two shots. Only two. It was like the pop of firecrackers followed by a thudding echo and then a growl just this side of a roar and a gargling scream cut short.

I heard the sound of running feet first. I touched Dennis's arm and moved a little closer to the trail. A panicked runner was coming back our way, his breath sobbing as he ran headlong, luck and adrenalin keeping him going. Running at that speed in the night, he could collide with a tree and knock himself cold.

He slowed a little as he came up the little rise to where we waited. I could see that he was now hatless and unarmed. I stood, grasped his collar, swept his feet out from beneath him, as I covered his mouth with one hand and rolled back off the trail with him beneath me.

Rifle in his hands, his back against my pine tree, Dennis took up a position to watch in case anyone or anything had been in pursuit.

The moonlight shone on the panicked runner's face. It was Greg. His eyes were unfocused. I took my hand from his mouth. The way he was breathing, he wasn't able to scream. I slapped his face gently.

"Greg, Greg," I said softly.

He shook his head as if trying to wake up from a nightmare. The hardness was gone out of him like the stuffing from a toy lion. He was barely holding onto his sanity.

"Your crew?" I asked.

"Dead," he said, his voice like dry leaves. Then he made a choking sound and tried to swing his head to the side. I saw what was coming and moved off him. He rolled to his knees and vomited.

When he was done disgorging dinner, I took him by the shoulders and pulled him up. There was no resistance. It was like handling a sleepwalker.

Dennis handed me the roll of duct tape he'd placed in his small pack along with extra ammunition and a cache of Hershey's bars. Trust Dennis to bring the barest essentials.

I taped Greg's ankles and his wrists, then ran a few loops of tape between them so he couldn't get his wrists up to his mouth to try to work himself free. We sat him back against a medium-sized birch and wrapped the tape around both Greg and the tree. It was a mean thing to do. But we hoped the tree might someday forgive us.

I didn't cover Greg's mouth.

"Greg," I whispered, "If you are very, very quiet, maybe nothing will find you. Okay?"

Greg nodded and kept nodding. His eyes were open very wide.

"Don't leave me," he whispered.

"It's okay," I said. "I'll be bok!"

"Or Mozart," Dennis added.

49

Turn to go straight,
go back to arrive

Two shots had been fired. Maybe they had struck home. Maybe one or more of our original adversaries had been wounded or killed. Maybe snakes have wheels.

"Back to plan A?" Dennis asked.

"We had a plan A?"

Kidding aside, it was time to get serious. Flank the enemy before the enemy flanks you, and then set up our own ambush.

There's a story we Penacooks tell—from back in the seventeenth century.

A hundred heavily armed white soldiers were manning Fort Number Four along the Connecticut River. One of their sentries looked out over the log wall and saw an Abenaki lurking in the trees.

"An Indian!" the soldier shouted. "Let us go and get him!"

"Be careful," said the Captain. "Those Abenakis be tricky devils. Here, take forty men with thee just to make sure."

The forty men went out. Soon there came the sounds of guns being fired, men shouting. Then the sole surviving white soldier came limping back up to the fort.

"T'was a trap," he cried. "There were two of them!"

Dennis and I went down the trail slowly, pausing and listening as we went. Everything we heard—and everything I sensed, using that other

196

way I had of feeling—told us that whatever had attacked them had moved on. But we still moved at a slow pace to the place where Greg and his companions had been ambushed.

It was easy enough to find and just where we'd expected it to happen. The first of them we came to, probably the last to die and the one whose scream we'd heard, was in the middle of the trail on his back. His face was gone, bitten off by jaws I didn't like imagining.

I'd seen something like that before in East Africa, in Kenya where the sound of a lion charging you is like the wind in the tall grass. Stephen, one of our Masai guides, had been attacked in his sleep by a hyena that had come into our camp at night. I'd heard the sound of its jaws crunching, wakened, and fired the shot that killed the hyena—but not soon enough to save Stephen's life. Of all the large mammals, none can exert more pounds per square inch in their bite than a hyena, enough to crush through the leg bone of a water buffalo. But whatever had taken this man's life, not in Africa, but here in the mountains of Ndakinna, probably ran a close second.

The next two men had died differently. One still held his rifle. A convulsing finger had accounted for the two shots. The other, his night vision glasses knocked askew, lay across the other man's legs. Both of them had been deeply ripped across their throats and chests as if by long claws.

Steel claws, I thought.

Someday I may explain how I knew that, tell about the Society of the Leopard and a Nigerian encounter with some of its members that I'll never forget. But not now.

We didn't follow the trail any farther. We cut below the brow of the hill through the valley below until we reached our original destination, a wide meadow that had probably been a beaver pond before silt filled in its water.

Dennis went up the big pine tree at the near edge of the meadow. It was easy to scale, having been set up for climbing by deer hunters. Two-by-fours had been nailed to the trunk to make a ladder and a platform blind built thirty feet above the ground. When he got up there, he rested his rifle on the railing of the platform, looked over the sights, and then flashed me a thumbs-up. The moonlight was more than bright enough for Dennis to see nearly the whole meadow over the open sights.

There were a few small trees here and there in the tall grass and one large fallen one near the center of the meadow fifty yards away. Aside from those blind spots, it was not a hard area in which to find a shot for a marksman as good as my big buddy.

I avoided those trees as I made my way through the hip-deep grass, which seemed much deeper now than it had during the daylight. I was quiet as I walked, perhaps no longer quiet enough. I could feel myself being watched.

I consoled myself with thoughts of what a good shot Dennis had always been. At the age of fourteen, he'd been able to jerk his .22 rifle up to his shoulder to hit a Coke bottle hurled spinning high up into the air. I never saw him miss. Not once.

That was when I heard the sound of the wind in the tall grass. I pivoted and saw something as it came bounding at me from the place where it had lain in concealment behind the large fallen aspen. In the moonlight it looked as big as a moose. But I knew my mind had to be exaggerating its size. It probably didn't weigh much more than two hundred pounds.

It was the biggest dog I had ever seen, like a cross between a Rhodesian Ridgeback and an obese St. Bernard, and it was bounding through the grass toward me, less than a hundred feet away and closing that distance fast. Eyes glittering in the moonlight, huge jaws agape, it was not coming to play catch. I rolled my shoulders and bent my knees.

Dennis, I thought, *you can shoot now!* as the joke about the guy who walked into a bar flashed through my mind.

This guy walks into a bar with a Rottweiler on a leash.

"Hey," the guy says to everyone there, "I'll bet a hundred bucks my dog can beat any dog you got."

"I'll take that bet," says an old man sitting at the bar. "My dog's out back."

They go out back and there's this big, short, ugly yellow dog tied to a telephone pole.

The guy with the Rottweiler laughs. "Hell, Pop, there's no way that mutt is going to beat my dog. My dog's killed a hundred other dogs so far. I don't want to take your money."

But the old man insists. So they unleash both their dogs. The Rottweiler dives in at the short yellow dog and **Wham!**, *just like that, the yellow dog bites the Rottweiler in half.*

"Holy Christ," the guy says to the old man, "What kind of dog is that?"

"Well," the old guy says, "before I cut his tail off and painted him yellow, he was a crocodile."

One more leap and the thing would be on me—and still Dennis didn't shoot. In the split second before its jaws closed on my throat, I cartwheeled to the side. I felt the hot moisture from the huge dog's jowls on my cheek, but its teeth missed me and the claws of its front foot did no more than rip the fabric of my black T-shirt, right through the middle of NEVER TOO OLD TO MUSS THE CUSTER.

Before the dog's feet struck the soft earth, I had grabbed at the ball-shaped clasp on my heavy belt, twisted it, and pulled out the chain.

That belt had been a gift to me from Sifu Huang. It was one of the hundreds of ingeniously hidden weapons that Oriental masters have devised over the centuries. In this case, it was the simple but deadly device of a weighted ball at the end of a thin, incredibly strong steel chain. There was time to slip my hand into the loop at the end of the chain, spin it twice to gather momentum, and then strike. I missed the dog's head, but it yelped as the ball glanced off its side. That meant I must have hurt it some, sort of like bopping a bear with a broomstick.

The dog turned and reset itself, crouching, swaying back and forth as it did so, bearing those formidable fangs. Its growl sounded as deep as a jet engine warming up. It wouldn't have to grab me by the throat. With those jaws, just a crushing hold on an arm or a leg would be enough. The pain would be paralyzing. Then it would shake me like a terrier shakes a rat.

I began swinging the ball in a whistling arc, making a figure *8* in front of me, weaving a net of defense, my left arm held out to the side for balance.

The image of Dennis leaning back in the tree stand, pigging out on Hershey's bars, feet up, gun cradled in his lap, came into my mind.

Dennis, you really can shoot now. Really.

Especially because our pas de deux was about to become trois.

A bare-chested man whose size matched that of his attack dog had just appeared at the edge of the meadow, and was moving purposefully my way. His hands glittered in the moonlight, but not because he was seeking to emulate Ringo Starr.

50

Soft against hard,
wind against stone

The muscles in the dog's haunches tensed—it crouched slightly and drove in at me. But I was ready and this time the ball struck home just above the right eye and a bit to the side where the bones of a canid skull come together and are the weakest. The CRACK! was like a pistol shot heard at close range and I felt bone give way. The huge animal collapsed, its legs beneath it, dead eyes still open, gaping mouth touching the toes of my right foot.

I stepped to the side and turned, whirling the ball as I did so. The big man I'd seen at the far end of the meadow had come at a dead run and was only twenty feet away. But he stopped as I faced him, spinning the chain in quick, deadly circles.

The man's face looked familiar to me. It was not because I'd seen him before, but because I'd seen similar Polynesian faces. In his eighteenth century-voyages, Captain Cook and his sailors were amazed at the size and the agility of some of the people they encountered. They saw men almost seven feet tall who could catch a spear hurled at them or float atop the waves on top of a slender piece of wood.

Captain Cook's own amazement was brief. His encounter with those bellicose islanders ended with Cook's demise when he was introduced to the business end of a war club. What a way to treat a tourist! After all, his arrival heralded nothing worse than diseases that killed 90 percent of the islanders, followed by colonial rule lovingly designed to destroy their culture.

The nobility of the islands of Hawaii were the largest Polynesians of all. Ali'i Nui, they were called. Men and women alike averaged over six feet in height, had the girth of trees, and often weighed well over three hundred pounds.

Today, many of those Polynesians who have inherited their genes for growth and battle can be found not on palm-lined beaches but in the football trenches as linemen for American college teams or various NFL squads. Like my pal Kamehameha Tanaka, who turned his 6'8" frame to the gentler martial arts after blowing out his ACL and blowing a career with the Chiefs. It was Kamehameha—named for Hawaii's greatest warrior king—who taught me what I know of Polynesian history and culture.

There was little doubt that the man who loomed over me was Polynesian, not only from his size, but also from the traditional tattoos on his face. The look on his patterned countenance registered pure homicidal rage.

He raised his hands to display what I thought I'd seen before—two sets of razor-sharp steel claws forged onto devices like brass knuckles, his fingers curled between them into fists. Clenched double handfuls of death. Aloha, indeed.

Yoo-hoo, Dennis. You really, really can shoot now!

Let's try logic. That might work. Yeah, sure.

"Look, Lothar," I said. "My friend has a rifle pointed at you."

Lothar favored me with a broad smile. Maybe he was pleased at my knowledge of comic strip trivia, pulling the name of Mandrake the Magician's massive companion out of my hat like that. But, then again, maybe not. With what might best be described as a roar, he charged in at me with those lethally loaded paws.

Have you ever seen an old man on the floor of a kendo dojo with a bunch of highly trained hotshot swordsmen? It's something to see, unless you happen to be (as I was) one of those know-it-all young guns.

Bop! He pops you on the head with his bamboo sword before you are halfway into your attack.

You get ready to—bop! He's just popped you again.

It's called seeing ahead: knowing what your attacker is about to do before he does it himself. It's one of Musashi's "Three Methods to Forestall the Enemy."

I'd never become as good as one of those old men, but I was good enough to not be there when those steel claws dissected the air. Lothar had moved a little bit faster than I'd expected, though, and my steel ball struck him a little too far back on the left wrist to break the joint. However, it numbed his hand enough to make him drop the claws held in it.

He was not smiling now as he glared at me, the two of us moving like a cobra and a mongoose. He waved his clawed hand back and forth, back and forth, then spun unexpectedly and swung down. He was better than I had expected, good enough to catch the steel chain and sever it. The steel ball went flying off into the night like a small planet broken loose from orbit.

I took a halting step backward, then another. My bad knee felt as if it was about to give out on me, the weapon I'd counted on had been broken, and for whatever reason, Dennis still hadn't taken a shot and probably was not going to fire now.

Lothar was smiling again. I wasn't.

That was when the voice came to me. It was that ancient voice I sometimes feel as much as hear, a voice that was within me and beyond me, held in the earth beneath my feet, carried by the wind, shared by the whispering of the trees.

Grandson, that voice said, *I gave you my strength in the dream we shared. This one does not have our strength. Do what you must.*

So, instead of circling or running, I attacked. My high left arm block caught his right wrist before he could strike with the steel claws. As my right foot kicked his left knee hard enough to splinter a small tree, I wrapped that blocking arm around Lothar's tree trunk of a forearm and jerked upward. His right elbow dislocated at the same second his kneecap broke. The hard shuto strike against the side of his neck with my right hand probably wasn't even that necessary. But it felt good. His face hit the ground next to the head of his dog. He was still breathing, but he didn't get up.

I used what was left of my severed chain to tie his wrists together. It would be secure enough for now. He wouldn't be walking again soon. I stood up and began to limp back toward the tree stand at the meadow's edge.

"Dennis," I called. "Dennis!"

A surprisingly weak voice answered back from somewhere below the tree stand.

"Here!" it said.

I ran as best I could to the base of the tree. Dennis was there, but he was not alone. He lay atop the twin of the dog I had left in the field behind me. That second dog was not moving, nor was it ever going to move again with a broken neck. Dennis was holding his right arm, which was bleeding. I tore the rest of my T-shirt off, helped him sit up, and wrapped the wound. It was deep, the flesh torn, but there seemed to be no arterial damage. By the time I was done, Dennis seemed stronger.

"I think I got a cracked rib," he said. He put his hand up to his face, feeling for the glasses that had flown off in the fall. I'd already found them, the bright moonlight reflecting off their thick lenses.

"Here," I said, handing them to him.

Although there was a large smudge resembling the print of a dog's pad across one lens, Dennis didn't bother to clean them. He hooked the end pieces over his ears, ignoring the fact that the nose pads and temple arms had been bent so that the glasses sat on his face at a forty-five degree angle. Then he heaved himself to his feet like a killer whale breaching out of Puget Sound.

He squinted up into the tree.

"Gun's still up there," he said.

"You mean you jumped down onto that dog from all that way up?"

"Not really," he said. "We did it together." He touched the dog with his foot. "Spot here landed on the bottom."

"Out, out, damned . . ." I began.

"Don't go there," Dennis said, gingerly touching the makeshift bandage on his arm. "Damn thing surprised me. Had my arm in its mouth before I even knew it was there. I just never knew that dogs could climb trees."

"This one can't anymore," I said.

I retrieved Dennis's gun and pack. We used the remainder of Dennis's duct tape to further truss up our Polynesian playmate and left him there.

By the time we were done, the sun had risen. We traced the footprints of Lothar and his man-eaters to the state road. The tracks of a sports utility vehicle were still there, but whoever had left him off was not.

Then, avoiding the blockade around the camp, we made our way back to report to Mikwe.

It was time for the denouement.

51

Light makes shadow,
light unmakes shadow

There were a lot of shocked faces when we walked back into the camp. Perhaps it was because they hadn't realized just how debonair two guys like us could look in our current state. Bruises, bandages, limps, and hound-dog grins—all we needed was a fife, a drum, and a flag bearer.

But I knew that the surprise for at least three of those who viewed our return was colored by some serious misgivings.

Dennis was immediately herded off by Katlin—interesting how a woman one-quarter of a man's bulk can move him about the way a border collie bullies a flock of sheep. She took him to her first-aid station to clean out his wound and apply a proper dressing.

Proper dressing was on my mind, too, and so I went to our tent. Time for a new T-shirt. I chose NEXT TO THE LAST OF THE MOHICANS.

By the time I finished changing, combing my hair, and plucking my whiskers (no need to shave if you've got tweezers), Dennis was at the door flap. He had a spanking clean dressing on and looked paler and more drained than he had when I helped lift him off the flattened corpse of the Hound of the Baskerville's understudy.

"Man," he said, "that Katlin!"

I smiled at an image of her determined expression as she cleaned, scoured, scrubbed, and disinfected my pard's torn arm while he gritted his teeth.

"Time to call all the suspects into the library," I said.

Of course, we met first with Ely, Nick, and Pete. They nodded at our simple instructions, to be carried out while everyone was in the meeting tent. I also took Mikwe aside to suggest a few things. I could have done them myself, but I wanted him to be the one. Our brief tutorial went well and the gleam that was in his eyes when we were done was interesting. Perhaps nonviolence was not his calling after all.

It took half an hour to get everyone together. One person, in particular, almost missed the meeting. He was heading into the woods "to take a leak" when Pete intercepted him.

"But with your pack on?" Pete said, as he slipped it off Sammy Loron's shoulder.

As I summed up the events of the night before, I looked around and saw, just as expected, three nervous sets of eyes. Mikwe stood to my right. His arms were folded in front of his chest.

"Our problem," I said, "was figuring out who was responsible for setting it up. It had to be someone in the camp. But who?"

On cue, my hoped-for help appeared at the back of the crowd. It was Pete Cook holding something up in his right hand. A second later, Ely and Nick Sabattis arrived next to him. They hoisted two more such objects, each a tribute to modern electronic miniaturization, plus—in Nick's hand—a bottle of hair coloring. The three of them looked at each other and grinned. For a minute I thought they were going to break into an old-time victory dance.

"Mikwe," I said. It was his cue.

"Come forward," he said in a deep voice. Pete and Ely and Nick made their way to the front as Mikwe waited. It was a good moment. Effective theatre.

"But there was not just one person trying to destroy what we are doing here," Mikwe said.

He gestured to the three men who held up their prizes of war, the three cell phones that they had found concealed in the personal belongings of Sammy Loron, Mook Glossian, and the large middle-aged Penacook woman who was now being propelled forward, her arm twisted behind her back, by Katlin. Although that woman had been calling herself Wapitisis, or Little Elk, I knew her by another name. Molly Ann Boulet. The younger half-sister of Chief Polis. Her face twisted with anger, she hissed like a snake as Katlin held firm to the armlock.

Although it was not possible for Molly Ann Boulet to make a break, the two others chose that moment to go for it. They didn't go far. A sudden exhalation of breath was the counterpoint to Ely's fist driving into the stomach of Sammy Loron. And when Mook Glossian tried to dart away from Mikwe's side, his escape ended in a nose-first landing. Mikwe had executed the foot sweep I'd shown him to perfection.

I stepped in front of Mikwe as he reached for Mook. From the glow in my childhood friend's eyes, he might just have been able to handle Mook at that moment, but I didn't want to take the chance.

"He used to beat me up when I was a kid," Mikwe said. He looked ready to do a stamp dance on Mook's cranium.

"Past tense," I said, grabbing Glossian's thumb with one hand and his throat with the other. All the better to help him to his feet, of course.

"Which one first?" Ely said, pointing to the three cell phones that had now been placed on the small table set up at the front.

"Which one is yours, Mook?"

Mook Glossian tried to squirm free.

"Fuck you. I don't have a phone."

I applied a little more pressure to thumb on throat.

"Which?"

"That one, that one!"

Pete Cook picked it up and handed it to Mikwe.

"Redial," I said.

Mikwe pushed the button and put it on speaker. It rang but once before being picked up.

"Agent Baxter here." Pause. "I said this is Baxter. This you, Glossian? I need a status report."

Mikwe pushed the reset button. No further explanations needed. We would learn later that Mook had cut a deal six months earlier when he was caught with a shipment of angel dust that would have sent him and his biker buddies off to make license plates in the state crowbar hotel for many, many moons. The state cops had dealt him off to the feds, who had just the perfect job for him. Who but a Penacook drug mule transporting angel dust would be better suited to be morphed into a mole, infiltrating what feds had classified as an Indian terrorist organization?

Angel dust, or PHP, was first used as a large-animal tranquilizer before people started sniffing it. It was a nice irony. PHP was the same stuff they used to tranquilize grizzly bears at Yellowstone Park when they had to relocate them away from tourists. Except those bears kept coming back for more. Forget the garbage, we need a fix! And the more often they were tranquilized, the meaner they got. It is one of the little side effects that angel dust also has on homo not so sapiens.

"Now for number two," I said, looking at Sammy Loron. I'd suspected Sammy ever since noting that his footprints matched those that had led Dennis out of the camp to that aborted mid-day ambush.

Ely pushed the redial option on pseudo-Sammy's cellular unit.

It reached the switchboard of the Snowflake Corporation. Which, it later turned out, had been involved heavily of late with a group of new immigrants whose operating base in New York is known as Little Odessa. Those Russian mafia contacts were equipped to provide all the cut-rate button men and moonlighting flatfeet that any heartless multinational could ever want to employ. My biker welcoming squad at the Albany airport was among their roster of one-way escorts for hire.

Once again, we would only learn Sammy's backstory weeks later. Sammy was not even his real name. Try Ricco Carlotti, an Italian whose thick blond hair looked pretty Indian when he kept enough dye on it to hide the paler roots of his deceit. He'd worked for the Royal Canadian Mounted Police by infiltrating Native protest groups in Canada. It was there that he'd gathered the credentials that let him in among the Children of the Mountain.

Which left Molly Ann. She had not stopped hissing the whole time. Her face reminded me of the story about the time Gluskonba was treated rudely by a group of very mean people. He patted each of them on the back and they started to shrink and turned into toads. Molly Ann looked to be halfway through that metamorphosis. She squirmed free from Katlin, raised her clawlike hands in front of her face, and tried to lunge at Mikwe, who simply stepped back and let Ely and Pete grab her.

Once again, Mikwe pressed redial. The signal from Molly Ann's phone bounced from transmission tower to switching office to land right in the lap of Chance International, the very company that was just itching to back a Penacook casino once we received recognition. A Penacook nation that could be headed by Chief Paul Boulet—Molly Ann's son—after the elimination of any other chieftaincy. The murders had been her plan, the person we called Lothar someone she had known during the years when she was much better-looking, living in Las Vegas and hobnobbing with professional athletes.

Ironically, the same sort of angel dust once transported by Mook was what our big buddy Lothar liberally dosed himself with each night when he went out in his guise as the angel of death. Lothar's real name, by the by, proved to be Packy Palehua. He was a former professional wrestler known as The Hawaiian Hammer when part of the World Wrestling Federation. Actually, he was a *former* wrestler because too many of the people who had shared the stage with him in well-rehearsed mock combat had ended up with serious injuries that were far from fake. The Chenoo spirit truly was in him. And his two best friends? They were identified as a breed of dog thus far unclassified by the AKC. Their origin? No one knew.

And that was it. I looked at Mook Glossian and then at Mikwe.

Mikwe nodded. "Let him go."

As soon as I released him, Mook stumbled away from us, looked back as if about to say something. For a moment I saw something in his eyes that made me sad. Traitor he had been, but a part of him had really wanted to be Malsum, a man who could have some pride. Then his eyes grew dark and he turned to lope down the hill toward the waiting authorities.

Mikwe dialed Baxter's number yet again. It was time to fill in the feds on what had happened, including the loss of three of their agents, the other bodies they would find in a certain beaver meadow, and the two guilty parties we had to hand over to them.

It took several days to straighten it all out. Part of that time Dennis and I had to spend in custody, enduring one interview after another about our roles in everything that had happened, being accused of conspiracy, of interfering in ongoing investigations, being threatened with serious jail time, and so on. It was nothing I hadn't been through before and in the end it was decided to cut us loose.

We went back to the Mountain to find that the occupation was being ended and that everyone would soon be leaving. It had been decided that the Children of the Mountain had made their point and that, because of the ample, extremely positive publicity, our Penacook Nation was now much more likely to gain federal recognition and win court cases for the return of some part of our traditional land.

Dennis and I struck our tent and stowed our things away into our packs. While Dennis was carrying the tent to his jeep, now parked down the hill where the law enforcement blockade had been, Katlin came up and gave me a big hug.

"Invite me to the wedding," I said.

"It's a deal," she agreed, hugging me harder before letting go—and then walking away.

I had knelt down to pull out a tent peg we'd missed when I sensed someone behind me. I thought it was Katlin, but it was Ruth. She was standing with one hand on her hip next to my backpack. Too bad she wouldn't fit into it!

"Going somewhere, sailor?" she said.

"Guitar school," I said.

She put a piece of paper in my hand. A phone number and address. Hers, of course.

"Okay?" she said.

"Okay," I answered. And then she kissed me.

And I kissed her back.